ALL OF ME

AN ALPHA BILLIONAIRE ROMANCE (THEIR SECRET DESIRE BOOK THREE)

MICHELLE LOVE

MEGAN LEE

CONTENTS

Made in "The United States" by:

Ivy Wonder & Michelle Love

© Copyright 2021

ISBN: 978-1-64808-797-4

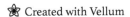 Created with Vellum

BLURB

All I wanted was to start over, somewhere quiet, somewhere I
didn't have to be me.
Tiger Rose, Hollywood movie star.
She's someone I don't even recognize as me anymore.
And now I found my haven...
And found *him*...
Lazlo. He's the last person I should fall for. He's from the
entertainment world too...
But that face, that body... and his good, good heart. I can't resist him...
But can I risk my new-found peace for him?
My body says *yes... yes...*
Yes...
But I'm scared to love again, scared to trust...
Can Lazlo break down the wall I've build around my heart?

CHAPTER ONE – EVERYTHING CHANGES

HE LEVELLED the gun at her and she knew this was it. "I thought you loved me," she said in a calm voice. Only a slight quiver at the end gave away her heartbreak.

"I do," he nodded, his eyes soft, "but I have to do this."

She drew in a deep breath as he fired, then crumpled slowly as the bullet ripped through her abdomen. Her legs gave way and she sank to the floor.

He put down the gun and came to her, cradling her in his arms. She felt his tears drip down onto her face. "I'm sorry, I'm so sorry..."

"It doesn't matter," she said, her voice weakening as she bled out, "it's all over now."

"I love you," he said, beginning to sob, but she shook her head.

"Love doesn't do this, my darling... Love doesn't do this." She gave one last shuddering gasp of pain, then went still.

He clutched her to him and gave a howl of bottomless grief.

"And cut! Good job, people." The director and his team clapped the actors, and Tiger opened her eyes and grinned up at Sifrido, her costar.

"Douchebag."

"Drama queen." He helped her up as they laughed and high-fived each other. Sifrido nudged her with his shoulder. "And lucky, too, to be finished early. So, what's next for you?"

"Hanging with my brother." Tiger smiled back at her friend and costar. She and Sifrido had worked on many movies together now and had been close from the start. She enjoyed spending time with him and his wife Lucy when they were in the same place, which was rare if they weren't working, and it was with half-regret now that she told Sifrido that she was going out of town. "Apollo is between jobs and wanting to spend some quality time with his big sister. So, we're going to the Olympics for a week with no internet, no cellphones. We bought a small cabin up there."

"Nice." Sifrido nodded approvingly. "Washington is one of my favorite places."

Tiger smiled at him. Sifrido's wife, Lucy, and his biological son Nicco, both taught at a college in Seattle. "Then I have the Malevolence press junket for a month. First here, then London and on and on." She grimaced and Sifrido laughed.

"You're really not used to them by now?"

"I just don't like being around that many people for that long. Thank God Teddy will be there to make me laugh."

Tiger said goodbye to her friend and went to thank the director. Cosimo DeLuca was one of her favorite people, and he frequently cast Tiger in his movies. He had been responsible for her first break in the industry ten years ago, and she remained utterly loyal to him, even doing small cameos for free and for no credit if he needed it.

He looked tired now as she went to find him in his trailer. Biba, his gorgeous wife, was with him, and she greeted Tiger with a hug. "You were incredible as always, Tiggy."

Tiger smiled at them both. "I hate to do this, but I have to say goodbye for a while. But promise me, when we're all free, we'll meet up for dinner at least?"

Cosimo, a devastatingly handsome Italian in his late forties with bright green eyes and dark curly hair, grinned at her. "It's a date. Just let us know when you're free, Tig, and we'll make it happen. And thank you for this... Not every actress would come in for a part where they were killed off in the first act."

Tiger laughed. She looked down at her costume, covered in the corn syrup they used for fake blood. "Are you kidding? A great death scene? Give me more."

Biba chuckled. "Actors."

"Actors," greed Tiger with a nod. She bid them goodbye and went to her trailer. Peeling off her ruined dress, wrinkling her nose as the syrup stuck the fabric to her skin, she removed the small 'blood' bag taped to her skin by the props people and stepped into her shower.

She took her time, enjoying the hot water cascading down her skin. Drying herself, she took a critical look in the mirror. She had never been one of the skinny actresses; she refused to lose weight for any role that required her to be unhealthily thin, and she had retained her curves through hiking and swimming rather than dieting.

Her skin was porcelain, her hair a dark, dark brown and cut into a bob. Her large violet eyes and full mouth made her passionately sought after by beauty brands to be their spokesmodel, but that wasn't Tiger's scene. She earned enough from her movies to make her financially secure and she wasn't a spendthrift.

Tiger valued her privacy more than anything. At thirty-two, she and her younger brother Apollo had been on their own since Tiger was eighteen, their parents both dying of cancer just a few months apart. Tiger and Apollo had been devastated, but she had known she had to step up to the plate and care for her fourteen-year-old brother. She'd intended to go to college but had been scouted by an elite model agency and started to get jobs right away. Her extraordinarily photogenic features helped make her an overnight sensation, and when she was offered her first film role, Tiger found her true vocation.

She'd proved all the doubters wrong by putting in a supporting performance that attracted awards buzz, and she'd even taken home a few of them. Since then, she had been in demand, which had made life for her and Apollo a whole lot easier. Her brainiac brother was able to go to Harvard—something of which Tiger was envious—but she was able to pay his way easily, and he swore he would one day pay her back.

Apollo was her best friend, her buddy. With his light brown hair and green eyes, he was popular with the opposite sex, but it was his warm, kind, loving character that drew people to him. He was more outgoing than Tiger, and although she didn't like to admit it, Tiger had learned a lot about being social from her younger brother, and it helped her overcome her natural shyness.

Now she hurriedly dried her hair and shoved it up into a messy ponytail, leaving her face free of makeup. She donned old sweats to be comfortable for the flight from Los Angeles to Seattle and packed up her belongings. She never brought much to set, just her books, laptop, and precious photos of Apollo and her friends.

THE FLIGHT to Seattle was mercifully quick, and as Tiger hurried through the Arrivals lounge, she scanned the crowd for Apollo. Soon enough, she saw her lanky brother, leaning nonchalantly against the wall at the far end of the hall. Tiger gave a whoop of joy and ran to him.

Apollo swept her up into a hug. "Oof, big sis."

"Ha ha, shut up." She punched his arm lightly as he put her down, and he took her bag from her. "You look good, Pol."

"I know," he said cockily and grinned. "And looking forward to our trip. Can you even imagine what those trails are going to be like? I hope you're fit, sis."

Tiger made a face, then laughed. "Hey, as long as there's plenty of food."

"Always."

They got into Apollo's car and he pulled out of the parking lot. "So... what happened with David?"

Tiger rolled her eyes. David Bao was her very recent ex-boyfriend, a sensationally attractive Korean-American actor who had loved her and who she... liked. There was no other word for it; David had been more invested in their two-year relationship than she had been, and eventually Tiger had to admit to herself that it wasn't fair on David. He was perfect: kind, funny, gorgeous—the full package—but Tiger just couldn't give enough of herself to him.

When she broke up with him, David had been devastated but accepting. "Just promise me, you will try to love someone someday." He'd told her softly during their tear-filled breakup. "You're too special not to be with someone."

TIGER HAD PROMISED him but she knew she had been lying. Something was broken inside of her, she thought, that she couldn't trust enough to love, to give herself over to someone, and what was frustrating was that she didn't have any clue as to why. She hadn't been abused as a child or assaulted as an adult. Yes, she'd put up with her fair share of harassment and inappropriate casting couch proposals over the years, but she'd maintained a reputation for never being one of those actors, someone who would sleep around for parts.

She would also speak openly about that side of her craft in interviews, naming the worst offenders. It had cost her roles, sure, but it had also increased industry respect for her.

Now, as Apollo drove back to his apartment in the city, she grinned at her brother. "Not much to tell. He's doing okay, as far as I know."

"And you?"

"You know me."

Apollo's mouth set into a hard line, and Tiger was surprised to see him shake his head. "What's up with you?"

"Tigs... David was a good one."

"I know, but at the end of the day..."

"You couldn't let yourself love him."

Damn, Apollo knew her too well. Tiger looked away, out of the window. "It is what it is, Pol."

"You're thirty-two, Tigs. Isn't it time you figured this shit out? Why does this happen all the time?"

"Just leave it alone, Pol. I'm happy being single."

"And I'm all for that... but I don't think it's just a case of you liking your own company. There's a block there and I cannot figure for the life of me what it is."

"Seriously, why are you asking me this now? I thought we were here to enjoy a vacation together..."

"I met someone."

Tiger's eyebrows shot up and she saw that there were two spots of pink high on her brother's cheeks. "You did? That's wonderful."

Apollo nodded and couldn't help the smile breaking across his face. "She's wonderful. Nell. She's a postgraduate at college."

"Cute?"

"Beautiful. All dark hair and dark eyes and the longest legs you'll ever see."

Tiger smiled at the love in her brother's voice. "How long have you been seeing her?"

"Six months."

Tiger was shocked. "Six months? How come you haven't mentioned her before?"

Apollo was silent for a few moments as he concentrated on his driving. "Tig... she's pregnant. Three months."

2

CHAPTER TWO – YOU SAY

TIGER GAPED AT HIM. "WHAT?"

Apollo nodded. "And, believe it or not... it was planned. Tigs... Nell and I... we're getting married. Soon."

Tiger was devastated. "Why did you keep this all from me? Did you think I wouldn't support you?"

"I know you would have, I know. Except... sometimes, you still think of me as a fourteen-year-old, and just sometimes you can be a bit..."

"What?" Tiger felt hurt, shockingly so. They had always been so close and now what? Apollo didn't need her anymore?

"Smothering. No, that's not right. Overprotective. Especially with my girlfriends."

"If you're talking about Liz, that's because she was an evil demon from hell."

Apollo grinned then. "In that case, you are correct, but sometimes, just you being who you are, Tiger Rose, can be intimidating for them. Not that Nell will be, but I didn't know that at the start of us. So, I kept it from you." He suddenly pulled the car over into a parking lot and switched off the ignition. He turned to look at her. "Don't get me wrong, Tigs. I adore you, I love you, and you are the best thing in the world. But you paid for everything, you gave me everything, and now I need to... God, I don't know. This needs to be mine, you get me?"

"I get it." But she didn't. She looked away, out of the window, blinking back tears. Apollo felt overshadowed by her? God damn it. She'd tried not to let that happen and besides... "Listen, you didn't get into Harvard because of me, Pol, you did that on your own."

He smiled kindly at her. "With your money, Tigs. I'm sure the fact I had the funding in place helped immeasurably with the offer of a place."

Alright, he had her there. But Tiger sighed. "Do I at least get to meet her?"

"After our vacation. When we come back to Seattle. She's spending the week with her folks in New Orleans while we're away; she didn't want to crash our vacay."

"That's thoughtful." Tiger shook her head. "Pregnant?"

Apollo nodded and she could see the joy in his eyes. "Honestly, Tigs, I never knew I wanted kids until I met Nell. She's the one, you know?"

But Tiger didn't know, and her heart ripped open with loneliness. She had known, of course, this day would come, when their little family unit would be invaded by someone else...

...invaded. What the hell is wrong with you, woman? Invaded. Tiger pulled herself together and smiled at her brother. "I'm delighted for you, Pol. Really."

He shot her a sideways look and a grin. "Nice try, sis."

"I mean it."

He patted her hand. "Thank you. Now, let's talk vacay."

THEY SPENT the night in the city. In the morning, Tiger padded into the kitchen to see Apollo watching the television news intently. He turned to her with troubled eyes. "Did you hear?" He nodded at the screen. "India Blue is in the hospital."

Tiger's eyebrows shot up. "Oh, no..."

Massimo Verdi, one of Tiger's friends in the business, had been seeing India Blue for a while, and Tiger had been on a double date with them a few months back. She'd like India very much. "What happened?"

"She was abducted. They found her this morning with serious stab wounds."

"Jesus."

Tiger sat down and watched alongside Apollo as the report showed a very distressed Massimo arriving at the hospital along accompanied by a very tall, handsome man who looked stressed out, dark circles under his navy-blue eyes.

"Who's that?"

"I think it must be Lazlo Schuler, India's kind-of brother. It's complicated." Tiger had never met India's family, but she'd heard of Lazlo. He was India's manager and a brilliant one at that. But he looked devastated now, and Tiger's heart went out to him. "Poor things. I must send flowers to Massimo before we leave."

IN THE CAR on the way to the Olympic Mountains, Tiger couldn't stop thinking about Massimo and India. She knew part of her problem with never allowing anyone to love her was exactly this: the fear of the pain of loss. When their parents had died, it had been such an overwhelming, all-encompassing shock. An ordinary Saturday. Her mom and dad going to Walmart to pick up the weekly groceries. A logging truck with an exhausted driver turning onto the road, not seeing their small Volvo car traveling along the same stretch. It had been all over in a second, the police told them, their parents barely even realized what had been happening.

The pain was unimaginable, and when the then-eighteen-year-old Tiger had to identify the remains—because 'remains' were all that was left of her Mom and Dad—it seared the experience into her psyche. No. She had Apollo and that's all she needed.

One person to worry about constantly. One person to be scared of losing.

One to be overprotective of. Damn it. Look at Massimo and India. He was close to losing India in the worst way possible, and yet he showed up, he was there, he loved her regardless.

Her brother was right. It wasn't healthy, it wasn't sustainable, and now he had proved it. There would be a new life, her niece, that she would worry over.

And the woman her brother loved. Tiger trusted Apollo enough now to know that if he had made this commitment, then Nell was the one. A good person. A great person.

"You're right, Pol," she said softly as she drove and he turned to her.

"What?"

She smiled at him. "It is time."

"For?"

Tiger's grin widened and she nodded. "It is time for me to trust to love."

"Finally."

And they both laughed.

CHAPTER THREE - SMITHEREENS

ONE MONTH LATER...

THE PRESS JUNKET for her latest movie to be released had been long and arduous, but finally it was coming to an end. The last interviews were in New York at a Manhattan hotel, and Tiger found being interviewed in a small hotel room uncomfortable and trying, especially when she was asked the same questions over and over.

Thankfully, for the last interviews, she would be paired with her costar Teddy Hood. Teddy was going through a painful divorce, but he'd still stayed professional and cheerful throughout, doing his job, fulfilling his contract despite his woes. He confided to Tiger after each day that his smile felt false, that he felt as if he were playing a role, but hey, he said, "That's what I'm paid to do."

"You can always talk to me, Teddy," Tiger told him, kindly. "Anytime."

For herself, Tiger was looking forward to getting home to Seattle to finally meet Nell. They hadn't been able to make the meeting work before Tiger had to work, but this weekend was the time. She was nervous, but thanks to Apollo's machinations, she and Nell had at least talked over Facetime a couple of times, albeit casually.

Tiger decided to call Apollo now, between interviews. She'd just finished with a creep from a British tabloid, Grant Waller, whom she had never liked. The way his eyes roamed over her body, the way he always, always, asked her about her underwear, for chrissakes. The film had been a comic book-based superhero movie, and Tiger played one of the main heroes, clad in a tight leather suit. She'd played the role a couple of times now, and each time, Waller had asked her about what she wore under the suit. Tiger had been gracious and humorous at first, but this time, she had snapped back at him.

"How about we talk about your underwear, Mr. Waller? You seem to have a fixation with it, after all."

Grant Waller had smiled what he obviously thought was a charming smile, but it looked to Tiger like the grin of a snake. "I'm not the one on public show."

"Public show? Funny, I thought I was fully dressed throughout. Tell me, Mr. Waller, have you a mother? A sister?"

His smile had faltered a little. "Yes, why?"

"How would you feel about someone continually asking about their underwear?" She fixed him with an ice-cold stare and felt victorious when he'd backed off and asked another question. The interview limped on for another few minutes before the studio rep had called time. She hadn't bothered to shake Waller's hand afterward. Asshole.

Tiger talked to the rep for a few minutes, then excused herself to the hotel corridor to make a call.

"Hey, sis."

"Hey, loser. How's it going?"

Apollo laughed. "Since you last asked about two hours ago? We're doing good. We've got everything ready for your visit... or should I say, Nell has been tidying everything up fifty-five billion times because she's scared."

Tiger chuckled as she heard Nell in the background, protesting that Apollo was busting her. "Hey, tell Nell not to worry. When we're all together, I'll help her get her revenge on you."

"I will not tell her that," Apollo laughed, "Hey, listen, I—"

Tiger never knew what Apollo was about to say, because something, someone grabbed her from behind, and she dropped her phone. She was slammed full force into the wall of the corridor, and she felt hot breath on her ear. "Fucking stuck-up bitch," Grant Waller growled, his hands burrowing under her skirt, "Let's see how much of a whore you really are..."

Tiger struggled with him, crying out before he clamped his hand over her mouth. No. No, this wasn't going to happen...

But his strength was too much for her, and for the next few minutes, Tiger could only cry as Waller assaulted her. Only when he attempted to kiss her did she get an advantage, biting down on his bottom lip hard. She tasted blood as he screamed and pushed her away, slapping her around the face hard enough to knock her down. Tiger slumped to the ground as Waller walked away, wiping his mouth.

For a few long moments, all Tiger could hear was her own heavy breathing. She felt numb, shocked into incomprehension about what had just happened to her. Then, moving like an automaton, she stood shakily and straightened out her dress, her hair, wiped her mouth.

She checked her watch. Her final interview was happening right now. She walked to the designated room, barely acknowledging the studio reps or even Teddy, who shot her a concerned look as she sat down next to him.

"Hey, are you okay?"

Tiger looked at him blankly, not seeing him. The journalist was shown in and sat down and began to ask his questions. Somewhere inside her wrecked mind, Tiger knew she should be talking, but she couldn't form the words, couldn't understand plain English.

Suddenly Teddy stopped the interview and turned to her. "Seriously, this is off the record," he added to the journalist, who was looking equally concerned. She nodded, her eyes on Tiger. Teddy held Tiger's hands. "Tiger... honey, you're not okay, are you?"

She stared blankly at him and the felt something wet drip onto her neck.

"Jesus, you're bleeding..." Teddy looked at the reps, one of which quickly got on her cell phone to call for help.

Teddy pulled off his overshirt and pressed it to Tiger's head. "Honey, what happened? What happened?"

Finally, the dam broke inside of her, and she spoke, only in a whisper, but to her it sounded like a scream. "No... no, I'm not alright... I'm not alright at all..."

THE MOVIE'S director stood at the podium with one of the studio lawyers and held his hand up for silence. The congregated press gaggle silenced. The director nodded.

"As you know, the press interviews scheduled for this afternoon were cancelled at short notice due to an incident. We can now confirm details of that incident. At precisely three-ten p.m., a beloved cast member was violently and sexually assaulted by a member of the tabloid press."

A furor broke out amongst the journalists, but the director wasn't finished. "This is unacceptable and horrifying. An arrest has been made, and we will be pressing charges against that journalist. The incident, while not witnessed by anyone in person, was captured on the hotel security cameras and was audibly witnessed by one of the cast member's family. We want to ask you, out of respect, not to try and speculate which cast member was the victim of this horrific attack nor invade their or their family's privacy."

"Can you confirm whether the cast member was male or female?" A question from the back.

The director glared at the whole pack. "What did I just say? The cast member is being cared for, and you will not invade his or her privacy. We will update you on the case when we have more."

. . .

TIGER WATCHED the news conference dispassionately from her hospital bed. Along the bottom of the screen ran the words, 'Backslash Studios abruptly cancels press interviews in wake of serious 'incident.' Police have made arrest. Man charged with serious sexual offenses and assault.'

That was her they were talking about. She felt numb, almost paralyzed. Apollo had been frantic, hearing her being attacked, and the police had told her they were flying both Apollo and Nell out to be with Tiger.

Tiger closed her eyes. There were so many people around her now that she felt she couldn't breathe. Grant Waller had been arrested, and she had been brought here where a laceration on her hairline was treated. Bruises were forming all over her body, but she couldn't feel the physical pain of them.

She waited until the others in her room were distracted before slipping out. She just needed a few minutes, just a few minutes peace to get her head together, and here, in this hospital, she felt safe enough to be alone.

She found a stairwell and curled up in a corner near a window. She heard a door well below her open but didn't hear anyone approach. It wasn't until someone far below her began to talk that she realized someone else was hiding out here, too.

"Jess? Jessie..." A man began to cry quietly, and the heartbreak in his voice made her eyes fill with tears. "It's okay. India's okay... it's just... I needed to talk to someone. I'm sorry if I've filled up your voicemail, I don't want to intrude. I just... Massi is so destroyed by this that I don't feel I can fall apart. Gabe is... Gabe. India's awake and she's trying to make jokes all of the time, but... I'm a wreck, Jessie." He laughed softly. "God, do me a favor, would you delete this? I'm just rambling like an idiot, but you're the only one I can share with. Everyone needs me, Jessie and... God, I'm sorry. Ignore me. I love you. I'll call you later."

Tiger heard him flicked his phone off, then heard the door open. "Mr. Schuler?"

"Yes?"

"Ms. Blue is asking for you."

"Of course."

The door squeaked again, and then Tiger knew she was alone in the stairwell. Lazlo Schuler. He sounded as wrecked as she felt right now. Tiger wondered if, like her, all he wanted to do was run away, leave everything and everyone behind, cocoon herself away from all the hurt and the pain in the world.

Because that was all she wanted to do now. The studio had released her from performing the rest of her public relation commitments, probably worried about being sued out the wazoo for not protecting her. So, she was going home, back to Washington, but not to Seattle. She knew exactly where she was going to go, somewhere no one would find her in a hurry: the small house she'd bought quietly a few years back to be a bolt hole. It would be perfect for her now. Apollo didn't need her in Seattle; he had Nell and the baby.

It was time for Tiger to finally be truly on her own.

4

CHAPTER FOUR - TOMORROW

THREE YEARS LATER...

THE ISLAND, San Juan Islands, Washington State

LAZLO SCHULER PULLED his car off the ferry boat and onto the island. The trip from Seattle had taken longer than he had expected, and he wondered now how wise it had been to drive rather than catch a plane and rent a car.

Luckily for him, the house he had rented for the next month wasn't far from the ferry port and soon he was inside, waiting for the realtor to leave him alone.

That was why he was here, after all. To be alone.

Lazlo Schuler was tired. No, more than tired; he simply had nothing left in him. In the last few years, he'd almost lost his beloved sister, India Blue, for the second time, and their adored Korean friend to a psychopathic killer, almost lost another to a vengeful ex-wife, and had lost his close friend Coco to an unexpected pregnancy complication. He was tired of loss, of grieving.

And he was tired of work. He managed not only his sister's career but others in the entertainment business, and most of them demanded more time than he could give.

But not India. He would work twenty-four-seven for his adopted sister, but it was she who sat him down two weeks ago and had gently told him she was worried.

He had gaped at her. "Indy... you're worried about me?"

She nodded, her dark eyes full of love and concern. "For a long time now. You've been our rock, all of us. With what happened to Sun and me, for losing Coco, and what's just happened to Jess, you've been there for all of us."

"That's my job."

"But you never, ever ask us for anything," India said, a note of frustration creeping into her soft voice.

"I don't need anything, bubba. Now that you're safe, Jess is safe, I have no worries."

But even as he'd said it, he knew he wasn't convincing India because he knew it wasn't true. He wasn't doing okay, not at all. Sleep evaded him every night and to distract himself from the nightmares that plagued him, he would work. The clients who weren't personal friends were delighted, of course, but Lazlo was exhausted.

The final straw came when India played a curveball, and Lazlo came home one day to find his best friend, Alex Rogers, waiting for him.

Alex had been AWOL for a couple of years, ever since Coco Conrad, his roommate and the mother of his unborn child had died unexpectedly. Alex had been beyond grief and had disappeared back to his family in Canada. None of them ever thought they would see him again.

"But India called me and begged to come," he told Lazlo that evening. "Because she's scared out of her mind for you, Laz. Don't forget Indy knows the signs of a breakdown; she had that with Massi, and she got him through it. She sees the same signs with you, but she says you won't give anything away."

Alex talked to him over the next few days and convinced Lazlo to take a break. "Listen, I'll take over for you while you're on sabbatical. I'm not trying to steal your clients, but I need something to do. Hanging out with my family has been what I needed, but I want to get back to work. I'll even do it for free. It's not like I can't afford to. I'll just be a placeholder."

LAZLO TRUSTED Alex at his word and after that evening, he had slept better than he had in years. He knew he needed to get away, but he was still too loathe to leave the country in case India needed him. She rolled her eyes, but as they talked about various locations, it was India who had suggested Washington.

"Remember when we went on that shindig with Quartet? We all stayed in that hotel on San Juan Island? It was bliss and well out of the way, but not isolated. Those islands, man, that would be prefect."

Lazlo had agreed, and so now as he bid the realtor to his rental goodbye, he closed the door and went into the living room. He'd rented the place furnished because he didn't want the hassle of being in an empty house—he was there to chill, after all.

In the corner of the living room sat a few boxes he'd had shipped: mostly books he'd been meaning to read for a while. He retrieved his laptop from his bag and flicked it on, making himself a cup of coffee while he waited for it to boot up. He couldn't resist checking his emails but laughed aloud when he saw twenty emails from India, all of them reading the same thing.

Don't you dare, Schuler. Your out-of-office is on and I have spies EVERYWHERE.

Lazlo grinned and replied to one of them with:

You are scary, but I love you. I promise, no work, just play. Laz.

As evening fell over the island, Lazlo walked around the little neighborhood. There was a pathway down to the beach, and he went down to it, watching the sunset, scanning the water for any orca sightings.

He was about to turn around when he saw a figure further down the beach, a woman walking a dog. He looked away, not wanting her to feel threatened at all by a lone man staring at her, but her dog clearly had other ideas. He skittered up to Lazlo, yapping happily and jumping up for a fuss. Lazlo grinned and bent to stroke the black-and-tan spaniel. "Hey, boy."

The dog's owner hurried up to them looking harassed. "I'm so sorry."

"It's no problem." He looked at the woman curiously. Even though the sun was dipping below the horizon, she wore sunglasses, and her hair, long, almost to her waist, was a deep almost-black. There was something vaguely familiar about her, but he didn't want to intrude on her privacy.

She clipped her dog's leash onto his collar and nodded politely at Lazlo before turning around. Lazlo in turn walked back to the pathway that led to his street and went home. It was nagging at him who the woman reminded him of—she couldn't be more than thirty, surely? What he had seen of her face was lovely: the sweet flush of pink on her cheeks, the full mouth.

Lazlo chuckled to himself. He hadn't come here to find a woman, but maybe, actually, it wasn't a bad idea to get back out in the game. Nothing heavy, nothing that would require a commitment. But fun. Some fun.

That was a word he hadn't applied to himself in way, way too long.

TIGER LET Fizz off of his leash, casting a mock-stern glance at her dog. "What have I told you about jumping up, dude?"

Fizz, his mouth open in a wide doggy grin, panted at her, his eyes hopeful. Tiger rolled her eyes and dug a treat out for him from her pocket. "Not that you deserve it."

Fizz, satisfied, trotted away to his basket and flopped with a sigh into it. He was asleep even before Tiger had finished taking off her coat. Filling a kettle, Tiger set it to heat on the stove and found a clean mug, grabbing a tea bag from the little box. This was her little ritual. Walk the dog on the beach until the sun went down, a cup of herbal tea, a square of dark chocolate and a half hour of silence, sitting out on her deck, no matter how cold she got. Tiger preferred the fall, which it was now, when there were still warm days, but when the sun set, there was a bite to the air that she loved. It felt fresh, cleansing.

This whole island had been the best balm to her broken soul. The last two years, living here in virtual anonymity had been the relief she had needed after the trial of Grant Waller had dragged up the assault over and over in the press. Tiger had utterly bonded with Apollo's Nell after the woman had swept in like an avenging angel and taken care of both Tiger and her shocked, angry brother and kept them on an even keel.

Tiger had come to live with them for a few months, then when the furor had died down, she bought a place up here in the San Juan islands, far enough away that she didn't feel she was crowding her brother and his love, but close enough to travel to Seattle if they needed her. When her niece was born, Tiger fell in love straight away. Little Daisy was the light of her life, and she had found being with her made Tiger question more than anything if she really wanted to shut herself away or if there was something more.

And, she had to admit, she had been feeling the loneliness lately. Fizz helped; she'd rescued the dog from a local shelter a year ago and had never regretted it for a moment. Fizz was a bundle of fluffy love who was never but completely happy to see her and asked nothing but love—and food—in return. Fizz slept next to her in bed and woke her every morning with a gentle nudge of her muzzle and a tentative lick.

Tiger was also getting bored. She'd spent the last two years away from acting, catching up with all the other things she wanted to do in life, learning to play the piano, trying her hand at writing, blogging (under an assumed name, of course), and even taking a few evening classes in various topics. But during the day, she was slowly losing the need to be undercover. No one, so far as she knew, had recognized her. Her bobbed hair was long and wavy now and back to its natural color after years of being dyed and bleached and wrecked by different roles. She wore very little makeup, and because her screen persona had been very screen siren-esque and old film star-style, her natural look was so entirely different that she had started to relax around other people.

She had one coffee shop she was a regular at now, and the owner, a sweet woman around her same age, often stopped to chat with her. Tiger only knew her as Sarah, and she'd told Sarah her name was Tig. There was no hint of recognition in the other woman's eyes, and Tiger slowly became more comfortable with the other woman and thought she may have found a new friend. It was a nice thought.

THE NEXT MORNING, she took Fizz and walked to the small main street and into her coffee house. Sarah looked up from behind the bar and smiled. "Hey, hello. I was wondering if I'd see you today."

Tiger grinned. "I'm like clockwork. And besides, Fizz wants to see his auntie."

Sarah adored the small dog and came to fuss him now. "Listen, I was hoping I'd see you. Can you sit and talk for a little while?"

Tiger was surprised. "Of course."

"Tea's on the house." Sarah went to serve a customer, then brought two steaming cups of Earl Grey tea over to a table. Tiger thanked her.

Sarah smiled. "I have ulterior motives. Now, I'm going to have to overstep here, but I need to ask you something."

Tiger's heart sank but she nodded anyway. She liked Sarah, and she wouldn't lie if Sarah questioned her about her true identity.

Sarah drew in a nervous breath. "Now, not that I don't love seeing you every day, but I'm assuming since you're here when most other people are at work, you don't?"

Tiger grinned, relieved. "Not at the moment. I'm on a sabbatical that somehow stretched into a couple of years. Why do you ask?"

"Because, if you don't think I'm being out of line, I wondered if you needed a part-time job? It's just my barista Bella is off to college at Northwestern soon, and I thought I had a replacement lined up, but she called last night and told me she'd been headhunted by someone else." Sarah sighed, smiling shyly at Tiger. "You can say no, and I won't be at all offended. It's just, I like you, and I think we could have fun working together."

"I don't have any experience in barist...ing—is that the word?" Tiger laughed. "But I'd be happy to help, happy to learn."

Sarah's eyes opened wide. "Really?"

"Really. I had been thinking about what to do next, and I love this place." She looked down at Fizz, laying patiently at her feet. "Can I bring Fizz to work with me?"

"Of course!" Sarah looked close to tears, smiling widely. "God, I'm so happy, Tigs."

Tiger felt a wave of fondness for the other woman and her use of her old nickname. She clearly didn't realize who Tiger was. Who I used to be, Tiger thought now, nodding to herself. That was a million miles away, a million years. "I'm glad... hey, I'm excited about it. When do you want me to start?"

"Anytime in the next two weeks if that's at all possible. That's how long I still have Bella and between us, we can train you."

Tiger picked up her cup and clinked it against Sarah's. "Let's drink to it... boss."

Sarah laughed. "Ha. I like to think of it more as a partnership. Thank you, Tigs."

TIGER WAS STILL SMILING when she got home, and as she walked in, her cell phone rang. She saw it was Apollo calling her and she smiled. "Hey, bro, you called just at the right time. Guess who got a job?"

Apollo was silent for a beat too long, and suddenly Tiger sensed his tension. "What? What is it? Is it Daisy? Is it Nell?"

She heard her brother draw in a deep breath. "No, darling," he said gently. "No, we're all fine, don't worry. Tigs... it's Grant Waller."

"What about him?"

"Oh, Tigs... he's out of jail. They let him out early."

5
_____

CHAPTER FIVE – GLORY BOX

The Island, San Juan Islands, Washington State

TIGER WAS DETERMINED that the news of Grant Waller's release would not affect the new life she had been building here. Two days later, she reported for her first morning's work at the coffee house and was soon caught up with the training. Bella, the barista who was leaving for college, was as sweet as Sarah but also a hard taskmaster and so knowledgeable about her role that Tiger's head was spinning by the end of her first shift.

Sarah laughed as she came into relieve Tiger and saw her stunned expression. "Ah, you've been Bella-d."

"I never knew there was so much to learn. Or that there were so many different types of beans."

Sarah leaned in and stage-whispered, "Don't worry much about it. Bella's what we call a Bean-Geek."

"I can hear you," Bella complained coming out of the backroom, and Tiger and Sarah laughed. "Actually, Tigs did really well, great for a novice."

"Thanks, Bells." Tiger had enjoyed spending the morning with the teenager, was even touched when Bella had given her a badge shaped like a tiny chalkboard with 'Tigs' written on it in chalk. Little things in life. Three years ago, I was at the Oscars and now... God, I'd so much rather be here. "Listen, do you want me to hang out while you grab some lunch?"

Bella looked at Sarah who nodded, smiling. "Okay, thanks. Can I bring you both something? I'm going to the sandwich bar down the street."

She took their orders and disappeared out of the door. Sarah nudged Tiger with her shoulder. "So, you can be honest. You think you can do this?"

"I do, I really do. And Fizz is already whoring himself out to all of your customers." She nodded over to a table where a solitary man sat, fussing Fizz who was loving the attention.

Sarah laughed. "Good, maybe Fizz will bring in more customers."

"It's been pretty busy."

"It's a nice day, we always get more when the weather's nice. Tourists coming in from Seattle. Which reminds me, I never asked you... are you from Washington?"

Tiger nodded. "Seattle born and bred."

"What did you do before you came here?"

"Makeup artist," Tiger lied smoothly. She'd come up with a cover story that was believable from her time in the industry—after all she'd always been attentive in the makeup trailer and interested in the craft. "Sometimes I do guest blogs or articles for websites." Also, not an entire lie but close enough.

Sarah nodded. "I thought you might have been a model or something. You certainly have the looks."

Tiger hoped her face wasn't red. "Ha, thank you. So do you."

She wasn't lying about that. Sarah was gorgeous, all soft curves and dusky skin with long, dark brown dreadlocks that hung well past her waist. She'd told Tiger that her father was Creole from New Orleans and her mother had been of African-American descent. Sarah was thirty-six and had been married before, but her husband, Ben, had succumbed to cancer a few years ago, leaving Sarah alone.

Tiger had gotten to know her new boss even better over the past few days and had invited Sarah to come have supper with her when she was free.

After Bella returned, Tiger bid both her and Sarah goodbye and collected Fizz. She walked home, enjoying the fall afternoon. Fizz was busy sniffing various lampposts, collecting his 'pee-mail' as Tiger called it, but suddenly the dog's head came up, and he pulled Tiger along, dashing towards someone walking across the street.

"Well, hello, I recognize this little pooch."

It was the man from the beach a few days ago, and Tiger watched as he bent to fuss Fizz again. The dog was wagging his tail madly, and Tiger smiled, relaxing. Fizz was a good judge of character. The man stood and smiled at her, and Tiger felt a shock of recognition shoot through her.

"Hi," he said, holding out his hand to her, "Lazlo Schuler."

She shook his hand dumbly, waiting for the inevitable recognition to set in. Shit. Not now. Not after everything.

But Lazlo Schuler just smiled at her as she shook his hand and said. "Tig."

"Tig?"

"Just Tig."

"Okay then, Just Tig, and who's this?" He crouched down again and fussed the dog, stroking his silky ears.

"Fizz. I'm sorry, I don't mean to give you monotone answers."

Lazlo laughed and something inside Tiger's belly fluttered. Butterflies? Really? Not with this man, of all people. If he recognized her, he could expose her in a second.

"Are you new to the area?" She was damned if she was going to give herself away by acting weird. Nothing to do with the fact that he had really very kind and extremely sexy navy-blue eyes, that he was tall, very tall, and he had the kind of body she could imagine took many hours of working out to achieve.

Calm yourself, woman.

Lazlo shook his head. "Just arrived. Taking a sabbatical from my normal life from a while. I've heard it's restorative. Are you local?"

Tiger nodded, chewing on her lip. "I work part-time in the coffee house on Main Street."

"I know it. Very good coffee."

Tiger smiled. "Well, now that I'm working there, I'd try not to expect too much yet."

"Now, that sounds like a challenge." He looked around. "You live around here?"

She hesitated and he seemed to realize how that would have sounded. "Sorry, I don't mean to pry. It's just, I enjoy talking to you. I don't know anyone yet, and I was wondering if I could walk you home, if that's where you are headed."

Tiger hesitated. She knew of Lazlo's reputation as a nice guy, a gentleman, but by accepting his offer, he might wonder why she accepted so readily.

Luckily, Lazlo saved her. "Listen, forget that. Can I come into the coffee house and chat sometime? How about that? Is that safer?"

She smiled at him gratefully. "Thanks for understanding. I'd like that." What. Are. You. Doing? This man could blow everything...

...but God, his smile. "I work Thursdays and Monday mornings." She chewed her lip again. "And I walk the dog every evening on the beach."

Oh God, she really was going to do this, wasn't she?

Lazlo Schuler smiled. "Then I will definitely see you around... Tig."

"You will... Laz."

His grin widened, and their gazes met and held, and something undefinable passed between them.

Tiger said goodbye and she and Fizz walked back home. God, getting to know Lazlo Schuler was risky, way too risky, but there was something about him. She'd never forgotten his sorrow, that phone call to his friend that she'd overheard in the hospital the night she'd been attacked by Grant Waller. Lazlo's grief for his sister, India Blue, and the way he had been so open with his emotions... This wasn't a man whose masculinity was in doubt, and yet he could express his emotions so freely. There was something so appealing about that. She was still smiling when she got home.

LAZLO WALKED BACK to his rental, shaking his head. Well, that was unexpected. He'd known she looked familiar the first time they'd met briefly on the beach, but today he'd recognized her immediately.

Tiger Rose.

Holy hell. So, this is where she'd disappeared to. But Lazlo also recognized the fact she knew who he was and was scared he would expose her. He knew from India's nomadic existence when Braydon Carter was stalking her, the fear of being exposed, and his heart went out to Tiger Rose. She didn't want to be found, that was obvious.

But he was curious. So, he played dumb out of respect but still he couldn't help asking her if they could talk. And, he told himself, that it wasn't because Tiger Rose, without all the stardust surrounding Hollywood, was even more beautiful than he could ever have imagined.

He wanted to wrap that dark hair around his fist and draw her close, press his lips to that rosebud mouth. No woman had come close to having this effect on him for what seemed an age.

Bad idea. Bad, bad idea. If Tiger wanted to remain anonymous, she wouldn't want someone so close to her previous life near her with the ever-present risk of exposure. After all, she didn't know him. She didn't know he would never put her or her new life at risk.

But those eyes, that mouth... could he really be that unselfish and stay away?

No.

But he would do everything in his power to protect Tiger Rose. That much, he knew for sure.

6
_____

CHAPTER SIX – HOLD ME TIGHT

New York City

Grant Waller was angry. No, not just angry, enraged. He had worked at that damn paper for five years; they had supported him through the sexual assault trial, assured him his job would be safe when he was released from prison; and now, now, his editor had decided that he wasn't going to be able to rejoin his old news team. Well, fuck him, thought Grant, marching purposefully across the city, what does he know? Pol Flaherty's words came back to him.

"Grant, you're a good writer, but not a great writer, not an inspired writer. I need something different. Times have moved on since you were last on the job." Pol put up his hands, "I'm sorry, kiddo. It's no go."

Grant scowled to himself as he walked down Bleecker Street. He thought of the smug satisfaction on Flaherty's face as he fired Grant. Fucker, he thought, jumped-up little wanker. He stopped and took a deep breath. Pulling out his mobile phone, he tapped in his friend Doug's number. As he arranged to meet him, a seed of an idea came to him, and for the first time that day, Grant Waller smiled.

. . .

INDIA BLUE WOKE up late and rolled out of bed, still barely conscious. She and Massimo were in the city for an award show, and it had run pretty late, and they had been smashed by the time they came home, laughing and giggling. Couple that with some pretty major fucking in every room in the apartment late into the night and early morning, and India felt wrecked. Mostly, in a good way.

She brushed her teeth, cranking on the shower, then stripping off and stepping under the hot spray. She heard the TV turn on in the kitchen and assumed Massimo was already up and dressed. He always let her sleep late when she needed to but then made sure she knew she owed him a favor. India thought of that now and grinned.

They had been married for years now, but still every day he made her feel like a lovestruck teenager. After the years of terror and sadness, she was finally, truly happy.

Except for one thing. She still hadn't fallen pregnant. She saw the corner of the bathroom cabinet was open, saw the edge of the blue packages of pregnancy tests inside, and kicked the door shut with an annoyed foot. Stop fretting.

Massimo had told her that he was absolutely fine with not having kids, and for a couple of years it had been a relief. That was until her beloved Sun and Tae in Korea had decided to adopt a child together. Their little son, two-year-old Mika, was adorable, and the two men were absolutely in love with their child. When India and Massimo had visited Seoul in the summer, just seeing how Massimo was with the child, playing and tickling him, making him laugh, made her heart ache.

She hid the tears from him, of course, but Sun, her darling Sun, who never missed a change of mood, found her crying and hugged her. "It'll happen," he whispered as she sobbed quietly into his chest. "You were meant to be a mother, Indy."

When they'd come back from Seoul, India had asked Massimo if they could both go and get tested, and he had been supportive. "Piccolo, of course."

And the doctors at the fertility clinic found nothing wrong with either of them. "Even with the damage to your womb from the stabbing, it appears to be viable. Your periods are regular?"

She nodded. "Every twenty-eight days."

"Any painful symptoms, apart from the usual?"

She shook her head. "No."

"Then you should have no problem conceiving."

So why haven't I? She wanted to scream at him, at every doctor in the place, in the city, even at Massimo. It wasn't as if she and Massimo didn't have sex every day, sometimes multiple times. Their sex life had never been better. They even frequented an exclusive sex club now and again, enjoying the frisson of being caught, fucking openly and exploring each other's kinks.

India went into the kitchen and found Massimo reading the newspaper. She slid her arms around his waist. "Hey, hubs."

"Hey, wifes."

She kissed his shoulder, then pretended to bite down on it, making an animal noise. Massimo laughed. "Feeling freaky?"

"Always. Also, hungry and not just for your cock."

Massimo snorted. "Are you still drunk?"

"Possibly." India pulled open the fridge and studied the contents. "Is it appropriate to have fried chicken for breakfast?"

"I won't tell."

India pulled out the tray of chicken drumsticks and set a pan on the stove. "Protein. Have you eaten?"

"Oatmeal, but if you want some company... Anyway, it's close enough to lunch time."

India glanced at the clock. It was just past eleven a.m. "Man, I did sleep late."

Massimo wiggled his eyebrows at her. "Well, I was 'up' all night."

"What are you, twelve?" But she giggled at him. She started to fry the chicken. "So... seeing as we have some time off before we both have to work again... what shall we do? Vacation?"

"If you'd like." He narrowed his eyes at her then. "But if you mean going to visit Lazlo in Washington... no. Leave him alone."

India pouted. "I just worry."

"I know, but he only just got there. Let him settle in before we descend on him. You know wherever we go, a fleet of press goes with us. You were the one who told him to get away—so let him."

"Fine."

"Stop sulking."

"I'm not. Well, how about we go to Italy, see your mom, see Gracia and Kyu?" Gracia was Massimo's younger sister who lived with her boyfriend Kyu in Rome.

"They're all on a cruise in Greece. I thought you knew this?" Massimo frowned. "You've been doing that a lot lately."

"I've been doing a lot of what lately?" India was only half-listening, absorbed in preparing their meal. She tipped the chicken out onto a plate and burned her fingers in her hurry to eat it. "Ouch."

Massimo sighed and handed her a knife and fork. "Doofus. You've been forgetful."

"About what?" But she grinned to show she was kidding. "I have to admit, I have been a little unfocused lately. I was in the studio the other day and completely forgot I had already recorded an entire song. Jimmy looked at me like I was a loon."

"Well, that's a given," Massimo smiled. "Are you sure you've been feeling okay?"

India nodded. "Oh, yes, there's nothing wrong with me. I guess I just need to concentrate, but to be honest, my heart hasn't been in music for a while."

"That isn't like you."

India shrugged. "Mass... what else is there for me to do? I've had successful albums, and they were the ones I wanted to write and record. I've collaborated with almost all my favorite artists. I've sold out stadiums. God, I sound big-headed, but I've done everything I ever wanted to do."

"Except some collaborations. I know you've mentioned a few you always wanted to do. Pearl Jam, The 9th and Pine—Bay Tambe is always talking about working with you in her interviews."

India looked blank. "She is?"

Massimo frowned. "Yes, darling. Seriously, you forgot that? You hero-worship Bay... you're telling me you forgot she returns the love?"

"I guess... it slipped my mind." India looked away from his penetrating gaze. "Mass, I promise, I'm fine. Let's not worry about silly things like me forgetting something like that. It's not like Bay and me are besties, we've only met a few times."

Massimo nodded, but India could tell he was preoccupied and she sighed. "Babe, we've spent the last few years worrying about each other's health. Now is the time not to. I'm absolutely healthy; all the doctors we've been seeing would have picked up on anything wrong with the number of tests we been having." She smiled at him then went to kiss his cheek. "If you'd like, I can prove just how well I am..."

He finally smiled. "Well, if you can still walk after last night, I must be doing something wrong..."

"There was nothing wrong with you last night." She grabbed his hand and guided it under her robe and between her legs. "Get me good and wet, Verdi."

"Such a dirty girl," he sighed, but he kissed her, his fingers stroking her clit, then sliding into her, stroking her, feeling her getting damp for him.

India sighed happily and leaned against him, cupping his cock through his trousers. "I'll never get tired of this."

Massimo gave an animal growl of desire and suddenly swept her into his arms and into the bedroom. India giggled as he pulled at the belt of her robe with his teeth, then, when he pushed the fabric aside, she gave a little gasp as his mouth found her nipple, and he began to tease the nub, his tongue flicking around it as it hardened.

"Oh, Massi... my life began when I found you."

He lifted his head and grinned at her, his startlingly green eyes twinkling at her. "Hush, woman, I'm giving you my best moves."

She laughed and soon they were making love, India clamping her legs around his back as he thrust deeper and harder into her with every stroke. She clawed at the hard muscles of his back, urging him on, kissing with a feral-like intensity as if she wanted to devour him.

No, she would never get tired of this, of him, of them... if they never had children, it was okay. They had each other, and for India, that would always be enough.

"So, you want me to do what? Find Tiger Rose?" Doug rolled his eyes at his old friend. He's known Grant for years, always had his back, but he knew trouble when he saw it. "Man, you've just done time for that bitch. You wanna to go back to jail that bad?"

"I'm not going to do anything to her, jackass, don't be crazy. I just want to know where she's hidden herself away. Then maybe I can ghost write a piece on her. Get myself some work."

"But why her, of all people? She's a poisoned well, Grant. For you, especially. Pick someone else. Everyone knows that when Tiger Rose announced her retirement, she meant it. She doesn't want to be found. Leave her alone."

Grant's too-light grey eyes were dangerous as he looked at his friend. "No. Look... that bitch put me away. For two long years, Doug."

Doug downed the rest of his beer. "You attacked her, Grant. I don't blame her. If anyone deserves revenge, dude, it isn't you. You did that to my sister? I'd put you in the ground."

Grant stared at him for a long moment in silence, then a hint of a smile flicked the corner of his mouth. "How is your sister, Doug?"

Doug put his glass down and stared back at his friend. The two men glowered at each other, then Grant grinned and held up his hands. "I'm yanking your chain, buddy."

Doug looked away before giving him a weak smile, and Grant knew his friend had caught the implied threat. "So, what?"

"So, I just need to find where she went. Who she is with, if anybody. An address is all I need. Then your job is done. I'll pay you, of course."

"With what?"

Grant just smiled, and Doug paled. "Fine. I'll get back to you."

He got up and left quickly and Grant chuckled to himself. He liked Doug, but if he had one weakness, it was his younger sister: a delicate creature called Janey. Janey had a king-size crush on Grant, had since she was a teenager, and she would be his with just a snap of his fingers. Grant was pretty sure she was still a virgin, and he wasn't at all interested in her. She was way too pale and quiet for him. But he would happily deflower her and break her heart if Doug let him down.

Now that he was alone, he eyed up the women in the bar. Not many caught his eye, but then he had particularly tastes. Ah, who was he kidding? He only wanted one woman, the woman who he'd spent his nights in jail thinking about. The woman he both lusted after and hated.

Tiger Rose.

She haunted his dreams. He'd kept up with what had happened to her after his trial, how she'd won an Oscar, but soon after had announced she was done with public life. The press had hounded her through a few false starts as she tried to start a new life somewhere, but eventually they'd moved onto another celebrity, and Tiger Rose was free.

And somewhere...

He knew she had family somewhere in the States, and he couldn't imagine that she would leave them alone. A brother. Some dumb name. Their parents had certainly been hippies, calling their daughter Tiger and their son... Jesus, what was it? Some Greek God name...

Who cared? It would make him easier to find and Tiger easy to get to. Then he would expose her new life, make it impossible for her to settle down and be happy. He, Grant Waller, would make her life a misery.

Grant might have gone home alone that night, but he went home smiling.

CHAPTER SEVEN – HOLD YOU IN MY ARMS

THE ISLAND, *San Juan Islands, Washington State*

TIGER WAS both disappointed and relieved when Lazlo Schuler didn't show up at the coffee house the next time she was working. A pit of tension had been lodged in her chest, but by the time Bella came in to relieve her, she felt a tug of sadness. Maybe she had put him off.

"You okay?" Bella smiled at her, and not for the first time, Tiger realized she would really miss the younger woman when she left the following week. She instinctively hugged Bella now, who looked surprised. Tiger wasn't the most effusive, physical person, but she felt she wanted the other woman to know she was a friend.

"I am, thank you, Bella. For everything. Promise me you'll keep in touch when you go, won't you? I feel I've found a real friend in you, and in Sarah. That's not... that's not something I'm used to."

Bella raised her eyebrows. "That surprises me."

"It does?"

"Yup. You're a sweetheart."

Tiger laughed. "Ha, not all the time."

"Who is? But you have a warm heart, Tigs. I can also tell you don't think too well of yourself and it intrigues me."

Tiger smiled a little awkwardly. "Are you studying psych?"

Bella grinned. "Yes, actually, but this was just an observation." She seemed to hesitate. "Tigs..." She glanced around the coffee house, then beckoned her closer. "Tigs... I know."

"You know? What?"

Bella smiled kindly. "Tiger."

A wave of hot embarrassment and fear washed over her. "God."

"Don't worry, I haven't said a word to a soul and I won't. I get it. There was a movie on Netflix the other night, and I just happened to look up at the right moment. I think it was one of your first—Dark Angel?"

Tiger nodded. "A bit part at the most, and you spotted me from that?"

"Like I said, I looked up at the right moment, and it was just a very slight motion you made, a gesture." She swept her hand up, drifted it across her throat slowly then tucked a lock of hair behind her ear. "You do that a lot. It's like you're thinking, then making a decision."

Tiger didn't know what to say and Bella laughed. "Sorry, I'm fascinated with people's singularities, their gestures, the mannerisms."

"You will be great at psych," Tiger said finally, laughing softly. She smiled at Bella. "Thank you for not telling. I just want a new life."

"From Oscars to serving coffee?" Bella shook her head. "How does that feel?"

"You want to know the truth? It feels like I'm finally free."

THERE WAS a kind of relief to think that someone knew, that with Bella she could be herself, could relax and not have to be on guard. During Bella's last week at the coffee house, the two of them became closer and Tiger wondered, when Bella had gone, if she should confide in Sarah. Sarah was the sweetest person she had ever met, and Tiger trusted her implicitly. She would like to have someone, at least here in her new home town, who she could be completely herself with.

But then something happened that made her question whether she ought to. Two women, one dark, one blonde, came into the coffee house chatting easily, and Sarah had gone very quiet after they'd been served, thanking them politely.

Sarah tugged Tiger into the back. "Oh my God," she whispered, "do you know who that is?"

"Who?"

"Them!" Sarah motioned unsubtly to the table where the two women were talking and laughing. "That's Bay Tambe and Kim Clayton."

The names sounded familiar. "That's..."

"The singer and the guitarist from the 9th and Pine." Sarah's face was red, completely starstruck. "I know they live around here, but I never expected... I cannot wait to tell Bella." She gave a muted squeal and Tiger knew, as much as she loved her friend, she could never tell her who she was. Sarah couldn't keep a secret to save her life.

Tiger was amused but dismayed. Damn.

They had a small party for Bella's leaving, and although she was flattered to be asked, Tiger made herself useful by providing food and drink and making sure everyone was tended to. Eventually Sarah pulled her into a seat. "Tigs, you've done enough. Work's over, relax."

She hooked an arm around Tiger's shoulders and Tiger had to laugh. Sarah was a little tipsy it seemed. "Now, Tigs..." Sarah nodded over to the corner of the coffee house where Bella was talking to her friends. "Bella's really leaving us, the ratfink, so it's just you and me now. Are you sure you want to do this?"

Tiger touched her wine glass to Sarah's. "One hundred percent. Thank you for the opportunity, Sarah, I mean it. It's been a lifeline."

"Aww." Sarah hiccupped and Tiger laughed.

"I think I'd better walk you home, Sarah."

. . .

AFTER DELIVERING Sarah safely to her own home, Tiger walked through the quiet streets. She reveled in the silence; only the faint wash of the water and the ferries drifting in and out of the harbor broke it. She breathed in the fresh air, only stopping when Fizz needed to pee or to sniff a passing post. This really was a haven, she thought, looking around. There was no one else on the street, a few blocks from her home, but then again, it was after ten.

A movement in one of the house's windows caught her eye, and she saw Lazlo Schuler in his living room, walking around, his phone to his ear. He was laughing, his handsome face lit up by his smile, and Tiger felt another jolt to her soul. God, he was drop-dead gorgeous, wasn't he? She couldn't tear her eyes away from him, then she gasped as, suddenly, he saw her.

Lazlo raised his hand to her, and Tiger could think of nothing else to do but return the gesture. She saw his talk into the phone, then put it down and walk away from the window. As she saw his shadow loom near his front door, she had to make a decision right there and then.

Stay or run.

"Hey, there... Tigs."

She was caught, there was nothing more to be done than greet him. "Hey, Lazlo. I'm sorry, I promise I wasn't spying."

Lazlo was coming closer, and she caught a trace of his clean, spicy cologne which sent her senses reeling. "It's okay. Lighted windows on a dark night always make one wonder what's going on behind closed doors." He smiled down at her, and Tiger couldn't keep her eyes from dropping to his mouth, wondering what it would be like to feel them against her lips, her skin, her body.

Lazlo's eyes were on hers as she looked up, and she could feel her face flushing red. "Hey," he said gently, then looked down as Fizz jumped up at him, breaking the tension. Lazlo laughed and crouched down to fuss the dog and Tiger breathed again. Damn. No man had ever had this effect on her, even the multiple actors and directors who'd declared their attraction to her over the years. Lazlo Schuler was all man, his masculinity obvious in the way he carried himself, and yet there was something gentle about him.

He looked up at her now. "Would you like to come in for a drink?"

Say no. Say no right now and leave. "I'd like that." I'd also like your cock inside me. Stop it! Tiger argued with herself in her head as she followed him into his home.

The house was furnished sparsely but it suited him. On the table was a stack of books, three old coffee cups, and a notebook. Lazlo gathered up the coffee cups with a sheepish smile. "Sorry, Have a seat. I have some beer or scotch or..."

"Beer's fine."

He brought two bottles and a glass for her, but she drank out of the bottle as he did. "So... how was your day?"

"Good." She chuckled a little. "I'm sorry. I feel awkward at having spied on you."

"Spy away, I have no secrets."

Tiger tensed a little but then relaxed. If he knew who she was, he either didn't care or knew she wouldn't want him to reveal it. "Anyway, I'm sorry. But I'm not sorry to see you again."

Lazlo smiled at that. "Me neither. Look... I'm out of practice at this whole thing, but I still know what it's like to want to get to know someone better."

"I know the feeling." God, she wanted to kiss him, even just to touch the smooth skin of his face. He seemed to sense she didn't want to talk and instead he gently took her beer from her and set both bottles down on the table.

Tiger was astonished she didn't feel any nervousness as he took her in his arms and pressed his lips to hers. His kiss was gently and far too short for her liking, but as he drew away, she saw the question in his eyes.

"Yes," she said in a whisper, "yes, Lazlo. Yes..."

He kissed her again, this time with more pressure, with his tongue seeking hers, and it was as sweet as she dreamed it had been. Tiger's hands moved of their own volition, sliding into his short-cropped hair, tugging slightly on it as his arms tightened around her.

The kiss seemed to go on forever, but finally, desperate for oxygen, they had to break apart. Tiger laughed as they both panted. "Wow... wow."

"Seconded." Lazlo grinned at her. "I've been wanting to do that since we met."

Tiger nodded. "Me, too..." She drew in a deep breath. "God... Lazlo..."

"Tiger."

She had known, somewhere deep inside, that he knew, so when he said her name, it wasn't a surprise or a shock. She looked up into his dark navy eyes and nodded. "Thank you, Lazlo. For not... you know."

"You came here to start again," he said softly."

"I did." She studied him. "Why did you come here, Lazlo?"

He chuckled. "To get away, to take a break. And I'm glad I did." He leaned in and kissed her again. "Sorry, but I needed another."

Tiger laughed and sat back on the sofa, feeling relaxed in his company. "I don't mind... but I do want to say, God, this is... I can't stay tonight, if you understand me?"

"I do, and there's no pressure to do anything you don't want to." He sat back with her. "In our old lives, our old industry, we know how the game works. I'm very open for doing things the traditional way this time."

"Our old lives? I thought you were just on sabbatical."

Lazlo laughed. "I don't know. I've been here for a few weeks now, and I'm rethinking a lot of things. I honestly didn't realize..." He stopped, shaking his head. "Ha, this is strange. I haven't had someone to talk to for a while."

"Not India?"

"There things I can't talk about with Indy. Can't or won't. She's been through enough."

Tiger smiled. "I get it." She hesitated then smiled at him. "I have a confession. The day I was assaulted, I had to spend the night at the hospital. It was the same hospital where India was."

Lazlo nodded. "I know. Your security team head came to see me to coordinate. I thought that was very considerate."

"I hope we were no bother,"

"Not at all. I'm so sorry about what happened to you, Tiger. I could have killed Waller for that."

Tiger sighed. "Believe me, there's a queue. I found out a few days ago he was released."

"God damn it." Lazlo stroked his hand into her hair, and she leaned against it. There was something so familiar, so comforting about him as if, because their worlds had overlapped, that they had already known each other for years.

"Laz, I have a confession. The night I was brought in to the hospital, I had to get some space and I went to hide in one of the stairwells. I thought I was alone, but then I heard you, talking to someone called Jess. I didn't want us to be friends and have you not know that. I wasn't snooping, I swear. You sounded..." She sighed. "Like I felt. Broken."

"I was," Lazlo nodded slowly, but she could see there was embarrassment, too. So, he wasn't completely confident. That was comforting. "But it wasn't the time for me to be unravelling. Jess, my friend, she talked me down, thank God."

"Is she... I mean I don't want to get in the middle of anything..." Tiger found herself more unsure of herself than she had been in years, but there was something about this man.

Lazlo grinned. "Nope, Jess and I never were lovers. She's married to Teddy Hood now."

"Oh, she's that Jess." Tiger grinned then. "I know she went through some crap, but I will be forever grateful to her for handing Dorcas Prettyman what she deserved. Vile, vile woman."

Lazlo nodded, but his smile faded a little, and Tiger remembered that Jess had been seriously injured by a man sent by Dorcas. "God, Lazlo, I'm sorry, that was so insensitive. Is Jess okay now?"

He nodded, but she sensed a change in atmosphere and cussed herself. "Listen, Lazlo... what you went through with India, with

Jess... the losses you've endured... I'm not surprised you're seeking some sort of peace. I know the feeling."

Lazlo reached out and stroked a finger down his cheek. "You know what I want? Fun. Silliness. I had to grow up quickly when I was young, and there's a whole lot of things I never got to do. Hang out with friends, spend days just reading." He nodded at Fizz who was curled up on Lazlo's feet asleep. "Getting a dog and going hiking. There have been vacations, of course, but I always, always take my laptop with me and work. It drives India mad."

Tiger smiled at him. "Well, then... what better time than now to redress the balance?"

"Wanna help me out with that?"

She laughed. "You've got a deal. I have to warn you though... hiking is my jam, and most people that come with me on a trail... they don't make it back. I'm hardcore, man."

Lazlo laughed loudly. "That sounds like a challenge." He nodded and smiled. "The real challenge will be keeping my hands to myself."

"Anticipation, remember? We're going old skool..." She trailed off, sniggering slightly. "But that doesn't mean you can't get to first base at least."

Lazlo grinned wickedly and leaned over to kiss her again, sliding his hand onto her stomach, stroking her through her blouse. Tiger wriggled with pleasure, getting closer to him, trailing her hand up his thigh but stopping before she reached his groin. Lazlo sulked when she removed her hand, and she laughed. "First base, remember? Now... I'd better go home before we break all the rules."

He offered to walk her home, and this time she agreed. "Not that I couldn't look after myself," she said with meaning, and Lazlo nodded.

"Oh, I know. I just need to know where you live, so I can arrange to be outside by accident, like you did earlier." He winked.

Tiger laughed and swiped at him. "That was an accident."

"Sure," said Lazlo, teasing her, and making air quotes, "an 'accident.'"

Tiger was grinning widely. "Doofus."

"Stalker."

"Ha ha, you wish, Schuler."

Lazlo chuckled and took her hand. "Come on, Tiger Rose. Let's take a stroll."

It felt good to hold a man's hand, to hold his hand, and when they reached her house, he made no attempt to invite himself in. He just kissed her gently and said, "Goodnight, Tiger Rose."

"Goodnight, Lazlo Schuler."

Tiger went inside and saw that he waited until she waved to turn away and walk back to his home. Fizz watched him go, too, and Tiger was touched that her dog seemed to be as enamored of Lazlo as she was. When Lazlo had disappeared from view, she smiled to herself and bent to fuss Fizz. "Come on. Bedtime."

And when Tiger went to sleep that night, she wished that Lazlo's arms were wrapped around her and his lips were against hers.

CHAPTER EIGHT – INTO YOU

New York City

Doug came through for Grant the following week. "The brother is in Seattle. He's got a kid now, and he's getting married soon."

Grant smiled. "And what big sister would miss her beloved brother's wedding? That's good work, Dougie, thank you."

Doug looked uncomfortable. "Like I said before, Grant, I really think you should leave this girl alone. She obviously doesn't want to be found. I could find no address for a Tiger Rose anywhere in the States. I'm assuming that's her real name which says to me she's changed it and doesn't want to be found. She could have even had surgery."

Grant snorted. "You can't hide that kind of beauty."

"With surgery you can hide anything. She could have cut her hair, dyed it, wear contacts, and that might be enough. If she's in a small town, they won't expect a movie star to come rolling in. She could be anywhere."

"But she'll be in Seattle when the brother gets married. Did you get a date?"

Doug shook his head. "The kid is young though. Can't imagine Tiger will want to miss out on the kid's cute years."

"No. Which means she's probably not a million miles away." Grant chewed this over for a few minutes. "Well... if you have the brother's address, that's a start."

Doug handed over his notes, and Grant handed him a wad of money. "Thanks for this."

Doug got up to go, then turned back. "Grant? If you do anything to harm Tiger Rose..."

"Say hello to your sister for me, would you?" Grant interrupted him, his smile not reaching his ice-cold eyes. "Tell her I hope she's doing well."

Doug said nothing more but left. Grant smirked. He loved yanking people's chains, but the threat of Doug's words meant he had to reassert himself. He looked down at the address on the paper.

Apollo Rose and Nell Lewis, Apt 1448...

Maybe it was time he paid Washington State his first visit.

~

SEATTLE

TIGER LIFTED Daisy into her arms and swung her around, making the two-year-old giggle and scream with joy. "Daisy, Daisy boo," her aunt cooed, making Apollo and Nell laugh.

"Honestly, you are a mushy mess," Apollo shook his head at his sister, "What's gotten into you?"

"What do you mean? I always play with Daisy Boo like this."

"Yes," Nell agreed, "but you have shining eyes and your cheeks are pink. You've met someone."

Tiger chuckled and hid her smile in Daisy's hair. The girl wriggled in her arms.

"Auntie Tiger, can we get some candy?"

Tiger was about to thank Daisy for changing the subject, but Nell took her daughter away from her. "In a minute, Daisy. First, Auntie Tiger has a question to answer."

Both Nell and Apollo fixed her with amused glares. Tiger sighed and held up her hands. "Fine. Yes. There's someone, but it's very new. Very, very new as in it only really started last night."

"Who is he?"

Tiger smiled to herself. This would shock her brother. "Lazlo Schuler."

"Lazlo Schuler? The Lazlo Schuler?" Apollo gaped at her. "What? How?"

"Believe it or not, he rented a house on the island. He recognized me when we first ran into each other, but he kept it to himself."

Apollo was still looking stunned. "Well, good on him... but what are the chances he'd pick the same island? Is he on vacation?"

"Sabbatical. Apparently, India Blue ordered him to take some personal time." Tiger chuckled at the thought of it. She'd met India a few times and liked her immensely but she could imagine her ordering her brother around. "Anyway, we're going to be hanging out when I'm not working—"

"Wait, working?"

Tiger grinned. "I work part-time in a coffee house on Main Street."

Her brother and almost-sister-in-law gaped at her, then looked at each other. Tiger chuckled. "I know. But you know what? I'm happy."

"Then that's all that matters."

Tiger smiled at her brother. "Thank you. I know it might seem... I don't know, I just like the simple life these days."

Later, as she ate with her family in their apartment in the city, Nell asked her the question she had been waiting for. "So, you don't miss it? Acting? The publicity?"

"I definitely don't miss the publicity or the endless press or not being able to eat what I want. Actually, I always ate what I wanted, but I like not having to think about it or justify it now." She laughed, then her smile faltered. "And I don't miss the creeps. Pol, Nell, I never told you this, but Grant Waller was merely the tip of the iceberg. The amount of times I was asked for sex in exchange for roles, or it was implied I had to be 'grateful' for what my own hard work got me."

Apollo nodded. "You never said, but I assumed. With everything that's come out about #metoo..."

"It's rife, it's endemic, and God, I am so glad I'm far, far away from it all."

Nell patted Tiger's arm sympathetically. "I know, sweetie, but do you miss the acting part?"

Tiger considered. "The craft? Yes. Yes, I do. Diving into another personality, a character, and disappearing? Yeah, I miss that part. But I made my decision and I'm finally finding peace. That's worth the sacrifice."

~

THE ISLAND, San Juan Islands, Washington State

SHE TOLD Lazlo what she had said the following day. It was their first official date, and they were hiking up Young Hill on the north end of the island. Tiger had promised Lazlo incredible views, and as they walked, Fizz scampering happily in front of them, sniffing everything he could find, they chatted easily.

Chatted and flirted. Tiger was glad that none of the red-hot attraction had dissipated between them because they had pressed pause on getting intimate. In fact, every time their hands brushed or their shoulders nudged, Tiger felt a rush of pure desire shoot through her entire body. When Lazlo turned to talk to her, his eyes would drop to her mouth as she spoke, his tongue licking his bottom lip slowly, mesmerizing her until she forgot what she wanted to say. Tiger was sure her face was red, because it felt like it was on fire every time he looked at her.

And despite her warnings that she really liked to hike, he was a lot more athletic than she was, and he grinned as she lagged behind as they reached the summit of the hill. "What was that you were saying about being hardcore?"

He ducked away as she swiped at him, grinning. "I have cramps, jackass. I have an excuse." She panted and bent double, and he rubbed her back.

"You should have said so, I would never have dragged you along..."

"...dragged?"

Lazlo grinned. "Hey, look, I'm being all New Man about your menstrual cycle. Don't I get credit for that?"

"Hipster."

He laughed. "So, I don't get credit. Okeydokey."

Tiger stood up and giggled. She stood on her tiptoes and kissed him on the mouth, brief and sweet. "You do get credit."

He slid his arms around her waist and held her close. "I can make you feel better."

"You already do." Tiger nuzzled her nose to his and laughed, shaking her head in wonder. "Why is this so natural? I swear, Laz, it's like I've known you forever."

"I know what you mean." Lazlo took her hand. "Come on, doofus, let's go find someplace to sit and have some water."

They found a place to sit where they could look over the view. Lazlo settled Tiger between his legs and she settled back against his chest. Lazlo kissed her temple. "Do you want some Tylenol?"

Tiger shook her head. "Nah. Fresh air and hugs work, too."

"They do?" He tightened his arms around her and she turned her head for a kiss.

"From you, yes."

There was a pause, then they both laughed. "Are we revoltingly mushy?"

"We might be. I don't care, though, do you?"

Tiger smiled. "Nope. I'm enjoying this old-fashioned, not too kool-for-skool thing we have going on. You know what I'd like to do?"

"Does it involve us being naked?"

"Well, yes, but also...you're such a pervert."

Lazlo threw his head back and laughed. "No, seriously, what?"

"I love Seattle, but I've never done the tourist thing there. Like the underground tour or even going to the top of the Needle. Nothing."

Lazlo half-smiled at her. "And you want to?"

Tiger flushed a little. "I thought it would be a cute—and chaste— date. Is it lame? I want to do things that people wouldn't expect a movie star—or ex-movie-star—to do. Hang out, eat crappy food, laugh at silly things. Everyday stuff, you know? Nothing polished or scheduled to the nth degree."

"I get it."

"So?"

He pressed his lips to hers. "No schedule. That sounds like heaven to me. I can't think of a day in the last ten years when my day wasn't regulated. At least before I came here."

"And met me."

"And met you." He stroked a hand gently down her hair. "Let's do this."

THEY HIKED BACK down the hill and back at Tiger's little home, they ordered pizza and argued good-naturedly over what movie to watch on Netflix. It was so easy being with Tiger, Lazlo wondered to himself, that he wondered why he had held out for so long on finding someone.

But then he was a fatalist—he truly believed he had meant to come here, meant to meet her, just her. That she'd witnessed from afar his pain over what had happened to India just made him feel a connection to her. They'd both been having one of the worst days of their lives. He just wished she'd made herself known—maybe he could have comforted her, too.

Having won the argument over the movie they selected, Tiger fell asleep in his arms halfway through, and he quietly flicked off the television and just held her. When she stirred an hour later, she smiled up at him sleepily. "Sorry."

"It's no problem."

Tiger sat up and stretched, before looking at him from under her lashes. "You know, it's late."

"I should go."

Tiger put her hand on his leg. "That's not what I meant. I mean, I know we're... waiting. And even if we weren't, my menstrual cycle is acting like some sort of medieval chastity belt, but..." She bit her lip. "If you want to stay, you could."

Lazlo half-smiled. "Tiger... if I shared a bed with you... I'm still a man. It would be exquisite torture."

"Are you a masochist?" Tiger brushed her lips lightly against his, grinning wickedly. Lazlo slid his hand into her hair.

"In this, as in all things, context is key." He kissed her, being a little rougher than he would normally, answering her question. He saw the fire ignite in her eyes. "Oh, you like the idea?"

She nodded, then drew away. "But like you said... anticipation."

He groaned feeling his cock press painfully against her jeans. "You are a sadist."

Tiger laughed and got up, pulling him to his feet. "How about I promise you, when things get... more intimate between us, that I'll let you switch the roles. And by switch, I mean..." She mimicked cracking a crap against his butt, and Lazlo grinned.

"I will keep you to that promise."

They walked to her front door, and she kissed him goodnight. "I'll be thinking of you... when I'm naked and in bed."

"Devil woman."

Tiger smiled and Lazlo felt his heart beat hard against his ribs. She was beyond beautiful, and it was such a hard thing to leave her, but they had agreed. "Goodnight, gorgeous."

"'Night, handsome."

~

LOS ANGELES

. . .

As IT TURNED OUT, Grant didn't immediately travel to Seattle. He had rent to pay after all, and when a producer in Los Angeles called and requested Grant come out to see him, all expenses paid, Grant had to accept.

Dex Loomis was a high-level producer at one of the biggest studios, and as Grant was shown into his office, he stood and shook Grant's hand. "Mr. Waller, thank you for coming."

"You're welcome, although I'm at a loss at what I can do for you. You need a journalist?"

"You're a writer, yes, but that's not why I called you." Dex looked at his assistant. "Thanks, Mike, can you give us the room?"

The assistant melted away and the two men were alone. Dex smiled at Grant, but the warmth did not extend to his eyes. Dex was tall, florid, and pudgy, not older than forty, but with a pallid, sickly complexion that made him look like he spent all day, every day inside. His muddy brown eyes searched Grant's face in a way that made Grant feel uneasy.

"So, Grant Waller. How was prison?"

Grant sighed. "Exactly how you'd think it was."

"She really did a number on you, huh? Tiger?"

Grant said nothing—what could he say? He'd attacked her, she's gone to the police, he'd gone to jail. The story was well known. "Mr. Loomis, if I could ask—"

"I bet you want revenge, huh? A little payback?"

"What if I do?"

Loomis smiled. "I'm in a position to help you out with that."

Grant sat up. "What?"

"I'm saying to you that I can help you deal with her."

Grant's eyes narrowed. "Forgive me, Mr. Loomis, but why the hell would you want to help me take revenge on Tiger Rose?"

"Because you're not the first man she's set up with her innocent Little Miss act."

Ah. Grant hid a smile. So, Tiger had turned this dude down, too. He sighed. He'd hoped he was coming here for a real job, a shot back into the industry. "I honestly don't know what you're asking of me."

Loomis opened a drawer of his desk and took out a check. He slid it across to Grant. It was made out to cash and was for such an eye-popping amount that Grant frowned. What the hell?

Loomis was watching his reaction. "Grant—I can call you Grant, right? Good. Grant, Tiger Rose has gone to ground, and I want you to find her."

"She has a younger brother in Seattle."

"That much I knew, thanks. This money is for you to go there, stay until she shows up, then I want you to—"

"What? What do you want me to do, Mr. Loomis?"

"Dex." Loomis smiled that queasy smile again. "I want you to make Tiger Rose's life is hell. She retired for peace, for happiness. I want you to make sure she never finds it. Do you understand me?"

Grant was smiling now. "Dex, I'm already there. Before you called, I was planning to go to Seattle anyway."

"Well, my money will make things easier. You'll have an apartment rented for you and access to any surveillance equipment you need. I want you to drive Tiger Rose out of her mind, and I don't care what you need to do to achieve that end."

Grant nodded slowly, then met Dex's gaze. "And in the end? What do you want to achieve, Mr. Loomis?"

The two men stared at each other, then a smile crept across Loomis' face. "I think we both know, don't we, Grant? This studio owns the rights to many of Tiger's movies. Imagine how good tragedy could be for business."

"What did she do to you, Dex?"

Dex's eyes were cold. "That's not your concern. Just get it done. But make her suffer first, and by that, I mean, in the worst ways possible."

Grant shook Loomis' hand. "You can count on it."

IN AN HOUR, he was on a plane to Seattle.

CHAPTER NINE – HEAVENLY DAY

NEW YORK

INDIA SPOKE QUIETLY to the maître d' of the restaurant, but then she saw Bay wave at her from a table and she thanked the man, hurrying over to her lunch date. She'd only met Bay a few times, but the other woman still gathered her into a hug and India smiled. Bay Tambe was one of the biggest music stars on the planet, but she had always remained as humble and sweet as she had when she'd been discovered. Her dark hair and eyes twinkled at India now. "You're looking well, Indy."

"I am, I'm good."

They chatted as they studied the menus and after they'd ordered, India noticed Bay seemed a little nervous. "What's up?"

Bay grinned a little shyly. "Well, I come with an ulterior motive, Indy, not that it isn't always good to see you. But I have a proposition."

"Let's hear it."

"A joint tour. A world tour. You and the 9th and Pine. We alternate headlining and also collaborate. Heck, I'd love it if we did the whole gig together. But it's been something I've been kicking around for a while, and I spoke with Kym and Pete and they agree. We're all, for want of a better word, bored. That sounds incredibly ungrateful, but what I mean is, we want to mix it up a little. Do something different and I have always wanted to work with you." She smiled sweetly and laughed softly. "I'm rambling."

"No, it's okay." India was thinking now. It certainly sounded appealing and hadn't she been saying the same thing to Massimo about losing her passion for her craft? Working with Bay and the rest of the band would surely be the thing she needed. And Massimo had movies lined up for the next year. It would mean spending time away from him, and the thought of that made her feel sick, but she was a grown up. She smiled at Bay now. "Bay, that's an incredible offer, but I'll have to talk to Massimo about it. I'd certainly like to work with you."

Bay looked pleased. "We could even record an album together. I bet we'd have fun writing together."

INDIA WENT HOME to the apartment in Manhattan they had bought. Their true home was upstate, a gorgeous home on the banks of the Hudson, but they had also invested in a palatial apartment where they and their family and friends made use of the easy access to the city.

Massimo was being interviewed by Vogue in the living room, and India crept silently to their bedroom, not wanting to get caught by the journalist. She changed out of her dress into a comfortable sweatshirt and loose pants and sat on their bed cross-legged, opening up her laptop.

She smiled when she saw she had an email from Lazlo.

HEY SIS, just wanted to let you know that I'm going to be staying here for a while longer. I kinda met a girl...

...but I'm not ready to talk about her yet, so forgive me. Coming here was your idea, so I have you to thank. I really needed this.

Having said that, you know where I am if you need me. Give my love to Massi and don't forget Jess and Teddy are coming to New York next week.

I love you,

Laz

INDIA SMILED. He's met someone... at long last. She had a million questions, but she knew to respect Lazlo's privacy. God knows he'd done it enough for her over the years.

She flicked to her schedule for the next few months. Nothing planned. Her last album had been a couple of years ago, and she knew her fans were expecting something new, but the truth was she had been suffering from writer's block for a while. Writer's block and forgetfulness. Not a good combination.

She heard Massimo's voice as he bid the journalist and photographer goodbye, and she got up to call him. "I'm home, baby, in the bedroom."

She heard his low chuckle. "Always what I want to hear."

India grinned as Massimo came into view, sauntering confidently towards her, exaggerating his moves until he got near her and picked her up.

India giggled as he dumped her on the bed and immediately covered her body with his. "Hey cutie."

India ran her hands over his face and into his hair. "Hey, gorgeous. Finished flirting with the journo?"

"I think he was into me, but I still prefer you," Massimo grinned down at her, his hand slipping under her sweatshirt, stroking her belly. India wriggled with pleasure and kissed him.

"Want to?"

Massimo grinned. "Now you know the answer to that is always going to be yes."

"Even when I'm old and saggy?"

"...when? Ah, ah, okay! I'm sorry, I didn't mean, ouch, ouch..." Massimo laughed as she attacked him, rolling him onto his back and straddling him as she pretended to punch him out. He gripped her hips. "These sweatpants haven't got easy access," he grumbled, and grinning, India rolled off of him and stood up, stripping quickly. Massimo watched her as she tugged her clothes off, kicking out of his own.

India straddled him, cupping his half-erect cock in her hands and stroking the length of it. Massimo gazed up at her as she touched him, his own hand snaking between her legs and his fingers beginning to caress her clit.

India gave Massimo a slow, sexy smile as she rubbed the tip of his cock up and down her slit, making him feel how wet she was getting for him. His free hand swept over her belly, gentle, loving, wondering at the softness of her skin.

India guided him inside of her and they began to move together, rocking and sighing with pleasure as they made love. India impaled herself harder onto him with each thrust of her hips, her head flung back, her dark hair streaming down her back, her full breasts moving with her.

Massimo never, ever got tired of looking at his beautiful wife. Even after all this time, she was the most glorious woman he had ever seen, and now she was completely healthy, her skin glowed, and her body was curvy and lush. Even the scars from the stabbings she'd suffered were fading.

India came, shivering and trembling, gasping his name and as he too reached his peak; he groaned as he pumped creamy, thick cum deep into her belly.

They lay together for a while afterward, not wanting to move from the bed, and India told him about Bay Tambe's offer. "That's a great idea," he enthused, sensing India was looking for his—not approval, as such—but his support. "I can see you're interested."

"It would shake things up a bit and I have been looking for that. But it would mean spending a long time apart from you."

"In blocks, not the whole time, and hell, we've done that before. We've made it work." He studied her. "So, what's changed?"

India looked away from him. "It would mean postponing... I

mean, we've been trying... and to think of putting the baby thing on hold again..."

Massimo cupped her face in his palms. "Indy... we have to face the fact that we might never be parents. We've been trying for months. We can't put our lives on hold for it. If it happens, it'll happen. If not... we have options."

India's eyes were full of tears. "Every night," she said in a low voice, "just lately, I've had this dream. This curly-haired little boy with bright green eyes running around. At home on the Hudson or at your mother's place in Italy. Every night. It haunts me, Massi. The thought that I gave birth once, and it was the child of a man who tried to kill me twice. The thought of never giving birth to your child, the child of the love of my life... it isn't fair."

She dashed her tears away with an impatient hand. "I know I should be grateful that I'm here to have this conversation. And I am, my darling, I really am. But when I see Jess with her kids, or Sun and Tae with Mika... God. It's an ache. A real ache."

"I know, darling. For me, too." He gathered her in his arms. "Look, how about this? Do the tour, the record with Bay, and meanwhile, we'll spend as much time as we can trying. We'll make time for each other even if our schedules are tight. We always have before. Then, when we're done, if we haven't conceived... well, then, maybe we'll have to look at other options."

India nodded and curled herself closer to him. "I know. I know that's a great plan, it's just... I wanted to have your baby. I wanted to feel him or her moving inside me for nine months. To know we made them."

"Baby... we'll have kids, and even if they're not biologically ours, then we'll nurture them so well they won't know the difference."

India nodded and kissed him again, and they began to make love once more, although Massimo knew, in his heart, that this particular discussion was far from over.

SEATTLE

. . .

THE TOUR GUIDE kept shooting them confused looks as they walked through the underground tour of the city. "I think he recognizes you," Lazlo whispered to Tiger who grinned and shook her head.

"I think he has the hots for you, Laz."

"Either that or he can tell that I really just want to get you naked."

Tiger kissed him, giggling. They had been like this all day, flirting nonstop as they took advantage of every tourist stop in the city. Tonight, they were meeting up with Apollo and Nell for dinner, and Tiger couldn't wait to introduce Lazlo to her brother and his love.

After the tour, they rode the monorail to the Seattle Center and took the elevator to the top of the Space Needle. Stepping out onto the viewing platform, Lazlo wrapped his arms around her as they took in the view. The day was cold, but the skies were clear, and both the Olympic Mountain range and Mount Rainier, the imposing, magical volcano, looked painted onto the sky.

"God, it's beautiful here," Lazlo said, his breath coming out in steam, so cold was the air up here. "I never thought I'd need to be close to mountains, but now I've seen them... New York seems a long way away."

"Los Angeles, too," Tiger agreed. "I never liked living there, but you know as well as I do that in my former occupation, that's where the work is. Sometimes, you know, I wish I had the confidence to do what Gary Sinise and his friends did with the Steppenwolf. Open my own theatre, put on the productions I wanted to, give young actors a break, something to put on their resumes."

"Why don't you?"

Tiger smiled up at him. "I'm too chicken. Plus, I'm enjoying my anonymity too much. I enjoy not being Tiger Rose too much."

"Is Tiger your given name or a nickname?"

"It's my real name. I should change it, except I love it. It's a link back to my hippie parents."

"Were they good parents?"

Tiger nodded, tears in her eyes, but she was smiling. "The best. The very, very best."

"I'm so sorry, Tigs."

She leaned back against him. "It is what it is. Apollo and I... We muddled along. When I got scouted, I was so set on going to college that I nearly turned down the chance to model... except I knew that me taking the job, earning real money, would be better for Apollo. And it was the right decision."

Lazlo pressed his lips to her temple. "There's no reason you can't still go back to college. You're what? Twenty-two?"

"Ha ha, flatterer. But you're right, it's an option." Tiger gave a little snort. "It's not like I can't afford it."

"I knew it!"

They both jumped as a woman's voice broke through their conversation. "I knew I knew your face. I was just saying to Matty, that woman looks like that model girl."

Tiger braced herself and plastered on a pleasant smile. "It's nice to meet you."

"Can I get a selfie with you?" The woman was already digging into her purse for her cell phone, and Tiger cast a panicked look at Lazlo. He gave her a smile and mouthed, "It's okay."

Not wanting to be rude to the woman, Tiger posed with her, smiling, and the woman thanked her kindly. "Thank you. Gosh, I never thought I'd meet Shalom Harlow of all people! Thank you. Enjoy the rest of your day, Miss Harlow."

The woman and her companion moved off leaving Tiger blinking behind them. She looked at Lazlo who was laughing. Tiger grinned with relief. "I look like Shalom Harlow?"

"A little," Lazlo was still chuckling. "Same bone structure. I think you're far more beautiful."

"I wish..." Tiger giggled. "I'm flattered by that. And at least, if she Instagrams it, my name won't be tagged. Poor Shalom, though."

"I'm sure she'll be okay," Lazlo said sagely and laughed. "Come on, Shalom. Let's go meet your brother."

. . .

TIGER TOLD Apollo and Nell the same story, and they laughed over it, but Tiger was a little bemused when Apollo seemed standoffish with Lazlo at first. She nudged her brother when Apollo asked Lazlo what his plans were for the pair of them. "Dude, what are you doing?"

Apollo grinned sheepishly. "I don't know how to do this. You've never brought a boyfriend home before. Aren't I supposed to give him the 'if you hurt my sister' speech?"

Tiger rolled her eyes and Lazlo grinned. "You go ahead and give me that speech," Lazlo said to Apollo, clapping the other man on the shoulder. "You have the right."

Apollo grinned back at him. "Nah... somehow I don't think I will have to."

After that, the evening was nothing but fun. Lazlo was a hit with her brother and Nell, but especially with little Daisy who insisted on bringing Lazlo every one of her toys to show him. He was endlessly patient with the little girl and talked to her without being condescending. When he pretended to eat her feet, she shrieked with laughter, and Tiger, watching them, felt something shift in her soul. This man... he made her heart ache with...

...love.

No, it wasn't possible. Not this quickly. It had only been a few weeks, and they hadn't even slept together yet. But Tiger, once she realized what the emotion was, had no doubt in her mind. She had fallen in love with Lazlo Schuler.

On the ferry ride back to the island, Tiger slipped her hand into Lazlo's and smiled up at him. "Laz?"

"Yeah, baby?"

"Did you like my family?"

"I adored them. I adore you, Tiger Rose."

She gazed up at him. Oh, how I love you... "Lazlo? Would you stay with me tonight?"

He looked down at her and smiled, nodding. "I would like that."

. . .

IT SEEMED to take an age to get back to her place after that, and as they walked slowly to her bedroom, Tiger found she was trembling as if this were her first time.

She gave a shaky laugh as Lazlo closed the door behind them. "I don't know why I'm so nervous. I'm not a virgin."

"If it helps... I'm terrified," Lazlo admitted. He came closer, sweeping her hair back over her shoulder. "I really don't want to mess this up. I want you so badly, Tiger Rose, and waiting for this night has been both thrilling and maddening."

He bent his head and kissed the curve of her neck softly. "Tiger..."

She let out a shaky breath, closing her eyes as he found her mouth. Then he took her hands, turned them over and kissed the inside of each wrist. "Tiger," he said again softly and she opened her eyes. "Tiger... I have fallen in love with you. I didn't want this night of all nights to pass without you knowing that."

"Oh, God, Lazlo, I love you... I think I knew it from the start and I... God... I have never felt like this about anyone. I didn't think I could ever trust again, never trust a man. What Waller did to me... and fuck, how I hate bringing that scum up at this moment, but what he did... I felt frozen. Shut down. I didn't think I'd ever let another man touch me. But, you, Laz... you..."

His mouth was rough against hers then, and their hands were busy undressing the other. The heat between them grew in intensity, and they tumbled naked onto the bed together, kissing, clawing, and grabbing at the other as if they were wild things.

Lazlo's mouth hungrily sought hers, then moved down her body, sucking and teasing each of her nipples, trailing down her flat belly, then as he pushed her thighs gently apart, his tongue lashed around her clit, making Tiger gasp and moan.

She tangled her fingers in his hair as he teased and made her writhe, then gasped out, "Move around so I can taste you, too."

With much laughing and some awkward shifting, Lazlo turned around so she could take his cock into her mouth. She swept her lips over the wide crest, stroking her fingers up and down the hot length of it. He was very well endowed, bigger than she'd even dreamed about, and the thought of it deep inside her made her even more eager to make him harder. She licked the salty precum from the tip, then teased it, gratified to hear his soft groan.

She felt her senses heighten, her skin blazing as they continued to pleasure each other, and by the time she was almost peaking, Lazlo pulled out and turned. He rolled a condom down his straining cock, and Tiger was almost screaming with anticipation as finally, he thrust deep inside her. If her body was on fire before, now it exploded with ecstatic pleasure, and she urged him deeper and harder as they fucked. Lazlo's hands pinned hers to the bed, their gaze never parting as they moved together.

Tiger came so hard she burst into tears and clung to Lazlo as he, too, reached his peak. She couldn't stop the tears, but she was smiling through them, kissing him, telling him she loved him over and over again.

Eventually, they had to draw apart, and after Lazlo had been to the bathroom to take care of the condom, he came back to her arms. Tiger kissed him, pressing her naked body against his, not wanting to be apart for a second.

Lazlo stroked his hand down her body. "Man, you are a one gorgeous woman, Tiger Rose. I've been dreaming about this body for so long."

"And it didn't disappoint?"

Lazlo looked at her askance. "Are you crazy?"

Tiger grinned. "Nah, just fishing for compliments. I'm glad, Laz... God, what a night."

"Not over yet... unless you're tired?"

Tiger snorted. "Are you kidding?" She nuzzled her nose against his. "Promise me you'll never stop fucking me."

"Even at the coffeehouse? In public?" He grinned down at her as she rolled her eyes.

"I was trying to be sexy," she complained but laughed with him. "But now you mention it... sex in public? Kinda hot."

Lazlo propped himself up on his elbow. "Kinky. So, tell me, Tiger Rose, what is your kink?"

"You." She shot it back at him and laughed when he kissed her. "But now that you ask... I think you promised me some sort of, how can I put this, punishment?"

"Ah." He suddenly turned her onto her stomach and slapped her butt hard. "Like this?"

Tiger wriggled with pleasure. "For now... but I expect you to be more forceful..."

He spanked her again, leaving a red handprint on her skin. "You like?"

To answer him, Tiger launched herself onto him, pushing him onto his back and straddling him. They made love again, this time getting rough with each other, talking about what they'd like to do to each other.

It was almost dawn before they finally fell asleep. They were woken a couple of hours later by Fizz barking at the door, wanting to be let outside for a pee, and as Tiger followed her dog into the garden for some fresh air, she felt something she hadn't for an awfully long time.

Happy.

10

CHAPTER TEN – FALL INTO ME

Seattle

Dex Loomis had called him two nights ago. "She's in Seattle—and she's not alone."

"How do you know?"

"An intern spotted her photograph on social media. It had been mislabeled as Shalom Harlow, but we've had face recognition software installed for... well, multiple reasons." Dex chuckled and Grant's nose wrinkled. Loomis was a creep and a predator, but he was funding Grant, so he couldn't exactly tell the guy to fuck off.

And who was he to talk? "So, this photograph?"

"Yeah. It was a candid taken by a fan, I assume, but in the photo, Tiger was with a man I recognized. Lazlo Schuler."

Grant felt a thrill go through him. "India Blue's brother?"

"You sound like you have history with him."

Grant smiled grimly to himself. "Oh, I do. Serious history."

"Well, don't lose focus, Waller. Tiger is the target. Now that we know for sure she's in the area, it shouldn't take you too long to find her and begin your campaign. Have you got any ideas?"

"I'm formulating."

Dex laughed but there was no humor in it. "Don't get too comfortable there, Waller. I'm generous, but I know when people are taking advantage. For example... how was the hooker you hired last night?"

Grant tensed up. "You're having me watched?"

"I made an investment, Waller. Of course, I keep tabs on it. I don't mind the hooker, just don't think I won't want some return."

"I won't."

"Make her suffer, Grant. That was the deal."

"Believe me. I will."

GRANT MADE himself some hot coffee and sat down at the table, his laptop open in front of him. Dex's intern had sent him the link to the Instagram photograph, and as he opened the page, he snorted to himself. Yep, there she was and with Lazlo Schuler in tow. Fuck, that would complicate things.

Grant and Lazlo had had run-ins before, mostly when Grant was pursuing stories on Lazlo's sister, India Blue. He'd gotten way too close to her for Schuler's liking, especially given what had happened to her later on, the same day he'd assaulted Tiger Rose. That was his one regret. If he hadn't wanted to avenge his hurt pride after Tiger went for him in the interview, he would have been front and center on the showbiz story of the year.

Instead he'd been languishing in jail. Another reason to hate Tiger Rose. And now she was fucking Schuler? God damn it. Grant was pissed but then as he drank his way down a bottle of scotch—a good one, thanks to Loomis' money—he began to see the bright side. What better way to pay both Tiger and Schuler back? Fuck their relationship, whatever it was. He'd screw that up for them, and if Grant did what Loomis wanted him to do in the end... well, Schuler would be devastated all over again.

Good. It made the thought of murder more palatable. Not that it was something Grant was considering. Destroying Tiger's peace of mind was all he wanted, and that would be easy enough to achieve. He couldn't bring himself to kill someone... could he?

Grant shook his head and poured himself another drink. Nope. That wasn't his jam at all. Dex Loomis was a psycho, and Grant would cut and run long before it got to that point. Dex could do his own dirty work. He wondered again what Tiger could have possibly done to Dex to make him want her dead. She was a ballbuster, yes, but...

Fuck this shit. He grabbed the bottle and took it to bed with him. Tiger Rose could wait until the morning.

THE ISLAND, *San Juan Islands, Washington State*

SARAH GRINNED at Tiger as she reported for work two days later. "Have you been with that lovely man of yours?"

Tiger laughed. "I have."

"When are you going to bring him to meet me?" Sarah scooped her long dreadlocks back into a ponytail and tied them back as she talked. The coffeehouse hadn't opened yet, but they could still see a few people outside, waiting for Sarah to go unlock the door.

She rolled her eyes, laughing as she went to let them in. "I swear they get earlier every day."

Tiger was at the coffee machine ready to start, taking the time to wipe everything down. She glanced up as the first customer came to the counter—and laughed. Sarah looked at her askance, but Tiger winked at her and went to serve the customer. "And what can I get you, sir?"

Lazlo grinned back at her. "An Americano and a hot date with the barista, if it's on offer?"

Tiger put her hand on her chest. "Well, the cheek of him! Sarah, this customer is harassing me..."

Sarah, her eyes twinkling, had obviously guessed who Lazlo was. "Want me to throw his ass out, Tigs?"

"Of course." Tiger stuck her tongue out at Lazlo, who laughed. "Lazlo, this is Sarah, my boss. Sarah, this is Lazlo, my side chick."

Both Lazlo and Sarah grinned as they shook hands. "Finally, I get to meet you. You are the one putting that smile on Tigs' face, then."

"I hope so."

"Nope, that's my other side piece," Tiger stage whispered. The three of three joked around as the coffeehouse filled with people. Lazlo stayed for most of the morning, even helping out, and Tiger was glad Sarah didn't seem to mind.

Sarah sent the two of them off for lunch together, and they grabbed some food from the farmer's market and went to sit down by the harbor. Lazlo cracked open a soda and handed it to Tiger. "I hope Sarah didn't mind me crashing for the morning."

"She didn't seem to. I think she was quite taken. She'll be fighting me for you."

"Well, it's good to know I have options." Lazlo said with a completely straight face, then grinning when she punched his shoulder. He leaned over and kissed her. "Kidding."

Tiger leaned against his shoulder. "I love you."

"I love you, too. Listen, I know we seem to be going at hyperspeed..."

"Oh, yes," she interrupted dryly, "the weeks of not having sex was seriously rushed."

"Sassy," he smiled, "but let me finish. You might think this is quick, but I made a decision last night, and it could affect you if you wanted it to. If not, no harm, no foul."

"Now I'm curious." She studied his expression. "Go for it."

"Well... I renewed the lease on my place for another three months."

Tiger let that sink in. "You're staying?"

His eyes were soft as he looked at her. "Of course I'm staying, Tiger... of course I am. Do you honestly think I could ever go back to my old life now? And by that, I mean no pressure on you, or us, just that I wanted to be where you are and see where this goes. What do you say?"

Tiger felt her eyes fill with tears; they seemed to be doing that a lot lately but luckily from happiness rather than grief. "I say I'm in. All in."

They kissed again, not caring that people were watching them. Tiger touched his face. "You make me so happy, Lazlo Schuler."

"Right back at you, Funny Face."

SHE WAS STILL SMILING when she got back to the coffee house, but when she went to dump her bag in the backroom, she heard Sarah arguing with someone on her cell phone. Tiger was shocked to see the normally cheerful Sarah in tears. Tiger gave her privacy and went to serve the customers waiting at the bar, but when Sarah emerged, she went to hug her friend.

"You okay?"

Sarah shook her head. "The landlord. He's selling this place to a developer."

Tiger was aghast. "What? Can he do that?"

Sarah nodded, blowing her nose loudly and wiping her eyes. Tiger steered her into a chair and brought her some hot tea. There were only a few people in the place now, and Sarah poured out all the bad news to her friend. "We have until the end of the month, then he's selling. They're building luxury apartments or some such shit. God damn it."

"God, Sarah..." Tiger felt sick for her friend, and to a lesser extent, for herself. The world had shifted again. "There must be something we can do."

Sarah laughed without humor. "Well, unless you have a spare few million laying around."

Tiger felt her face redden. Oh God. Oh God... "Maybe we can find financial backers?"

"You are sweet but coffee houses are a dime a dozen around here. Why would anyone back this one?" She drew in a deep breath. "Nope. We're just going to have to find new premises."

"I can help."

Sarah smiled at her, wiping her damp cheeks with a tissue. "I know. I'm so glad I have you here, Tigs, I really am. This would be so much harder without you here to support me. You know... Ben found this place for me. I'd dreamed of opening my own place. I was a nurse when we first married, but I lost my passion for it and wanted something closer to home. Ben worked from home, you see, and I hated being away from him for long hours."

She cleared her throat, obviously trying not to cry again. Tiger squeezed her friend's hand. "Lazlo has some contacts, I'm sure. I'll see what he can find out for us."

"I'd be grateful."

LAZLO CAME to pick her up as the coffee house closed. Sarah had gone home a couple of hours ago, and as Tiger let Lazlo in the locked door, she saw him raise his eyebrows at the tense look on her face. She told him about the landlord.

"The thing is... I could save it. I could buy this place from the developer, many, many times over. But to do so... would expose me. I feel wretched even using that as an excuse. I would do anything to help, but the thought of this little bubble being wrecked..." Her voice wobbled. "That's so incredibly selfish of me."

"No, it isn't. You came here for anonymity, for peace. After what happened to you, no one would blame you for wanting to protect that."

"But she's my friend."

"And you can't save everyone." Lazlo stopped suddenly, and gave a soft chuckle. "Damn."

"What?"

"India's words coming back to haunt me. Baby, I understand, I do. I spent years trying to do the same." He took her hands in his. "Listen... maybe we can find a way to help Sarah out anonymously. We can look into it, certainly."

Tiger smiled at him. "You really are the best, you know?"

He kissed her. "As long as you think so, beautiful. Come on, I'll help you clear up then we can go home."

THEY MADE quiet enquiries about the developer over the next few days, and in the meantime, Tiger helped Sarah scout out new properties on the island. On the fourth day, Tiger, skimming through listings on a realtor's website, came across something that made her heart pound.

A few blocks away, still situated on the waterfront, was an empty old movie house. Tiger read through the listing. It had fallen into disrepair, but the owner, an elderly widow, had refused to sell it. But when she passed on, her son had put it up for sale.

Tiger went out on her own to see the property the following day. Although it was dank and spider-webby, she could see the potential in it. The realtor was a sweet, kindly-faced old man who showed her around.

"It used to be a vaudeville theater when I was a kid," he said. "See, all the old stage lights are still in place, though they weren't used for years." He smiled at her. "You say you're looking for premises for a new coffeehouse? Well, the space out front certainly lends itself to that, but it would be a shame if the stage wasn't used for performances. Perhaps you were thinking of starting your own company?" His eyes twinkled at her, and Tiger realized he had recognized her. She smiled shyly.

"I wouldn't presume, but it's a dream. Although, I came here for... peace."

The old man tapped his nose. "I can keep a secret, Miss Rose. But personally, I would love to see it."

Tiger thanked him and told him she would call him soon with an answer. She drove home and parked in front of her house.

As she got out of her car and let Fizz out, she nearly jumped fifty feet in the air as a cacophony of voices yelled hello at her. Tiger clutched her chest and turned to see Apollo, Nell, and Daisy on her porch. "Oh, my God, I nearly died. What are you doing here?"

But she was smiling, delighted to see them. She swung Daisy into her arms and kissed Nell's cheek. "We're playing hooky," Nell told her. "Someone—" she cast an eye over to her grinning partner, "has a cold. A cold."

"Ah, man flu?"

"Yup."

Apollo grinned, looking remarkably well for a man with a cold. "And I thought to myself, who better to share my snot with?"

"Eww, Daddy!" Daisy wrinkled her nose as Tiger made a face.

"Daddy is gross," Nell chuckled, not phased at all, obviously used to Apollo's sense of humor.

"Come on in before you all freeze then."

THEY WENT INSIDE, not noticing the man sitting in the car across the street, watching them. Grant Waller watched them in silence, then started the car and moved away before anyone could spot him and report him to the neighborhood watch he was sure existed in this kind of place. He could barely believe that this was where Tiger Rose had hidden herself, and yet... it was prefect. He had to give her that.

He hadn't thought it would be this easy to find her, but he'd gone to the brother's apartment this morning to see the entire family loading themselves into their car and decided on instinct to follow them. Halfway on the journey to the San Juan Islands he wondered if he was being led on a wild goose chase, but no. This was where Tiger Rose had exiled herself to.

Grant snorted as he drove back towards the ferry port. It was hardly the type of place she was used to, and he wondered if she behaved like a diva here, wanting all the attention. He shook his head. He knew the answer to that. There had been a reason Tiger was so popular in Hollywood—she was always warm, friendly, and a consummate professional. She arrived on time, knew her lines, and didn't stand for any of her costars behaving badly. She'd even dressed down a few of them who had screamed at the crew.

So, he imagined she was well-liked here—which was a problem.

She'd be well protected by her new friends as well as Lazlo Schuler. Her brother, too, was an imposing man, at least six-two and well-built.

Grant drove onto the ferry, parked the car, and then went up to the ferry lounge to grab a drink to ease the boredom. He strolled along the deck, then pushed into the lounge—and recoiled. Lazlo Schuler was sitting in the lounge, alone at a table, scrolling through his laptop. Grant ducked back around the corner just as Lazlo looked up in his direction, bothered by the rush of cool air from the door Grant had opened.

Fuck. The last thing he needed was Schuler recognizing him and warning Tiger he was in the area. He'd never get near her. Cussing, thinking about the drink he could now forget, Grant went back down to his vehicle and waited out the trip. His senses were heightened though—what if Schuler had seen him and was looking for him?

He didn't relax for the whole journey back, and when they arrived at Seattle, he had to duck his head as he saw Lazlo get into the vehicle just ahead of him. Grant fumbled around on the back seat of his old Chevy—Loomis hadn't sprung for a new car—and found a musty old cap. He pulled it down over his eyes.

It seemed obvious to him that he would follow Schuler to wherever he was going, but he frowned when he saw it was a realtor. Surely Schuler's business was in New York and Los Angeles? Grant knew he worked closely with Jess Olden, one of showbiz's busiest lawyers. At his own trial, he had been relieved when Jess Olden wasn't on the opposing team. He would have gone down for a lot longer if she had been.

He forced his focus back to the task at hand. Really, it didn't matter what Schuler was doing—Grant's focus should be Tiger and that was all. But if Lazlo was buying property here... they must be serious.

More obstacles. Well... he'd start small. Follow her for a day or two. See how she spent her day. Was it worth renting a motel room on the island? He thought so.

He went back to his apartment and packed his stuff up. He placed a call to Dex and told him he'd found Tiger. "Good," the producer sounded in a hurry, "now make her life hell."

TIGER WAS ALMOST bereft when Apollo and his family left later that day. She pleaded with them to stay, but Nell had work in the morning and the commute was too much for her. "But I promise we'll come stay when we have more time," she said to her almost-sister-in-law, seeing her disappointment. "You're building a beautiful life here, Tiger. I'm so happy for you."

When she was alone, Tiger tidied her house and took Fizz for a walk on the beach. Her phone buzzed as she was almost back at her home. "Hey, baby."

"Hey, gorgeous. I have good news."

"About the development?" Tiger felt her heart leap, then sink when Lazlo spoke again.

"Um, no, sorry. Apparently, that's watertight. I made the offer through my lawyer, but the developer isn't interested in money. He wants the property."

Tiger sighed. "Damn."

"But... if you want it, the movie house is yours."

Tiger gasped. "Really? They accepted our offer?"

"Seems you were quite the hit with the realtor... who happened to be the owner, too."

"What? That sly fox... he never said." Tiger laughed, remembering the old man fondly.

They talked a little more, then Tiger chuckled. "When are you coming home? I miss you."

"I'm on the ferry now. About forty-five minutes away. Listen," he dropped his voice lower, "when I was in the city, I picked up some things for us."

"Food?" Tiger was starving even though she had eaten a huge lunch with her family.

Lazlo laughed. "My little glutton. No, not food... some toys."

Tiger's body immediately responded. "Toys?"

"Exactly what you're thinking of, beautiful. Just a little...taster of what we could enjoy. How does that sound?"

Tiger's voice was thick when she replied. "Tell the ferry boat captain to speed things up."

Lazlo's laugh was low and husky. "Darling... I hope you have a lot of energy because you're not going to get much sleep tonight."

AN HOUR LATER, Lazlo walked up to her front door and saw the note.

Come on in, handsome...

He chuckled and pushed the door open. Inside the large hallway were strings of tiny white lights, casting a beautifully sensual glow, and as he looked up, he saw her. Tiger was on the stairs, stunning in a simple white dress with spaghetti straps. Her dark hair was pulled over one shoulder and her large eyes flickered with desire. Slowly, she drew her legs apart and hiked the dress up over her thighs. Underneath she was naked. "Welcome home," she said softly.

His cock reacted immediately, pressing hard against his jeans as his eyes slid down her body to the glistening wetness between her legs. Lazlo tugged at his tie as he approached, and when he reached her, he wound it around her wrists and pulled it tight. He bent down to kiss her once, briefly, then met her gaze. "Are you mine?"

"I am, all yours for as long as you want me." She said softly, but then laughed as he picked her up and threw her over his shoulder, carrying her up the stairs.

He laid her down on the bed and slowly undid all the buttons on the bodice of her dress. Tiger smiled sleepily up at him, her eyes drowsy with desire. "What did you bring me, my man?"

"Patience, woman," he said softly, smiling. "We have all night. Right now, I'm going to kiss every inch of your skin."

And he did, beginning with her mouth, then trailing his lips down her throat to her breasts and over the flat plane of her belly. "Open these beautiful thighs for me, Tiger."

She obeyed and he heard her gasp as his tongue found her sex, sweeping up and down the peachy folds of her cleft, then flicking around her clit. His fingers dug into the soft flesh of her thighs and she shivered with pleasure.

Lazlo made Tiger come hard, before he raised his head and grinned at her. "That was just the beginning of tonight's pleasures."

"It is?"

He touched the bindings on her wrists. "Are these uncomfortable?"

"Not in a way I find displeasurable."

He kissed her mouth. "I'm going to roll you onto your belly now, Tiger. Do you trust me?"

She nodded, her breath quickening, her face flushed pink. "Yes."

Lazlo left her then to retrieve the small bag he had brought home. From within it, he withdrew a blindfold and a small, thick black riding crop. Tiger's eyes lit up.

"Oh, Lazlo..."

He grinned at her. "You wanted kinky. How about we start here?"

"Oh, yes... please, Lazlo, please..."

He laughed and straddled her back. He was still in his jeans and sweater, but it turned him on to have her completely at his mercy, naked and vulnerable, willing to submit to him. His cock was hard against the fabric of his pants and all he could think about was fucking her, slamming his cock into that juicy, warm velvety cunt of hers... but he could wait.

For this, anyway. He gently blindfolded her, using the opportunity to kiss her sweet mouth as he did, then he trailed the tip of the crop down the length of her spine. "You want me to punish you, Tiger?"

She nodded, biting her bottom lip, then yelped as he whipped the crop against her buttocks. "More?"

"Yes, yes..."

He brought the whip down harder this time, snapping it hard against the back of her thighs and her body jerked. Tiger moaned so beautifully that Lazlo couldn't wait any longer. He unzipped his pants, kicking them off, and pushed her legs apart. "I'm sorry... I really can't wait a moment more."

He thrust deep inside her and she cried out with pleasure. He fucked her hard, pinning her to the bed, biting down hard on her shoulder as he did. Tiger urged him on, telling him to make her feel pain as well as ecstasy, spurring him on to go harder, deeper with every thrust.

They came together, almost explosively, laughing and gasping. Tiger asked him to use the crop on her belly, her breasts, and for the rest of the night, they played master and servant, torturer and victim, fucking with abandon.

Finally, exhausted, they collapsed on the bed. Lazlo unbound Tiger's wrists, kissing the red welts left there by his tie. "You should have told me they were rubbing."

Tiger grinned at him. "That would have rather ruined the mood of the role play, baby."

"Did you enjoy it?"

"It was thrilling."

Lazlo propped himself up on his elbow and traced a pattern of her belly with the tip of his forefinger. "And it was tame by most BDSM standards."

"I don't mind that. This is... the first time I've tried it. The first time I've trusted a man enough to try it."

Lazlo was absurdly pleased. "Really?"

"Really. I love you, Lazlo Schuler. I knew it almost right away."

He kissed her again and she cradled his face in her palms. "Laz?"

"Yeah, babe."

She hesitated then met his gaze. "You've renewed your lease for another three months?"

"I have. Why?"

She bit her lip. "Because I was wondering... this might be crazy-soon, but when that lease is up...maybe you'd like to move in here with me? If you're not back in New York, that is."

Lazlo was dumbstruck. "You want me to live with you?"

Tiger nodded. "I think we'll know in three months whether this thing is going to go the distance. Actually, I believe in my heart, very much, that this is it for me. You. You are it for me, my love, my person. I've never lived with a guy before, never wanted to. I know it's fast, that's why I'm saying three months. If we don't think this will work, then by then, we'll know."

Her voice was shaking, and she was rambling now, but Lazlo silenced her with his mouth. He kissed her until neither of them could breathe, then drew away. "Tiger Rose... I already know. I already know."

CHAPTER ELEVEN – NEVER BE THE SAME

The Island, *San Juan Islands, Washington State*

A WEEK LATER, Tiger went to see her lawyer in the city to finalize the purchase of the movie house. She wanted to know everything was in place before she told Sarah that they had new premises for the coffee house—if Sarah wanted them.

Tiger and Lazlo had talked, and Tiger had admitted she needed to trust Sarah with the knowledge of who Tiger really was. It was a gamble, yes, but Bella had known, and had told no one. "I just hope she doesn't hate me for not telling her sooner. Or that she'll think this is charity. It's not." Tiger told Lazlo over breakfast that morning.

Lazlo smoothed a hand down her hair. "It's a business investment. Sarah's not a child, she'll see it for what it is. Want me to come with?"

"Nah, I want to do this one on one." Tiger kissed him. "Oh, shoot, now look what I've done."

She had leaned over the table and her left breast now had the remains of Lazlo's breakfast smeared onto her t-shirt. "Damn."

"Sexy." Lazlo wiggled his eyebrows at her and she grinned.

"Weirdo. What have you got planned for today?"

"Well, believe it or not, work. At least, stuff for India. She's going on tour with The 9th and Pine and then recording an album with them."

Tiger raised her eyebrows. "Really?"

"You sound surprised."

"I thought she'd lost her mojo."

"I guess she found it." Lazlo smiled at her, and Tiger could see he was relieved that his sister had found her motivation again. "I think she was so caught up in trying for a baby with Massi, that nothing else mattered for a bit. I think I have Bay Tambe to thank for this."

"I know Bay," Tiger said, "she's a Seattle girl, too. I used to go by her uncle's motorcycle store when I was a kid."

"You were a biker chick?"

"Nah, but he made the most gorgeous Indian candies. And I think he was a little sweet on my mom. I remember Bay's brother, Dev. He killed himself a few years ago."

"Damn, that's rough."

Tiger nodded. "Anyway, I'm happy for India. Maybe I'll get to meet her soon?"

"Of course." Lazlo stroked her cheek but nodded at the clock. "You're going to be late."

TIGER FELT SO nervous as she arrived at work. In a few days they would be closing the shop down, and she could see from Sarah's increasingly fraught expression that it was weighing heavily on her. Her customers had pledged to remain loyal to her wherever she opened her next endeavor, but Tiger knew Sarah's confidence had been rocked.

She waited until lunchtime when the coffeehouse was empty to ask Sarah to sit down with her. Tiger wrapped her hands tightly together to stop them from shaking. "Sarah, you've become one of my closest friends," she started but stopped as Sarah groaned.

"Oh, God, you're leaving me."

"No, no, no, quite the opposite." Tiger took a deep breath in.

"Sarah, there's something you should know about me. My name... Tiggy... it's not my actual name. Close but not... Sarah, my name is Tiger."

Sarah grinned. "For reals?"

Tiger laughed. "For reals. My name is Tiger Rose."

She was silent then realization dawned on Sarah's face. "Oh, my God. You are. You're Tiger Rose, of course you are. Oh, God, how could I have not..." Sarah laughed then frowned. "But why didn't you tell me?" She groaned again. "Holy hell, I asked a damn Oscar winner to be my assistant in my coffeehouse? What must you think of me?" She dropped her head in her hands, and Tiger, who was chuckling to herself, took them.

"What I think of you, Sarah, is that you gave me a lifeline, something to focus on. Do you know I've been happier working here than at any time in Hollywood?"

"Oh, you're just being nice."

"I'm not, I'm really not." Tiger leaned forward and hugged her friend. "This is us. You've let me become part of this town in a way I could never have on my own. I came here for peace, and you helped me find it, and I love you." She took another breath in. "Which is why, I have something else to tell you."

"You're pregnant with Brad Pitt's baby?"

Tiger snorted. "Eww, and no. Sarah, since we found about losing this place, I've been hunting around, trying to find alternatives. Lazlo and I made an approach to the developer to see if he would sell to us so we could save this place. We tried, Sarah, but I'm so sorry, we couldn't make it work."

Sarah threw her arms around Tiger and burst into tears. "The fact you tried..." She couldn't speak for a few minutes, and Tiger rubbed her friend's back as she calmed herself.

"But... there is a property on the island that I think we, you and I, could make into something special. Do you know the old movie house down on Harbor Lane?"

Sarah nodded, dabbing at her eyes, and Tiger smiled. "Well, I bought it. For us, for you. We could make the whole thing into a coffee shop, or we could open a theatre and a coffeeshop. We could do whatever you liked."

Sarah was gaping at her now. "Are you kidding me?"

"Nope."

For a long moment, Sarah stared at her, then got up and began to pace. Tiger knew her friend needed some time to get used to the idea. Eventually Sarah sat down, her expression unreadable. "So, I would be working for you?"

Tiger shook her head and reached into her bag, pulling out a manila folder. "No. Sarah, these are the papers I had my lawyer draw up, transferring fifty percent of the movie house and its future business to you. No, Sarah, you won't be working for me, you'll be working with me. Partners. Together."

Sarah blinked. "I can't possible accept..." But her voice trailed off and Tiger smiled, knowing she had her.

TWO DAYS LATER, Tiger took Sarah to see the movie house, and it didn't take long before the two of them were excitedly making plans for the space. Sarah loved the idea of having a small theater company, and Tiger felt the excitement of possibly acting again in a production of her own. They talked about finishing the coffee shop first, and when they told their existing clientele about the new premises, their customers all vowed to follow them there, some of them offering their services to help renovate.

AFTER WORK, the day before their last day at the original coffee house, Tiger had to say goodbye to Lazlo. Lazlo was flying to New York to help India arrange things for her tour, and he would be gone for a few days. Tiger already felt the loss.

She sat in his suitcase sulking as he was packing, and he grinned at her. "You lunatic. You could always come with me."

He shooed her out of the case as he dumped a handful of clean underwear into it. Tiger sat cross-legged on his bed, watching him. "I would, but what with it being the last day tomorrow, I want to be with Sarah."

"Of course you do, and you should be." Lazlo smiled at his love, his blue eyes twinkling. "Love, it's only a few days and I'll call you every night."

"I know." Tiger chuckled. "I never thought I'd be the clingy type."

"You're not clingy, I'm going to miss you, too. It was always going to be weird the first time we're away from each other. This whole thing has been pretty intense."

Tiger smiled. "It has. I'm actually surprised at myself; I would have thought I'd have freaked out about that before now."

"Want to know a secret? Me, too. I've been on my own for so long that I thought that was it. A lone wolf."

Tiger sat up and kneeled so she could kiss him. "Yup. And I think I would have still been that way if it wasn't for you. Only you, Laz. No one else could have had this effect on me."

"Aww, shucks," he said but she could see he was pleased.

AFTER LAZLO HAD LEFT, Tiger clipped Fizz's leash onto him and took him for a stroll around the neighborhood that had become her home —her haven—and felt a contentment she hadn't felt for... ever? Had she ever felt like this?

Her relationship with Lazlo was so much fun, and yet it wasn't frivolous or shallow. Aside from the incredible sex, and they'd been experimenting even more with the paddles and crops and bindings Lazlo had bought to the bedroom, they talked about every subject under the sun, really random things, and Lazlo never ever treated her like a child. That was new for a man for her. She was either a child to be dismissed or merely a hole to be presented for fucking. Lazlo, and her new life here, made her feel like a whole person.

She wasn't meant to be working that afternoon, but she went along anyway. She smiled delightedly when she saw Bella chatting with Sarah. "Hey, what are you doing here?" She hugged the younger woman tightly, and Bella kissed her cheek.

"Cutting class. I couldn't not come back for the closing. It wouldn't seem right, no matter how sad I am. But Sarah's been telling me about the new place."

"It'll take time to get it ready, but we should be open in time for Christmas, the coffee house, at least." Sarah grinned at Tiger. "Thanks to Tiger."

"Ah, no, it's our baby, Sazzle."

"Sazzle?" Bella grinned at her two friends who laughed.

"Now I know Tiger is Tiger," Sarah rolled her eyes, "and yes, I still can't believe I asked Tiger Rose to come work for my pissant little coffee house..."

"...it is not pissant," Tiger and Bella said in unison and then laughed.

"Anyway, we've become even closer," Sarah said, her voice warming. "And Tiger's insisting on trying out nicknames. That's a new one for you."

"For me?"

Sarah's eyes were soft. "Sazzle was Ben's nickname for me. I love hearing it again."

Tiger squeezed her friend's shoulder and looked around. "Well, looks like everyone is trying to make the most of the last two days. It's busy! Need a hand?"

Sarah smiled at her gratefully. "You're the best."

Bella helped out, too, thankfully, as at early evening, there were no free tables and people were even doubling up to drink their beverages.

It was late November and the sun set early. After the rush, the coffeehouse began to thin out and Bella, who had a date, said goodbye. "I'll come back tomorrow," she promised and waved as she left.

Sarah went into the back office to do some paperwork as the final customers drifted out, and Tiger began to clear up.

She was sweeping a broom around the wooden floor when she felt the hairs on the back of her neck stand up. A scrap of newspaper lay on the floor, and on it, she could see her own photograph. She picked it up. The date read a few days after Grant Waller had attacked her, and the article detailing the attack was all right there. Who the hell would leave this here?

Had Sarah or Bella found it and forgotten to mention it? But when Sarah returned from the office, Tiger stuffed it into her pocket and didn't mention it.

Sarah smiled at her, not noticing the expression on Tiger's face. Sarah nodded to the window. "Looks like we have a straggler. Shall we be kind and let him in or is it too late?"

Tiger turned to look at the customer standing outside the door—and her heart failed. No. It couldn't be...

Grant Waller. The man smirked slightly, then walked away from the door, leaving Tiger wondering if she had seen things. Was it her imagination? How the hell would he have found her here?

"Oh, well, looks like he gave up." Sarah went back into the office, and Tiger darted to the door, pulling it open and looking out. The man was nowhere to be seen, and Tiger felt a wave of distress flood her. Was she going crazy?

She thought about the newspaper in her pocket. No, she'd been imagining it, still rocked from finding the article. Coincidence.

As she walked home though, Tiger felt on edge and watchful, ready for an attack. Fizz picked up on her mood and was alert, his ears pricked, his stride protective. That made Tiger smile a little. My little man. But for once, and silently apologizing to her feminist sisters everywhere, she wished Lazlo was here to walk her home like he did every night now.

At home, she locked and double-locked the door behind her and went to check all the windows in the house. It wouldn't hurt, she told herself, it's not paranoia, just common sense.

Still, she was jittery all night until Lazlo called. He could tell immediately something was wrong and she told him about finding the article. "It is strange, baby, but at least I can set your mind at rest about one thing. Waller is in New York. I had the misfortune of being at the next table at a luncheon today. The fact he still gets invited to functions after what he did to you..." Lazlo sounded furious, but to Tiger, it was a relief.

"Thank God. I'd rather just be paranoid about him than right." She chuckled slightly, then sighed. "Sorry, baby. I guess it just got to me."

"Completely understandable."

"How's India?"

Lazlo sighed. "There's something not right, Tigs, and I can't place my finger on it. She says all the right things, but there's something... missing. Her spark. Massimo has noticed, too, obviously, but he's at a loss. We both thought this tour had given her back her mojo and she's insisting it has, but... I don't know. I might be overthinking things."

"I wish I could help."

"It's okay, baby. India's a grown-up. If she's keeping something from us, it's for a good reason." He chuckled softly. "I miss you. Indy's guest room is really comfortable, but a bed feels empty without you in it now."

Tiger smiled down the phone. "I know what you mean."

They talked for an hour or so, then said goodnight. Tiger went to the kitchen to make herself some chamomile tea. She glanced back into the living room at Fizz who was sleeping soundly in front of the open fire.

As she grabbed the kettle to boil some water, she looked up and dropped the kettle with a shriek. Fizz was up immediately, barking, as Tiger rocked back.

There was someone looking in the window straight at her.

CHAPTER TWELVE – UNSTEADY

T IGER, panicked, grabbed a knife from the drawer and darted into the living room. She snagged her cellphone and called 911. She strained to hear if the intruder was trying to break in as she told the operator what was happening.

"We'll send someone out right away, ma'am."

As she waited, she went around to every door and window on the lower floor, knife at the ready, making sure none were broken or unlocked. She heard someone kick at the front door and ran to it to look out to see who her stalker was, but the front porch was empty.

Under the door, however, a piece of paper had been shoved. Tiger stared at it but didn't touch it. Fizz was still barking wildly, and Tiger scooped him up into her arms to calm him.

A few minutes later, she saw the police cruiser pull up to the sidewalk, but she waited until the officer was at her door before opening it.

The officer checked around her entire property, then came in. Using his pen, he flicked open the note that had been shoved through her door and then chuckled. He picked it up. "It's a food delivery pamphlet." He handed it to her.

Shame and embarrassment flooded through Tiger's body. "Oh, God, I'm so sorry."

"It's no problem, really. Better safe than sorry, but you do live in a safe neighborhood here." He bent down to fuss Fizz. "Good little guard dog, is he?"

"Not really," Tiger smiled, "but he can bark up a storm."

"Sometimes that's all it takes. Listen, you seem to have good locks and security here, ma'am, so I'm confident it'll keep out any intruders. But, if you're scared, or whoever it was comes back, call. Don't be embarrassed."

"Thank you."

SHE LOCKED the door after the deputy left and rubbed her face. How embarrassing. She looked down at the leaflet. Pizza deals from a local pizzeria. She hadn't used that one before, but she knew of it. God. What had the delivery guy been thinking, shoving his face into her window like that?

"Fuck." She screwed the leaflet up and dumped it in the recycling bin. They wouldn't be getting her business after tonight.

She picked Fizz back up and climbed the stairs to her bed, feeling foolish, but it didn't stop her from locking her bedroom door, too. Finally, just after two a.m. she fell into a fitful sleep, filled with nightmares and violence, and she woke, screaming Lazlo's name.

~

NEW YORK

GRANT'S CELLPHONE rang and his guy in Washington reported back to him. He'd found him at a local bar one night, the bartender remarking on his remarkable resemblance to Grant, and Grant had bought the young kid a drink. "How do you feel like earning some money?"

The kid who was trying to pay his way through college agreed, and Grant had him change his hair, dye it. The kid was thinner than Grant, and taller, but he looked enough like him to convince someone at a difference.

Convince Tiger—or at least freak her out enough she'd be unsettled. Grant had made sure he was at the function in New York—he'd found out through Doug that Lazlo Schuler would be there and had called in a favor with an ex-girlfriend to secure himself an invite.

Well, 'favor' might be a stretch. He had enough dirt on his ex that her newish billionaire husband would divorce her in a second if he knew she'd made her money 'yachting' for other rich guys before he came along. His ex had cussed and sworn at him, but Grant knew she was backed into a corner.

So, his campaign had officially started. The kid reported back that Tiger was freaked out twice on the same day, and that he'd planted the newspaper story in the coffeehouse. It would unsettle her, but this was just the beginning.

He'd found out that Tiger and the owner of the coffee house, a hot piece called Sarah something, were opening new premises in an old movie theater. They were renovating it. Funny how so many buildings that were being remodeled were full of security gaps. He was looking forward to tormenting Tiger.

Soon, the article he had written under an assumed name would be published, and the world would know where Tiger Rose had hidden herself away.

He'd called Dex Loomis, who had been dismissive of what he had planned. "This is all kid's stuff, Waller. She might be upset, but it's hardly going to wreck the life she has now, is it? Damn it, man, get creative. Even if you have to spill blood."

"What exactly did she do to you, Dex? What? Because I have to tell you, you sound very much like you want revenge for something. Did you try to fuck her and she turned you down? What?"

"That's none of your business. Just get it done."

He hung up before Grant could ask what he meant by 'it.' Grant had made up his mind he wasn't going to do time for Tiger Rose again, so harming her—again—wasn't an option. Once he'd had his fun and destroyed her peace of mind, Dex could do what he liked.

Grant went back to his apartment and packed his things. He was going back to Seattle ready to witness the shit hitting the fan when Tiger was exposed. Hell, he might even hang around afterward when Dex caught up to see the biggest story in showbiz if Dex murdered her. She owed him that, at least.

He was on the plane within the hour.

~

New York

LAZLO COULDN'T SLEEP. He was worried about Tiger being alone on the island, but more than that, he was worried about his sister. India wasn't herself. She was forgetful, vague and listless, but whenever he or Massimo tried to talk to her, she would shut them down and change the subject.

He glanced over at the clock. It was almost four a.m. He got up and went into the kitchen to grab some milk from the fridge and found India siting up. To his horror, she was crying, silent tears pouring down her face. He went to her immediately. "What is it, Indy?"

She looked up at him, a desperately sad look in her eyes and then leaned against him. Lazlo could feel her shoulders shaking as she cried.

When she'd stopped sobbing, Indy wiped her eyes, and Lazlo sat down with her, waiting for her to talk. India took a deep breath and looked at her brother. "I'm pregnant."

Lazlo blinked, then hugged his sister. "But that's wonderful! It's what you've always wanted, Indy..." He sat down slowly when he saw her shake her head. "What is it, boo?"

Indy dashed away fresh tears. "Two months ago, I had a letter. From my daughter's adoptive parents." Her lips wobbled, and she touched her fingers to them to quell the trembling. "She died, Laz. Some rare genetic disorder whose name I can't even pronounce. Something they can't detect before the child is born. She was fourteen, Lazlo, and she's gone. Just like that. My baby... Massimo's baby..." She put a hand over her belly, still flat at two months gone. "God, I want him or her so badly, but what if... what if we go through the same thing? What if we have this child, but it's taken away just as young? I don't think I could cope, or Massimo. We've lost so much, Laz. Coco... my mom. Almost Jess and Sun, too."

Lazlo wrapped his arms around his sister and held her not knowing what to say to her. Over her shoulder, he spotted Massimo in the shadows listening to them. By the expression on his face, Lazlo knew—India hadn't told him anything.

He nodded at Massimo to come closer, and Lazlo released his sister into her husband's arms.

India started a little when Massimo slid his arms around her, but then as she looked up into his eyes, she began to cry again, and Massimo drew her close.

LAZLO LEFT them alone and went back to his room. God, what a choice lay ahead of them. His heart hurt for his sister. It was too cruel after everything she and Massimo had been through.

He glanced at the clock again and he could wait no longer, even if it was early. He called Tiger in Washington and wasn't surprised when she answered right away. "I didn't think you'd be asleep."

"Even if I had been, I would still have answered. Well, you know what I mean," she chuckled softly, and Lazlo closed his eyes at the beautiful sound.

"God, I love you, Tiger Rose."

"I love you, too, big man. When are you coming home to me?"

"Soon, I promise. Tiger?"

"Yeah, baby?"

Lazlo hesitated for a long moment, but his heart was strong, and he knew what he wanted to say to his darling love more than anything else. "Tiger Rose?"

She chuckled again. "Lazlo?"

He drew in a deep breath. "I know we talked about living together, Tiger... but I want more. Much more."

"What do you want, my love?"

Lazlo smiled to himself. "I want everything, Tiger Rose, all of you. I want to marry you."

CHAPTER THIRTEEN – THIS MUCH IS TRUE

THE ISLAND, San Juan Islands, Washington State

TIGER WAS sure she still looked shell-shocked as she walked into work the next morning, Fizz scampering at her feet. She knew she was right when Sarah gaped at her. "What's up? Are you okay?"

Tiger blinked. "Apparently I'm getting married."

Sarah gave a whoop and came to hug her. "That's wonderful, Tigs!"

Tiger let her hug her and tried to smile back at her. She couldn't quite believe it herself, and it wasn't just because Lazlo had proposed over the phone. She'd said yes. She'd said yes. And it hadn't occurred to her for even a second to say no.

"Hey, come and sit, you look like you're about to pass out."

Tiger followed Sarah to a chair and sat, but she shook her head. "I'm okay, I'm just a little..." She laughed quietly. "Shocked at myself. I never was one of those girls who aspired to be married, never. And to even think... we've been together such a short while, and yet I know it's right, Sarah. That's what frightens me. How do I know that?"

Sarah grinned at her. "I think this calls for tea. Hang in there."

She went to fetch them both a hot cup of tea. Tiger sat patiently. The coffee house wouldn't open for another forty minutes, so she had plenty of time to gather herself. A movement caught her eye outside the window, and she looked up to see the man from yesterday, only now she could see, it wasn't Grant Waller. This man was younger, thinner, better looking. He glanced in and stopped, and Tiger was surprised to see a strange look on his face. It was almost... apologetic. Tiger frowned, and the moment was over. The boy disappeared from view.

Tiger sighed. All of that worry for nothing. A pang shot through her. She hadn't said yes to Lazlo because of last night, had she? No. In a strange way, she had been waiting for him to ask, and when he did, she hadn't been that shocked.

Her saying yes was the thing that made her rock back. But now she laughed softly to herself. She was marrying the man she loved with all her heart. What the hell was there to be shocked about?

Sarah brought the tea over and smiled, seeing Tiger's face lit up. "You look like you're glowing from the inside out," Sarah told her. "That man is good for you."

"You don't think it's too quick?"

"What's too quick? I knew Ben was the one three seconds after meeting him, and I was right. Your Lazlo... he adores you. No, Tiger, I don't think it's too soon at all. Not for you two."

THE REST of the day was a whirlwind of laughter and tears as they served their customers the last coffee in this building, and Tiger propped Sarah up when she got too emotional to talk anymore.

They closed very late, lingering over the packing up of the machines. Some of the clients helped them pack Sarah's truck up with everything they were taking with them, and Bella offered to drive Sarah home. Tiger hugged her boss who, from tomorrow forward, would be her business partner. "Will you be okay?"

"I will," Sarah nodded. "Onto new things."

"You betcha."

. . .

TIGER WAVED her off and walked home with Fizz. It was after midnight when she got home and despite herself, she still checked every door and window before going to bed. She crawled into bed and called Lazlo.

"Hey, fiancé."

He laughed. "Hey, wife-to-be... so I take it you didn't change your mind in the cold light of day?"

"Hell, no, you're stuck with me now." Tiger chuckled, then sighed. "It's been a strange day, high and low. I've been thinking about you all day. I can't wait to see you. Sarah and I are taking a few days before we start on the movie theater... I thought, well, if you don't mind, I might come out to New York and see you. If I wouldn't be intruding, that is."

"Baby, that would be perfect." He hesitated for a moment. "But perhaps I'll book a hotel room for us, rather than stay here. India and Massi are still... talking. It's a little tense here."

Tiger wasn't stung. "Of course, if it would be better for everyone. After all, the last thing they need is to feel as if they have to entertain, if you know what I mean."

"You're a sweetheart. Listen, I'll see if I can get us a suite somewhere. Somewhere soundproof."

Tiger laughed then, the release of tension welcome. "That sounds promising."

"New York is going to love you, but not as much as I'm going to, baby."

She giggled. "You'd better keep that promise."

"How soon can you get here?"

"I'll be there in the morning, baby. I can't wait."

Tiger went straight online after they said goodbye and booked the first flight she could get to New York. She booked coach—after all, people would be less likely to recognize her there—and packed her case before finally falling into bed.

. . .

SHE WOKE FEELING UNEASY. Her dreams had been full of those night-marish visions of violence again, and she showered and dressed, her stomach quivering with unease. Strangely, her parents were in her dreams, something that hadn't happened for a very long time, and she dreamed of the car wreck that had taken them away when she was young. She saw their mangled bodies, but in the dream, her mother opened her eyes and smiled the worst kind of rictus grin at her. "I'm dead, my darling, and soon, you will be, too."

Tiger had woken, sweating, and on the very edge of a panic attack, but she managed to deep-breathe her way out of it. After she dressed and fed Fizz, she called Apollo and asked him if she could leave her dog with him for a few days. She hadn't yet told Apollo that she and Lazlo were engaged, and as she stepped onto the plane to New York, she questioned herself as to why. Was she afraid of Apollo's reaction?

Thinking back to when he had told her that he and Nell were engaged and expecting Daisy, she didn't think so. He could hardly complain she was moving too fast. So why hadn't she told him? Was it because it was something so right, so precious, that she wanted to keep it to herself a little while longer? Maybe.

Sitting in coach, her cap pulled down low over her eyes, Tiger didn't see Grant Waller sitting across the aisle, shielded from her view by the female passenger next to him, but he had seen her.

He had followed her from her home this morning, surprised she was up so early, but when she reached the airport and headed for the New York flight, it made sense. She was going to Schuler. Given that Grant had only just gotten back to Seattle, it sucked that he had to get on yet another plane, but what the hell, he wasn't paying for it.

He followed her through the baggage claim and watched as she waited for her case. Her cellphone rang and she answered it, missing her bag as it sailed past her on the carousel. Grant didn't hesitate. He snatched up the case and began to walk quickly away before she could stop him. He was out of the airport in a flash and hailing a cab. He barked the name of a hotel at the driver and settled in. What was the point of that? he thought, looking at the overnight bag in his hands, but there was something so satisfying about knowing he'd inconvenienced her.

Maybe Loomis was right. Maybe this was all child's play. But, God, he was enjoying it.

TIGER WAITED for her bag for nearly thirty minutes, but then she had to find someone to help her. It was another two hours before the airline told her that her bag was missing. "We're so sorry, Miss Rose, but there's really nothing we can do. We'll look at the security camera footage because obviously, someone has stolen your bag."

Tiger gritted her teeth but thanked the representative. She walked out to meet Lazlo who was waiting for her, but as soon as she saw his face, she forgot about her bag. She threw her arms around his neck and kissed him. "Hello, baby..."

His kiss went on for what seemed an age and before long, they were breathless, knowing other people were watching them. Lazlo grinned down at her. "I guess we just went public. There are some very interested paps over there looking at you."

"I don't care. I love you." And she realized that was true.

IN THE CAB she told him about her bag. "Was there anything that meant a lot to you in there?"

She shook her head. "Not unless you count my old lady underwear."

Lazlo look mock-aghast. "Not the old lady panties? This is terrible."

Tiger grinned. "I'll be okay. I'll just have to shop for underwear while I'm here."

"Well, you won't need any for tonight if that helps," he leered at her, and she giggled.

"You'd better keep that promise."

Still, they stopped at a high-end store, and she bought what she needed: underwear, two pairs of jeans, a dress, and some loose comfortable tops. Lazlo told her the hotel was high-end and he wasn't kidding. All the toiletries she would ever need for a year, let alone a few days, were provided in the bathroom as well as fluffy white robes.

The bed was huge, and Tiger flopped down on it, remembering the plush hotels of her former life and wondered if she had ever appreciated them as much as she did right now. Probably not. She grinned and Lazlo asked her what was funny. She explained and he nodded.

"I know what you mean. Things are better if you don't have them all the time."

"Except you. I need you all the time." She trapped him by hooking a leg around his knee and pulling him down on top of her. "So, what's the plan for today, Mister?"

Lazlo was already unbuttoning her dress. "Well, Miss Rose, I intend to keep you busy—and naked—for most of today. Then, we've been invited to dinner with my sister and Massimo. They left the invite open so if you're feeling too nervous, we don't have to go tonight."

"No, I'd like to. Why wait?" Tiger kissed him. "Do they know we're engaged?"

"Not yet. I thought we'd tell them together."

Realization dawned on Tiger and she laughed. "What?"

"That's it. That's why I haven't told Apollo and Nell. We need to do it together."

"I'm glad you think so, too. Now, can we concentrate on the job at hand?"

Tiger snickered. "What kind of 'job' were you referring to? Because I'm happy to oblige..."

"My turn first." Lazlo buried his face in her neck, but she laughed, pushing him away.

"Oh, no, you always go first." She pushed him onto his back and moved down his body. "And then somehow we're fucking, and I haven't given you as much pleasure as you've given me."

"Not possible..." But he laid back and sighed happily as she freed his cock from his underwear and swept her lips over the wide crest of it. Tiger took her time, feeling every quiver down the length of it, feeling the hot blood pumping beneath the skin, making him hard as a stone.

"God... Tiger..."

She trailed her tongue up the shaft, flicking it over the sensitive tip until Lazlo was bucking and groaning under her. He made to withdraw so he could pleasure her, but she shook her head and he came into her mouth, shooting thick creamy, salty cum onto her tongue.

Tiger swallowed him down, moving up his body, kissing the hard ripple of his abs, sucking at each of his nipples, then fixing her mouth onto his, hard. His hands were in her hair then, pulling, gripping, winding the long dark hair around his fist. He flipped her onto her back, tugging her legs around his hips roughly, his cock thrusting deep inside her, his movements animal and feral.

He fucked her with abandon, his eyes locked onto hers as he pinned her to the bed and rammed his hips against hers harder and harder until she cried out both with pain and ecstasy. Her eyes were alive with desire. "Hurt me, Lazlo, make me scream..."

He tumbled her from the bed onto the floor, the carpet a luxurious shag pile, but still, as they wrestled with each other, Tiger felt the sting of carpet burn. It just made her more excited.

Lazlo flipped her onto her stomach and bound her wrists behind her back with the cord of a robe, pulling it tighter and tighter until her shoulders burned. He pushed her legs apart, gripped her pert, rounded buttocks, spreading them and eased into her ass. "I'm going to make you beg me to stop, baby girl."

"I'll never want you to..."

Tiger didn't know where the rest of the day went, but soon enough, Lazlo looked at the clock and sighed. "I hate to say this, but we're going to have to get ready if you want to have dinner with my sister."

They showered together, lathering soap over each other's bodies and fucking again, laughing as they slipped around on the cold, wet tile of the bathroom. In the cab to the restaurant, Tiger started to laugh when she saw that her wrists were red where he'd tied her up. "You'll have to tell them... God, what can we tell them?"

Lazlo was chuckling at her. "Believe me, if India asks, all I'll have to say to her is 'Christmas Eve, four years ago' to her, and we'll be fine."

Tiger raised her eyebrows at him. "Gossip?"

Lazlo grinned. "Let's just say India was in New York, Massimo was in Italy, and there was a really good internet service that night." He shuddered. "And she's loud."

"Dude!" Tiger was cackling with laughter. "You can't tell me that now, just as I'm about to meet her. Plus, that's your sister."

"I know," Lazlo rolled his eyes, "I'm scarred for life."

TIGER FORCED herself not to think about what Lazlo had told her when she shook hands with India Blue, and even though she herself was an ex-movie star, she still felt a little starstruck. She and India had met briefly before, a quick hello as they were passing at award shows, but India had always been warm and friendly, and that wasn't any different now.

"I'm so happy to finally meet you properly," India told her as they were shown to their table. "Massi has always spoken so highly of you, and I wish I'd been able to be around when you were doing promo for your movies together."

"I have always wanted to get to know you, too," Tiger admitted. "There are so many disingenuous people in our business, and you always seems one of the few people of whom no one had a bad word."

India flushed pink. "Thank you, that's a sweet thing to say. And you, too. I was talking to my friend Jess earlier today, and Teddy wanted me to say hi."

"He's a good man. If it wasn't for him..." She trailed off, thoughts of Grant Waller creeping back into her mind. She'd never forgotten Teddy taking care of her the day of the attack.

India squeezed her hand and bent her head closer. "Grant Waller is a scumbag. He actually reached out to me recently and asked to do an interview."

"I hope you told him no."

"I told him to fuck off and die," India said fiercely, then smiled sheepishly. "I really did. That asshole has a nerve. I'm so sorry for what happened to you."

"And I for you. Are you well now?"

India nodded, and she shot a look at Massimo who was deep in conversation with Lazlo. "We're... talking about children." She seemed to be about to say something else but stopped herself, and Tiger wondered what she was about to tell her.

But then Lazlo spoke up, lifting his glass and proposing a toast, shooting a glance at Tiger. He nodded and she realized he was about to tell them about the engagement.

Both India and Massimo looked delighted, and Indy hugged Tiger. "I'm so happy for you, and for Lazlo. If you knew how... just... God, I'm going to cry again." She dabbed at her damp cheeks with her handkerchief.

"She's a hormone machine at the moment," Massimo said, then when he realized what he'd said, he made a face at India, who rolled her eyes.

"Way to keep a secret, hubby." She smiled at Tiger. "Yeah, so we're pregnant. Well, I am, he gets none of the credit," she said, sticking her tongue at her grinning husband.

Tiger congratulated them both, but she couldn't miss that Massimo seemed more excited than India, and when finally they said goodnight, with India making Tiger promise to spend girl time together before she left New York, she embraced the other woman tightly.

Back at the hotel, Tiger asked Lazlo about India's reaction, and he explained about her first-born biological child. "She's scared it will happen again."

"I can understand that." She felt sad for India. "But we can't live life like some day we won't experience tragedy because we all know how that is."

"Yup. I think that's the reason Massimo is so positive, and don't get me wrong, India is coming around. She's actually two months gone already, but she didn't want to admit it until she'd decided whether to have the baby or not." Lazlo ran his hand through his hair. "They've been trying for a couple of years, and she thought it would never happen."

Tiger rested her head on Lazlo's shoulder. "I am happy for them."

"Me, too."

The atmosphere was different between them tonight, less animal, more tender. They took a long soak in the huge claw-footed bath tub, then went to bed, making love slowly, taking their time. Tiger clung to him, loving the feeling of his big body on hers, the hard muscles of his chest against her soft breasts.

Afterward they talked quietly. Lazlo brushed his lips against hers. "While we're here in Manhattan, what do you say we take a little trip to Tiffany's?"

Tiger grinned. "You romantic."

"You'll always outshine any precious jewel, but at least at Tiffany's, I know they'll be worthy of you."

Tiger snickered and Lazlo looked sheepish. "Was that cheesy?"

"Very, but I still love it." She giggled as he tickled her. "We have to tell Apollo and Nell the day we get back to Seattle."

"Agreed. Now, are you very tired?"

Tiger smiled, reading the lust in his eyes. "I'll never be too tired for you, baby."

And they made love for the remainder of the night.

14

CHAPTER FOURTEEN – BREATH CONTROL

SEATTLE

APOLLO ROSE OPENED the door of his apartment to see his sister and Lazlo outside. "Surprise!"

He gaped at them for a few seconds, then laughed. "Well, you got me. Come in..."

He stood aside to let them in, and Tiger hugged him as she entered the apartment. He kissed his sister's cheek. "We weren't expecting you for another few days."

"We came home early because we have something to tell you."

Nell greeted them, too, and Daisy waddled over to cuddle with her aunt. Tiger held her close.

"So, what's the news?"

Tiger glanced at Lazlo, and they both grinned before Tiger turned to her brother. "Please don't be angry or hurt... but Lazlo and I... we got married."

Apollo's mouth dropped open while Nell whooped and hugged Tiger. "Oh, darlings, that's wonderful."

Tiger turned to her brother. "We were shopping for engagement rings in Tiffany's, and suddenly Lazlo said, 'Why are we waiting?' I had no answer, so... we went to City Hall." She bit her lip looking at her brother, waiting to see how he would react.

Finally, Apollo shook his head, half-chuckling. "Well... damn. Congrats, both of you. Can't say I'm not shocked, but at the same time... I think I was half-expecting it." He shook hands with Lazlo, then laughed and pulled his new brother-in-law into a hug. "You promise to take care of her forever?"

"With all my heart, brother. Every second of every day."

"That's all I ask." Apollo grinned at his sister as he released Lazlo. "Come here."

The siblings held each other for a long time, Apollo whispering in his sister's ear. "I'm so happy for you, Tig."

"You must stay for the evening," Nell said, wiping a tear away, "I'm not saying we'll have a fancy time, but how does pizza and beer sound?"

"Perfect." Lazlo smiled at her.

In the end, Apollo insisted on at least running out to buy some champagne. While he was gone, Nell put Daisy to bed, and Tiger and Lazlo sat on the couch. Lazlo smiled down at his new wife.

They'd done exactly what they'd told Apollo they had done. Walking hand in hand to Tiffany's, they stopped outside and looked through the window at the engagement rings, but Tiger had been overwhelmed by them. "It just... it's not that they aren't beautiful, Laz, and I appreciate the thought, but it's not me anymore. My life isn't about the bling, the expensive clothes or shoes or jewelry. It's simpler than that. It's somehow purer, more honest. I don't care about baubles; all I care about is spending the rest of my life with you."

"Then why are we waiting?" Lazlo bent his head to kiss her. "Let's just take the leap. City Hall. You and me and two strangers for witnesses. We'll have a celebration with our families later, tell them we wanted the simplicity of a quick wedding before the judge. Indy and Massi will understand; Gabe won't even care about missing a wedding; they will all just be happy for us. What about Apollo and Nell?"

"The same, I think. Neither of them is into material things, and at least, we won't overshadow their wedding with a grand one of our own. We don't need it, do we?"

Lazlo shook his head. "So... we're doing this?"

Tiger grinned up at him. "Let's take the leap."

So, they were married two days later at City Hall, quietly; the vows taken were nothing flowery, but the depth of the feeling between them was obvious. Tiger couldn't take her eyes of this perfect man in front of her as they said the words that would bind them together. To her, nothing had ever been so right, so certain in her heart, as him. Lazlo Schuler. And now she thought back and realized their bond had been set that night at the hospital, when, although he hadn't known it, she had heard the raw honesty, the love in him, and had known he was a singular man.

As Lazlo predicted, Indy and Massimo were delighted for them, not caring about missing the actual wedding, and had taken them out for cocktails and dancing at a swanky place in Manhattan. They'd drunk mimosas and laughed until the early hours, then Tiger and Lazlo went back to their hotel and spent their wedding night making love, laughing and joking around.

The next night, Lazlo had suggested something that made Tiger's whole body ignite with anticipation. A club, an exclusive club that catered for the BDSM crowd. Lazlo suggested it over breakfast and Tiger readily agreed. "Damn, Laz... why didn't you suggest it before?"

"I just thought, seeing as we'll be going back to Seattle soon, we ought to take advantage of Manhattan as best we can."

"Ah, I see. Experiment but not on our own doorstep."

"Yup." Lazlo grinned. "Here, in Manhattan, we're kind of living the old life. Luxury hotel, expensive restaurants, high society. Let's take advantage before we go back to our quieter lives."

Tiger kissed him. "You're on."

So, that night, after eleven p.m., they took a cab to the club. Lazlo spoke quietly to the security guard at the door, and he stood aside to let them in. The club, set below ground, had exposed red-brick walls, and within them were set little alcoves, some curtained off, in which clients were kissing, fucking, and even whipping each other without any inhibitions.

Lazlo held Tiger's hand as they walked through the club, and there was only a little nervousness in her as he opened the door to a private room and led her in.

Inside, there was a huge four-poster bed at the end of which a wooden X-shaped cross stood. Tiger grinned as she saw the manacles attached to the top of it. "That looks like fun."

There was also a table, wooden, with manacles at one end where he or she could lie as the other fucked them. Tiger ran her tongue over her bottom lip as it curved up into a smile.

Lazlo chuckled. "There are so many toys in here, baby, and we can enjoy everything you want to."

Tiger walked slowly around the room, gently touching all of the paddles, crops, nipple clamps. She picked up a cock ring and smiled at Lazlo. "I'd like you to wear this."

"Whatever goes, baby." He walked to a closet and opened in. Inside hung various harnesses. Tiger saw Lazlo pick out one, a butter-soft leather one, and show it her. "And I'd like you to wear this."

Tiger smiled and slipped out of her coat. Underneath she was wearing a simple silky slip dress, and she nudged the straps from her shoulders, letting it slither to the floor. She wore nothing underneath, and she saw Lazlo's pupils dilate, heard his sharp intake of breath and she smiled.

He helped her into the harnesses and as he fastened it for her, she slid her hand down and cupped his cock through his pants. "I like being naked while you're fully dressed. I like being possessed by you, like this."

"Would you like to fuck first?"

Her answer was a smile, and her hands unzipped his pants and freed his cock from his underwear. It was already hard, but as she stroked it, she felt the hot rush of blood pounding through the veins, and it became rock-hard under her touch. "I love your cock," she murmured, "I love to touch it, taste it, feel it deep inside me. Take me on that table, Laz, take me and fucking drill this magnificent cock deep inside me..."

Lazlo grabbed her then, turned on beyond reason, and did as she asked, pushing her down onto the table, locking her wrists in the manacles and shoving her thighs apart so he could thrust his diamond-hard cock deep into her ready, wet cunt. Tiger gasped at the sudden violence but loved every moment as Lazlo's cock slammed into her, his fingers working her clit, his mouth rough on hers.

He made her come again and again, but refuse to let her off of the table until she was almost delirious with pleasure. Lazlo wanted to stroke her tenderly then, but she shook her head, instead rolling onto her stomach and fixing him with a demanding stare. "You know what I want, husband."

Lazlo grinned and Tiger rested her head on the table as he strolled to the cabinet and picked out a crop. It wasn't especially long, but thick, and as he cracked it against his palm, Tiger grinned to herself. The next second, she yelled as Lazlo brought it down hard against her buttocks, urging him to strike her again. He obliged as she moaned with pleasure. "Open your legs, beautiful."

Tiger spread her legs, and he cracked the tip of the crop against her sex and she shrieked.

"Too much?" Lazlo's voice was immediately concerned, but she shook her head.

"No... again..."

She heard his low throaty chuckle, then the crop was flicked against her clit and she came, hard, suddenly, moaning loudly. "God, Lazlo... don't ever stop loving me..."

"Impossible..." he said, breathing hard, and she turned her head to see him, one hand gripping his cock as he gazed at her body.

"Let me suck you," she breathed hard and he moved to the head of the table so she could take him into her mouth. Tiger hollowed out her cheeks as she tasted him, and when he came, she swallowed him down with obvious enjoyment.

He unfastened her wrists from the manacles and turned her onto her back, picking her up and carrying her to the bed. As she lay there, she watched him finally strip down and then his body was covering hers.

Tiger ran her hands down his thickly muscled arms. "Did I do okay?"

Lazlo chuckled. "Did I? Believe it or not, I'm new at this. You were amazing."

"So were you. God, what a rush... not that making love with you isn't always a rush, but Laz, that I can trust another person enough, that I can really trust you enough to do this... it's incredible to me. After what happened."

"What happened to you, what Waller did, that wasn't sex, it was violence. Not the same, not the same at all." Lazlo kissed her. "And thank you for trusting me. It means the world."

TIGER LOOKED up at Lazlo now, smiling and knew he was thinking of the same night. "Adventures together," she whispered, and he smiled.

"For the rest of our lives."

Nell came back in, glancing at the clock. "Pol's taking his time. Knowing him, he's driving around every liquor store looking for the most expensive champagne he can find."

A half hour later, she tried to call him but got no answer. An hour later, Tiger and Nell began to call around as Lazlo went out to see if he could find Apollo.

Three hours later, the police came to the apartment to tell them that Apollo had been in a hit and run.

CHAPTER FIFTEEN – CRUEL WORLD

Los Angeles to Seattle

DEX LOOMIS HAD BEEN apoplectic with rage when Grant Waller had called him to tell him that Tiger had married Lazlo Schuler. Waller had sounded almost as if he were mocking Dex. It had been a mistake to get the journalist involved.

Dex had thought, after Waller's attack on Tiger, that he'd found someone who shared his hatred of her, that he would be willing to facilitate what Dex needed from him: Tiger's demise.

He should have known he would have to do it himself. The trouble was he was just gaining traction on his career, and he worked for someone who, unusually for Hollywood, didn't stand for any scandal or misbehavior. None. A colleague had been caught with remnants of coke in a bathroom and had been fired on the spot. Remnants, not even a full line of the stuff.

So, if Dex wanted Tiger Rose dead, he would have to be careful about it. Leave no trail. So, yeah, hiring Grant Waller was a huge mistake. He would have to do this himself, but... he would test the water first.

Let's ruin the bitch's honeymoon period, he thought grimly. He told his assistant he would be out of town for a few days and drove to Seattle. Booking into a motel, using cash, he didn't want there to be a money trail back to him. He spent a couple of days camping out outside Tiger's brother's apartment, not knowing how he was going to play this. He'd bought an old car for cash from Craig's List, something that again, could not be traced back to him and was careful not to leave any trace of himself that he could avoid. He wasn't that worried; there was nothing anywhere that could raise any suspicion of him. His path had never crossed with the Rose family before, certainly not in a way that could link back to Dex.

Then he saw them arrive. Tiger and her new husband. Dex couldn't take his eyes off of her. She looked more beautiful then he'd ever seen her, her hair dark, long, and loose around her shoulders, her eyes sparkling, no makeup on that exquisite face. It made Dex's cock hard and his hatred palpable. He wanted to hurt her, emotionally as well as physically.

When the brother had set out alone in his car, Dex followed him. He was going from liquor store to liquor store ,and at the last one on the outskirts of the city, Dex saw his chance. As the young man walked back to his car, champagne in hand, Dex floored the gas and took him out with a glancing blow just as Apollo reached for his car door handle. Apollo was thrown in the air, slamming down with a sickening crunch onto the hood of Dex's car. Dex saw the shocked look in Apollo's eyes as they met Dex's, then the injured man's eyes closed, and he slid from the hood onto the ground.

Dex gunned the engine and sped out of the parking lot of the liquor store, glancing in his rearview mirror at the prone figure slumped unmoving on the ground. He drove for a while, changing directions until he finally came to a stop back at his motel.

Dex got out of the car and inspected the damage. There was blood smeared on the hood, and he grabbed a cloth from the back and washed it off. Otherwise, there was crumpled areas but nothing that looked out of place on the already battered vehicle.

Dex grabbed a handful of snacks from the vending machine and went to his room, dumping his food on the bed and flicking on the television. He changed the channel to a local news site and sat watching, mindlessly, waiting for any report of the accident. "Accident," he grinned to himself. He knew, in this day and age of instant media, that once news broke of the incident, that Tiger Rose's beloved younger brother was hurt or even dead, that she would finally be exposed.

He smirked and called Grant Waller. Waller sounded half drunk when he picked up the call. "What?"

"You might want to be nicer to the guy paying for that good liquor, Waller. Anyways, this is just a courtesy call. That article you were writing about Tiger? You might want to post it online or you'll be beaten to the punch."

Grant was alert then. "What the fuck are you talking about?"

Dex laughed. "You'll see." He ended the call and threw back another handful of chips. Tomorrow morning, he would go rent a car and drive down to his place in Lake Tahoe, stay there for a few days, establish an alibi. Not that he'd need one. Who the hell would suspect him?

He looked up at the television as the first reports of the hit and run started to come in. They didn't know yet that the victim was Tiger Rose's brother, that was clear, and maybe they wouldn't. No details of the victim's condition, but that could just mean they were waiting for the family.

Satisfied, Dex turned the television off and went to bed, falling quickly into a deep sleep, not caring that he almost certainly killed a man.

TIGER'S CHEST felt constricted and tight as the doctor explained what was happening to them. Apollo was in surgery now, and the doctor would not give them the odds of his survival yet, just saying his injuries were severe.

"As far as we can figure, he was almost certainly hit directly by the car. He has broken limbs, his left arm, right wrist and shoulder are fractured. But what concerns us is the internal bleeding. We're trying to stop it now."

Nell hugged Daisy to her, both of them silent and still. Tiger sat next to them, her hand in Nell's, the other in Lazlo's. All of them were dazed by the evening's events. It just didn't seem real. There were a lot of police officers there, too, and the lead detective told them they were treating it as an attempted murder. Tiger wanted to scream, but seeing Nell so devastated yet calm made her realize she couldn't lose it in front of her young niece.

Eventually, Nell called a friend to come pick up Daisy and take her home. The friend offered to take care of Fizz, too, but Tiger wanted him to be with someone he knew, but she couldn't bring herself to leave the hospital. She called Sarah and explained what had happened. "Is there any way you could come bring Fizz back to your place for a few days?"

"Of course, darling, I'm so sorry. Is there any news?"

"Not yet." Tiger felt her throat thicken and willed herself not to cry. "I'll call you when there is."

A few hours later, a senior nurse came to see Tiger. "Could I speak to you privately?"

Oh God. Tiger felt vomit rise in her throat, and the nurse put her hand on her arm. "It's not about your brother, Miss Rose, don't be alarmed. No, it's the press. They've found out your brother was the one in the accident, and there's a pack of them downstairs. Normally we would throw them out, but there's so many of them. Is there any chance you could speak to them?"

"I'll go." Tiger heard Lazlo's voice behind them, and she turned to see him looking at her with concern. Lazlo put his arm around Tiger and nodded at the nurse. "I'll go speak to them, ask them to act responsibly and respectfully. I'm sorry if they've caused a nuisance."

"Thank you, Mr. Schuler."

When they were alone, Lazlo pulled Tiger close, and she looked up at him. "Are you sure, Laz?"

He smiled and kissed her. "This is what I do, remember?"

"Not for me."

"Yes, for you. Of course, for you. We're a team now, remember? I'll go tell them we don't know anything. I doubt we'll be able to get rid of them entirely, but... we have to deal with the fact that our little secret is out now."

"Not entirely. They don't know I live here, too." But she knew he was right. "Well," she sighed, "it doesn't matter now. All that matters now is that Apollo pulls through." Even saying it made her voice crack and suddenly she couldn't breathe. She bent double and sucked in some air while Lazlo rubbed her back.

Finally, she felt better and stood. "Sorry."

"Don't apologize. How you're still standing is beyond me. When India... well. We shouldn't talk about that now, but just to say, you're my hero. Now, I'm going to go down and try to ease the standoff with the press. Will you be okay?"

Tiger kissed him. "Go. I'm going to sit with Nell and wait for the doctor."

Lazlo nodded and disappeared to the elevators. Tiger went back to the relative's room to wait with Nell. Nell was standing at the window, staring out at the dawn, and Tiger went to her side and slipped her hand into Nell's, feeling her friend squeeze it.

"He's not going to make it, is he?" Nell said quietly but calmly, and Tiger shook her head.

"He is, Nell. He'll pull through. He loves you and Daisy Boo too much to give up. He'll be fighting." She took a deep breath in. "And life cannot be this unfair. Our parents died in a car wreck. No, the pendulum has to swing our way sometimes."

Nell sighed and leaned her head on Tiger's shoulder. "I hope so, Tig. I can't imagine my life without him."

APOLLO'S SURGEON came to see them less than a half hour later. Lazlo was still not back from dealing with the press, but as the doctor came into the room, Tiger felt her heart clench with fear.

"We've stabilized him," were the first words out of the doctor's mouth, and Tiger felt Nell's body sag and held her friend up. The doctor sat down and took Nell's hands. "He's not out of the woods, but we've managed to repair the internal bleeding and his heart is strong. We gave him a CT scan, and there seems to be no brain injury, but obviously we'll know more when he's awake. It'll be a long road to recovery, but this is a good sign."

"Can we see him?"

"In a while. He's in recovery at the moment, and obviously, he'll be asleep for a time yet. But as soon as it's safe, you can sit with him."

"Thank you so much, doctor."

He smiled at them both, but then his expression turned serious. "The police will want to speak with him soon, too, if you consent."

"It's up to Apollo, if he can make that decision, but of course, anything we can do to catch the scumbag who did this."

"Quite." He patted Nell's hand and smiled at Tiger. "I'll see you both later."

"Thank you, doctor."

As he left the room, Nell leaned forward, putting her face in her hands and starting to cry, purely out of relief, and Tiger wrapped her arms around her and held her as she sobbed. A few tears of her own escaped, but she wiped them on the sleeve of her shirt. She didn't want Nell to feel alone right now, that she had no one to hold her up. She was her sister and she would do anything for her. Family is more than blood, she thought, leaning her head on Nell's, rocking her sister slightly to comfort her.

LAZLO CAME BACK to the room shortly afterward, and they told him the good news. He looked as relieved as they were, and Tiger realized just how invested he was in their family. It gave her strength.

The doctor allowed one of them to sit with Apollo a few minutes later, and having briefly looked in on him, Tiger told Nell she should be the one to sit with her brother. "We'll be right here when the doc allows us in, but he needs to be with his love."

Nell kissed her cheek. "I love you both so much."

"We love you, too, sweetie."

Nell went to hold her man's hand as he slept, and Lazlo took Tiger off to a private room. "Sweetheart, I have some news."

Her heart sank as she sat down. "What?"

"There's a story online. It basically outs you, your life on the island, our marriage, everything. Everything."

Tiger gaped at him. "What? How the fuck did they find out everything so quickly? This only happened last night."

"That's just it, baby. Apparently, the editor of the online gossip site has had this in his pocket for a few weeks."

"Who is the writer?"

Lazlo's face was grim. "That's just it. The editor owed me a favor and told me the writer got in contact with him a couple of months ago. Around the time Grant Waller was released from prison."

"Oh, fuck. So, he has been following me?"

Lazlo stopped. "What?"

Tiger sighed. "There was a couple of incidents, nothing heavy, but I put it down to me being paranoid."

"You didn't tell me."

"It wasn't a big thing, not then, but when you put it together with the sto—" It was Tiger's turn to stop talking, and she felt ice in her veins. "Oh, my God."

"What?"

Her hands were trembling. "What if... what if he... Apollo..."

Lazlo drew her close. "We'll tell the police and they'll question him. But I have to say, why release a story about you the day after he tries to kill Apollo? It would, and will, make him the prime suspect."

"I feel sick."

"Should I get the nurse?"

Tiger shook her head. "Look, God, although I hate the idea of being exposed, what can the story possibly say that would hurt me now? People have already found out I'm here, and they'll soon get sick of bothering me when they find out I'm just a coffee house owner now. All that matters is our family."

"I agree, but I'll help with the press side of things."

Tiger looked at him gratefully. "Guess your sabbatical is up."

"Guess so." He kissed her. "Talking of which, India called me when she heard the news. She said she and Massimo would get on a plane the moment you wanted them to be here for you. She loves you, Tig."

"And I love her. This has been a terrible day, but for one thing: Apollo and I really found out who our family was. That has to be a good thing for all of us."

Later, Nell came to find them and told them Apollo was waking up, and Tiger and Lazlo went in to see him. Although groggy and in obvious pain, he was still kidding around with them.

It wasn't until later when Tiger was alone with her brother that he became serious. Tiger stroked his forehead, noticing how clammy it was. "Pol? Did you see the guy's face?"

"Kind of, although I can't remember the details." He winced and Tiger saw him press the button that delivered morphine to his aching body. "I do remember that the car was aimed right at me. Right at me, Tig. I remember flying up into the air, then crashing down on top of his car. I must have wrecked the shit out of it, but he didn't stop."

"Did you tell the police all of this?"

"I did, but I couldn't tell them why."

"Why?"

Apollo looked steadily at her. "Why someone would want to kill me. Tig... I'm scared. I don't want to leave Nell and Daisy alone. Who would want to kill me, of all people? What the hell is going on?"

CHAPTER SIXTEEN – WAITING ON THE WORLD TO CHANGE

SEATTLE

GRANT WAS glad that he had a cast-iron alibi for the night someone tried to kill Apollo Rose. He spent the evening and most of the night drinking in a downtown bar, eventually leaving after the bartender called him an Uber. He'd been in that vehicle at the same time Apollo had been struck and injured, so there was a record. Still, it gave him a little thrill of both fear and excitement. He had no problem surmising that Dex Loomis had been the one to try and kill Apollo Rose—the question was—why?

And clearly, Loomis didn't care if his actions led straight to him, Grant. Asshole. He thought back now to see if any of the money could be traced back to Loomis and realized how clever the man had been. Even if he, Grant, were to implicate Loomis, there was no evidence. So, if Tiger were to be killed—and if Loomis had tried to kill the brother, it was a real possibility he would try to harm Tiger—there was no way he would be implicated.

Unless Grant could find out the reason why. After all, he was a journalist, right? This was his thing. If he could dig up a link between

Dex Loomis and the Rose siblings, then maybe he could head off any blame Loomis might want to frame him for.

He had to get out of Seattle, that was clear, but he didn't to alert Loomis to the fact he was now working against him; he'd continue to take his money and pretend to stalk Tiger, but now things had changed for Grant. Somewhere along the line, he'd lost the motivation to hurt Tiger. His schoolyard-stalking had spooked her enough, and now with her brother being hurt...

"Christ, Grant man, you're going soft." But Dex Loomis's mysterious campaign had reignited Grant's love for investigation, something that had been missing from his life since before his pathetic, nonsensical attack on Tiger Rose.

Because now he saw himself for what he was. A toxic male with a fragile ego. It was a hard look in the mirror, but having met a true psychopath in Dex Loomis, he could confront his own demons now, and he didn't like what he was seeing.

Jesus, what is this, a fuckin' psychology class? Grant got up and packed his things. He'd leave enough that it looked like he still lived there if Loomis' spies came calling. Grant had been through the apartment after Loomis had found out about the hookers and checked that there were no hidden cameras, but he found the space clear. So that meant, Loomis had people on the outside. If Grant could get a photograph of one of them, it might link back to Loomis.

That was a thought. Hmm. Maybe he should try and lead whoever was watching him on a wild goose chase to smoke them out. Could he risk going to the hospital where Apollo was? That would interest them, surely. He smirked to himself and grabbed his keys.

NELL HAD GONE HOME to tend to Daisy and bring her to the hospital to see Apollo. Lazlo was dealing with the press, and Tiger sat with her brother, holding his hand as he slept. He was definitely doing better, but the injuries, the trauma, and the medication wiped him out a lot.

Tiger was lost in her thoughts when she heard someone clear their throat at the door to Apollo's room. She looked up to see a well-dressed man she didn't recognize at the door. "Hi," he said softly, with a friendly smile, "I just wanted to stick my head in and say I hope everything is okay."

Tiger stood. Was this a journalist? The man was wearing an expensive suit, Saville Row, she guessed, and was handsome in a bland way. "Thank you, Mr..."

"Fenway. Harry Fenway. We worked together years ago on stage in New York. I was just an extra, and you probably don't recognize me, but my wife is here giving birth to our first child, and I heard you were here. I just wanted to give my best wishes. I don't want to intrude."

Tiger half-smiled. She got up and steered him from the room politely. "Just so we don't wake him while we talk."

"Of course. Like I said, I don't want to intrude."

"No, it's very kind of you. How is your wife? And the baby?"

"A boy. Our first," he said again, and Tiger noticed his eyes gleaming with joyful tears.

"I'm very happy for you."

Harry Fenway smiled. "You don't remember me, do you?"

Tiger gave him a sheepish smile. "I'm sorry, no, but I haven't worked on stage for, God, fifteen years?"

"I think it has been that long, I'm not surprised you don't remember. You were always very nice to us, though, so I wanted to say hi."

Tiger shook his hand, touched. "I appreciate that, and I hope you and your wife are very happy with your new baby. Do you live in the city?"

Harry smiled. "We live out in the San Juan Islands."

"Oh." She didn't tell him she lived there, too; she didn't know him well enough to share that particular piece of information. Hell, she didn't know him at all but he seemed genuine.

Harry nodded now. "I'll leave you alone now, but please, give your brother my best wishes. I remember him coming to the theater as a kid."

"That's kind, thank you. Great to see you again."

Tiger watched him walk away, raising a hand as he turned back to wave at the end of the corridor. Sweet guy.

DEX LOOMIS WALKED AWAY from Tiger, grinning to himself. So, it really was that easy to get near her then? Where was that husband of hers? He got his answer when he saw Lazlo Schuler in the elevator he was waiting for, and the man brushed past him as he exited. As the doors closed, Dex saw Tiger greet Lazlo with a kiss, her lovely face glowing with love.

Enjoy it while you can.

It seemed his plan to kill the brother had failed, but that was okay. It had given him the opportunity to see what kind of security Tiger had in place. He'd seen a few local cops, one or two detective types, but no bodyguards as such. Most unlike a Hollywood star, but then again, Tiger was no longer that star. She was a small business owner in a remote part of the world. Remote-ish. The address Waller had given him was for an island in the Sound. Maybe he should go scope it out, see if there were any weak links there, any ways he could get into her house, to get to Tiger when she was alone.

But when would she be alone now? The press had found out who she was, and although it was an annoyance, it also meant he would have some cover if he needed it. Telling her he lived on the same group of islands meant that if he were to 'accidently' run into her again, it wouldn't look suspicious.

And he fully intended to run into Tiger Rose again. Not least when he killed her. That was the day he was really looking forward to.

THE NEXT DAY, Apollo insisted Tiger and Lazlo go home and rest. "I'm doing okay, and you can't put your lives on hold any longer," he smiled at them. Despite being covered in bruises, black and stark against his pale skin, he looked better. His broken limbs would take time to heal, and it frustrated him to be so reliant on his family and the hospital staff, but Apollo was just relieved to be alive, that much was obvious.

Tiger thought about that as she and Lazlo took the ferry back to their island home. Leaning her head on his shoulder, she felt herself relax for the first time since Apollo's accident. Not accident, since someone tried to kill him. The police had made no progress except to find the car that hit Apollo, abandoned and burnt out. No trace of the owner, no DNA, anything. The liquor store's security cameras had only picked up the car hitting Apollo, footage the police had warned her against seeing, but Tiger had insisted in case she recognized anything.

It had killed her to watch it, but she'd kept her countenance until she got back to the hotel with Lazlo, and then she had sobbed out of grief, out of rage. "I want to kill whoever did it," she almost screamed as Lazlo tried to calm her down, "I want to tear them apart with my bare hands."

"I know, I know..." And the thing was, Tiger knew that Lazlo did know exactly how that felt, and although it made her feel guilty, she was glad she wasn't alone in this.

The weather outside the ferry was rough, the seas roiling, the rain lashing down. It was only just past noon, but the sky was so dark with angry purple and black clouds crowding the sky. The ferry lurched up and down, and she felt her stomach twisting with nausea. "Yuck."

She felt Lazlo's lips against her temple. "Okay?"

"Just a little sick feeling. It'll go, it's just the boat rocking."

"Ferry boat."

She grinned at him. "Nerd."

"Your nerd."

"You know it."

WHEN THE FERRY DOCKED, they walked quickly to find a cab that would take them to their home. Neither wanted to get soaked, but the rain was so heavy that even the short run from the cab to their front door drenched the pair of them.

Inside, they raced each other up the stairs and stripped off, shivering and laughing. Lazlo cranked the shower on and let the water heat up before they both gladly got in.

Things got sexy almost immediately as they soaped each other's bodies and kissed under the hot spray, and soon Lazlo was lifting her and impaling her with his cock as the water streamed over them. They fucked, as best as they could, in the slippery shower, laughing and joking as they did, before tumbling onto the cool tile floor of the bathroom and making each other come. Tiger smiled up at him as they recovered.

"This truly beats any fantasy honeymoon location. Just you and me on the bathroom floor with your big cock buried inside me."

Lazlo laughed. "My wife has the dirtiest mouth."

"Perfectly complimenting my husband's dirty mind," she grinned and kissed him. "We should get dressed though. I told Sarah we'd go pick Fizz up this afternoon."

IN THE END, Lazlo decided to go pack his things up and move them to Tiger's—now their—home while Tiger went to collect her dog. Sarah hugged her friend as Fizz went crazy, barking, his tail wagging delightedly as Tiger picked him up. "Hello, sweet doggie. Did you miss me?"

"I'll say he did," Sarah said fondly, "and I'm going to miss having him around. He's a little angel."

"Isn't he?" Tiger kissed her dog's silky head. "There's plenty of other pooches need rescuing."

Sarah laughed. "Maybe, maybe. How's Apollo?"

"He's getting there. I still don't think he knows just how much rehab is in store for him, but he's just grateful he's alive. We all are."

"Awful way to start married life." Sarah said with a sly grin. "It's okay, it was in the newspaper, is all."

"I was going to tell you, but then this thing happened..."

"Don't worry about it. And congratulations, I'm delighted for you." Sarah went to make them some tea. "I take it Lazlo will be moving here permanently then?"

"I think so. I hope so," Tiger laughed, "We're going to be living together at my place because I own it, and he only leases his, but we haven't thought further ahead than that. He knows my home is here on the island now, but his work might take him anywhere. We'll make it work."

Sarah studied her. "You know, this is the most positive I've seen you since you moved here."

"It is?"

"Yes. It feels like you're taking more chances, risking some stuff. It's inspiring." Sarah gave a strange little smile then, half-shy, and Tiger narrowed her eyes at her.

"What's up? What are you hiding?"

Sarah's cheeks flamed dark red. "I might have met someone."

"No way! I mean, sorry, I didn't mean to sound so amazed, of course you were always going to meet someone, but when did this happen? Details, woman, details!"

Sarah threw her head back and laughed. "Slow your roll, Rose. It just happened. Literally two days ago, but... it's been a while since a man flirted with me... no, I mean, really flirted, not just banter at the coffee house. I went to a bar across the island, during lunch, to see a guy I knew about something for the new place. While I was there, this guy started to talk to me, wanted to know about the movie house. He'd overheard me and was interested."

"...in what's in your pants," Tiger muttered, and Sarah laughed.

"And that's a bad thing?"

Tiger grinned. "Nope. So, what's he like? What does he do?"

"He's in construction—"

"—useful."

Sarah smiled. "He's tall, good-looking, and not married. So, he says. We're having lunch next week."

"Not rushing things?"

"Nope."

"Good for you. But still—you get yours."

Sarah grinned, going red again. "Talking of which... I suppose the honeymoon has been postponed?"

"No, we're still having one as such... just at home. Naked."

They both laughed, and Sarah hugged Tiger. "I really am so happy for you, and I'm glad Apollo is doing well. Listen, we need to start talking about the renovation when you have some time. People are already bugging me about when the new coffee house will open."

ON A WHIM as she drove home, Tiger made a detour to the old movie house. Because of the past couple of weeks, she had almost forgotten about it, but now as she stepped out onto the wet sidewalk and looked at it, she felt the excitement of it again. She and Sarah would build this place into something the islanders could enjoy and bring their families, too. She couldn't wait.

TIGER DIDN'T SEE the car parked across the street, its driver watching her intently. So, this was Tiger Rose's retirement plan? He'd let her have it. Let her build it just so he could burn it all down. Dex Loomis smiled bitterly to himself. You have no idea how I've suffered, Tiger Rose, but you will.

You will.

CHAPTER SEVENTEEN - DIAMONDS

The Island, San Juan Islands, Washington State

TO EVERYONE'S JOY, Apollo was released from hospital in time for Christmas, and Tiger and Lazlo insisted that the whole family come to stay with them during the holidays. Nell worried about being an imposition but admitted to Tiger that she was relieved in some ways. "As long as you're sure we won't be too much."

Tiger hugged her tightly. "I'm very, very sure. We're a family and with everything that's happened, we need to be together."

"We won't be imposing on the newlyweds?"

Tiger rolled her eyes. "Nonsense. Besides... the walls are pretty thick here." She grinned as Nell protested, laughing.

Daisy, of course, was delighted with the adventure of being away from the apartment and even more excited that she could play with Fizz all day, every day. Tiger saw that Nell was grateful that her little girl was distracted from her father's pain. Although Apollo was laughing and joking around, Tiger could tell he was suffering, and she did everything she could to make him feel included and not stuck on the outskirts of the celebrations because of his broken limbs. It killed her to see her younger brother so indisposed.

They invited India and Massimo to come to the island, too, for the festivities, and they readily accepted, although told her they would stay in a hotel on the island. "You already have a houseful, darling," India told her over the phone, "and we'll just get in the way. But we'll be there to help any way we can."

Lazlo drove to SeaTac to pick his sister and her husband up from the airport, and they all returned, telling Tiger and the others tales of trying to avoid the paparazzi who had gotten wind of the arrival of two huge stars.

"If you'd have been there, too," India laughed as she hugged Tiger, "I don't want to know what might have happened. God, how embarrassing."

Nell's eyes were huge as she was introduced to India and Massimo, and Tiger nudged her. "Are you starstruck?"

"A little." Nell gave her a wicked grin. "Funny how I never was with you."

"Cheeky."

"Diva."

Tiger and Nell laughed and went to join the others in the living room. India was already play-flirting with Apollo, making him laugh and Massimo roll his eyes. "Don't be fooled. This woman has a hero-complex."

Lazlo snorted and India grinned. "Look who's talking. Anyway, I'm so happy to finally meet you all—Tiger told me all about you." She winked at Tiger, then looked at Apollo. "She even told me some good stuff about you."

"Ha," Apollo shot back, "she must have been drunk."

THE JOKING around and laughing lasted all day. It was Christmas Eve, and when Daisy had finally been persuaded to go to bed, Tiger broke out the booze for the adults. Apollo sulked because his strong pain meds meant he couldn't drink, and India patted her small bump on her belly. "I'm with you, Pol," she said, already friendly enough with him to use his nickname. "We shall have to be the boring responsible adults."

The adults played a lewd but hilarious card game as they enjoyed their evening, but India couldn't help but notice that Tiger wasn't drinking either. When Tiger went to fetch more chips and salsa for them all, India followed her into the kitchen. "You're not drinking?"

Tiger shook her head. "Just don't feel like it. A little nausea is all."

India gave her a knowing stare and Tiger flushed. "The test says negative."

"But tests can be wrong."

Tiger nodded. "And it is early. My period is only three days late, and it's never been like clockwork." She caught India's hand. "Is this too far? For Lazlo, I mean. Everything has been at light speed and now... if I am pregnant... is this the straw?"

"What straw?" India was confused. "Tiger, Lazlo loves you beyond words. So, what if it's fast? Massi and I had to postpone our relationship because of outside forces, and it nearly killed us. And me, too, actually, ha ha. But, seriously, Tiger, these things happen when they happen. Stop applying dumb societal rules to your own life, you know better." She gave a sheepish grin. "Sorry, that was a bit much."

"No, it wasn't and thank you. I needed to hear that, Indy. Of course, this could all be moot."

India squeezed her arm. "Have you got more tests?"

Tiger nodded. "Squirreled away upstairs. I didn't want to either upset or excite Lazlo unless I'm sure."

India gave her a look and Tiger laughed. "You want me to take another now, don't you?"

Indy grinned. "Sisters, remember? We'll sneak away, pretend we're doing girl things. Hang on a sec, I'll get Nell, too."

"Good idea."

Nell looked confused as India asked her to join Tiger and herself upstairs, and all the men looked suspicious. "Girl things." India said with a firm voice and they grinned.

"Fine." And they went back to their game.

Standing outside the bathroom as Tiger went in to pee on the pregnancy test in private, India filled Nell in. "So, we're just... taking a test?"

"For now." India smiled at her, giggling when she saw Nell turn red. "What?"

"I cannot believe I'm standing here with India Blue talking about peeing on a stick."

Indy snorted. "Believe me, I'm nothing special."

"I disagree. You and Tiger... man. You know your song, Believing in Forever? That's my and Apollo's song. It's the song we have picked out for our first dance at our wedding."

India was touched. "Oh, wow, I am honored." She smiled shyly at Nell. "If you want the live version, I'd be happy to sing at your wedding."

Nell gaped at her and India laughed. "We are family now, Nell."

Nell was still shaking her head in disbelief when Tiger called them in. She was washing her hands, her eyes riveted to the test sitting on the edge of the sink. "Three minutes. I couldn't pee for a while."

"Stage fright?"

Tiger and Nell groaned at India's bad joke, but she grinned at them. "Just trying to make the time pass quicker."

She took Tiger's hand. "You okay?"

Tiger nodded. India smiled at her kindly. "Either way, it's okay, right?"

"Either way."

TIGER COUNTED DOWN the last seconds before she looked at the pregnancy test, then picked it up. For a second, she couldn't focus on it, but then it was clear. A smile broke out over her face.

"Pregnant," she said quietly, then whooped loudly.

Nell shushed her, but she smiled. "Daisy's asleep."

"Sorry... oh my God. Oh, my God, oh my God... I have to tell Laz." Tiger was so excited she almost fell down the stairs before India grabbed her. Indy was giggling at her excitement, and Tiger could tell she was delighted for her.

"Breathe, Tig. Nell and I will go ask Lazlo to come up to see you. Stay here." She hugged her quickly then she and Nell went downstairs.

Left alone, Tiger gathered herself, her hand over her belly. Was this real? She smiled, tears in her eyes, then Lazlo was coming up the stairs. His eyes dropped to her belly immediately and he stopped on the top stair. "Really?"

She nodded, the tears escaping down her cheeks and Lazlo was there then, lifting her up and spinning around. She shushed him, pointing at the guest room door behind which Daisy was sleeping, and with one slick move, Lazlo whisked her into their bedroom.

Closing the door behind them, he gazed down at her. Tiger tried to read his expression past the smile on his face. "Are you sure you're okay with this? It wasn't planned, I know, but we, well, we haven't exactly been careful."

Lazlo laughed. "Are you kidding? Of course, it's okay! More than okay... God, Tiger... we're having a baby?"

"We are..." She started to laugh, almost incredulously. "Man, we don't do things by half, do we?"

"Nah, but who cares? This is our family, this is our life now." His lips were on hers, then and there was no more need to talk.

They didn't go back downstairs but stayed in their bedroom, leaving their guests to figure out what they were doing. "They'll survive one more night without us..."

They made love slowly, their gaze never leaving the others, and afterward, Lazlo cradled her in his arms, his fingers splayed out over her belly. "How far along are you?"

"Well, it can't be more than a few weeks." Tiger chuckled. "And definitely not more than two months."

"Is that really how long it's been since we met? No, that can't be right."

They grinned at each other. "When you know, you know," he shrugged, and Tiger kissed him.

"This baby is going to be so loved… and so close in age to his or her cousin. That's kinda cool."

Lazlo smiled. "I'm surprised Indy didn't give it away when she came downstairs. I could see she was excited about something."

"I love her so much. And Nell, too. I never had sisters before."

Lazlo stroked her hair. "You don't talk about your parents that much. I'd like to know more about them."

Tiger nodded. "They were so in love with each other."

"Like us."

"Like us." She kissed him again. "Dad was a lot older than Mom, twenty years or so, but he'd never married before he met her. He was an appellate judge, Mom was a bookseller. He walked into her store one day and that was that. They married—" she stopped and laughed, "—they married three weeks after they met. Guess speedy weddings run in the family."

Lazlo grinned. "Did they have you right away?"

"No, about five years later. Then Apollo, obviously. Mom wanted more kids, but Dad said he was getting too old, and they should stop at what he called the perfect two. So, it was just me and Pol and we were all so happy, Laz, you have no idea. Then one day, they were coming home from a benefit function and boom. A van sideswiped them and it was all over. The other driver didn't even stop."

Tiger shivered involuntarily at the memory of identifying her parent's bodies, then she couldn't help but think of Apollo's broken body, the way he had been left to die outside that liquor store. "They never caught who did it. For a while, the police were looking at it as possible murder, you know, one of the cases Dad oversaw. Maybe someone wanted revenge for a conviction, or lack thereof." She shook her head. "I don't think it was that."

"How do you know?"

Tiger half-smiled. "Call it instinct. It was just dumb bad luck, is all." She snuggled closer to Lazlo. "But why are we talking about that now? We're having a baby, Lazlo."

Lazlo chuckled and kissed her. "We are. Our family, Tig. Our little family."

Tiger laughed. "How much my life has changed in just these few weeks. Unreal."

Lazlo rolled her gently onto her back and began to kiss her throat, sliding his hand under her t-shirt and stroking the non-existent bump on her belly. Tiger raised her arms and he pulled her shirt over her head, flicking the clasp of her bra so her full breasts fell loose. Lazlo's mouth found her nipple, and Tiger moaned softly as he began to suck and tease.

By the time they were both naked, he'd revved her up into such a state of excitement that she cried out when he thrust his cock deep into her, wrapping her long legs around his hips, tightening her thighs around him.

"I love you so much," she gasped as he drove her towards a shattering orgasm. Her back arched and she let out a shuddering cry of release as pleasure flooded through her body like a wildfire. "Oh, Lazlo... Lazlo..."

AFTERWARD, they lay talking softly and hearing the others downstairs obviously enjoying their evening together. "What a life," Tiger said, nuzzling her nose against Lazlo's. "I never, ever thought I could be this happy."

Lazlo kissed her. "Even when you were winning Oscars and living the high life?" He grinned, already knowing the answer.

"It was just the one Oscar, and you know what, that was an anticlimax. You win it and then think, well, what now? I was way, way too young to win an award like that. I was just the Flavor of the Month back then. Give me this life, now, with you."

She propped herself up on her elbow and studied him. "Laz... everything has happened so fast, and all we seem to talk about is what I want. What about you? You've found yourself with a wife and a kid on the way when you only came here for a sabbatical."

"I found my home," Lazlo said simply. "I found my place in the world."

Tiger's heart thumped against her chest so hard she thought it might burst from her chest. "You are the prefect man," she said, emotion making her voice sound thick."

"I'm not, but I'm your man and that's good enough for me. Okay?"

"Okay," she smiled and kissed him until they were both breathless.

INDIA AND MASSIMO stayed until almost one a.m. then went back to their hotel, promising to return the next day. As they got ready for bed, Massimo watched his wife as she smiled to herself, lost in thought.

"Penny for them."

India smiled at him and he saw excitement in her eyes for the first time in a while. "What?"

India chuckled. "Just... this is all perfect. Laz is happy, Gabe is... well, Gabe, but he seems happy and sober. I adore Tiger and her family... and you, my love. You are the best of it all." She slid a hand onto her rounded belly. "The three of us."

Massimo felt a weight lift from him that he hadn't known was there. "Oh, thank God," he couldn't help breathing out, and India smiled, tears in her eyes.

"I know, I'm so sorry, Massi. I was happy about the baby, I swear, it was just... I don't know. After wanting to get pregnant for so long... it just seemed like, I don't know, like I was being set up for a fall. That it wasn't real. I don't know why I felt like that, but I did. But, tonight, seeing how excited Tiger was to find out she was having a baby... it hit me. And God, I'm so, so happy, baby..." She was crying now but smiling as Massimo took her in his arms.

"It's okay, baby, I know, I know." He smoothed her hair away from her damp face and smiled down at her. "I promise, from now on, everyone's going to be happy. Everything's going to be wonderful."

BUT, of course, he was wrong.

CHAPTER EIGHTEEN – AN EMOTIONAL TIME

THE ISLAND, San Juan Islands, Washington State
Two months later...

TIGER WAS dabbing paint on yet another chair as she listened to her contractors working on the coffee house, or rather the newly named Wharf Picture and Coffee House. Tiger personally thought it was a bit of a mouthful for a name, but Sarah had her mind set on it. And, Tiger thought with a grin now, it had taken them weeks to find something they'd agreed on.

She had loved working with Sarah on this project. They challenged each other, and she loved that Sarah wasn't at all intimidated by who Tiger really was. Their friendship had transcended Tiger's past, and they had, through collaborating on the Wharf, become closer than ever.

Today, Sarah was at last bringing her new boyfriend, Johan, to meet Tiger. Sarah had been secretive about the man, cautious, taking things very slowly with him after her heartbreak over losing her husband, but now she was ready to begin to reveal her relationship to the world.

"You promise to like him?" She had asked Tiger yesterday afternoon before she left, and Tiger had rolled her eyes.

"I promise, Saz. Stop worrying, just bring the dude to meet us."

Tiger grinned to herself now, then looked up as she heard a car approach the site. Her smile widened as she saw it was Lazlo, who stopped the car and got out. "Hey, pretty girl."

"Hey, handsome. I thought you were in the city looking for offices?"

Lazlo had decided to move his business wholesale to Seattle, a move that India and his other business partner Jess wholly approved of, and he had been hunting for suitable offices. He kissed Tiger hello now. "I was, but I got a very interesting offer from Quartet. Tomas Meir heard I was looking for offices and offered me one in the Quartet building... along with a partnership in the company."

Tiger gaped at her husband. "What?"

Lazlo grinned. "I know. I was shocked as you. But he called me this morning and asked me to meet him. Seems Roman Ford is retiring and he wants someone with equal experience to replace him. I think Bay and India's friendship might have helped."

"Wow. Wow."

"I know."

Tiger blinked. "Did you say yes?"

"I told him I would have to discuss it with you first, but that I was interested."

Tiger gave a whoop and hugged him. "You want this. You have to do this!"

Lazlo laughed as he picked her up and swung her around. "I knew you'd approve."

They were still talking and laughing five minutes later when Sarah hailed them from along the roadway. She waved and Tiger broke away from Lazlo, smoothing her dress. "It's the new boyfriend," she hissed quietly at Lazlo, who chuckled.

"You make it seem like it's your own daughter bringing home a date."

"It's good practice," Tiger sulked, then grinned. "Hey."

"Hey, you two." Sara's face was flushed dark red, but she was still trying to give the impression she was cool. With her, a tall, well-built man smiled at them both. He had strangely 90s frosted tips to his light brown hair, but he had a pleasant face, if not handsome. Sarah introduced him to Tiger and Lazlo. "This is Johan Zimmerman. Johan, Tiger and Lazlo."

"Good to meet you both."

They shook hands with him, Tiger smiling at him, but she noticed out of the corner of her eye, that Lazlo's smile was cooler. She wondered why, but didn't have time to process as Sarah suggested they all go for a drink at the nearby bar.

Johan seemed, to Tiger at least, to be as smitten with Sarah as she with him. He treated her with respect and gentleness, and Tiger was relieved. Sarah deserved a good man.

Johan looked at Tiger now. "I hear you used to be an actress?"

"Used to be," Tiger said with a smile. "Not anymore."

"Why is that?"

"Just wanted to change direction."

"Did you find it difficult to get work? I know it's an unstable business."

Tiger's lips twitched. "Nope, just decided to change direction."

"Tiger won an Oscar," Lazlo's voice had the faintest hint of ice in it, and Tiger nudged him under the table.

Johan looked sheepish. "I'm sorry, I really don't know much about movies at all. Forgive me."

"Nothing to forgive. It's nice to finally be anonymous," Tiger smiled at him, wondering what Lazlo's problem was. He was usually so courteous to everyone that she couldn't fathom why he was reticent with this newcomer. Luckily Sarah didn't seem to notice, and it wasn't until later, when Lazlo was driving Tiger home, that she questioned her husband. "You didn't like him."

"It wasn't that," Lazlo admitted, "it was just I felt he was a little..." He hesitated and Tiger prompted him.

"What?"

Lazlo sighed. "Disingenuous."

Tiger's eyebrows shot up. "Really? You thought he was a fake?"

"God, I hate to think it, but there was just something about him... he looked vaguely familiar."

"You know him?"

"I can't say that. It may be just a resemblance to someone I once met." He shook his head. "I hope I'm wrong. I'm sure I am. Sarah seems happy."

"She does." Tiger put her hand on Lazlo's leg. "And it's not up to us to say otherwise."

"I know." Lazlo grinned at her. "And I never asked. How are you today? How's our baby?"

Tiger put her hand over her belly. "We're both good."

"Felt him or her kick yet?"

"Nope. Bit early for that."

Lazlo nodded. "Have you booked an appointment to see the OB/GYN yet?"

"Not yet. Like I said, let's just see how we go along."

Lazlo shook his head but Tiger just shrugged. She was pregnant, not ill, and she loathed seeing medical staff. Something about the smell of the medical centers reminded her of her parent's death. When Apollo—who was healing nicely—had been admitted, she had been too beside herself to notice, but if she didn't have to see the doctor until the last minute, she would. She knew the advice, but...

"Tig... for me. Just book an appointment."

She sighed. "Fine."

Fizz was jumping around in ecstasy as they arrived home and Tiger scooped her dog into her arms. "You'll always be my first baby," she cooed at the dog. "Yuck, Fizz, dog breath," she moaned as Fizz licked her cheek. She put the dog down and then noticed the note shoved through her door. She picked it up and opened the envelope.

"That's weird."

Lazlo stopped. "What?"

She handed him the envelope. It was empty. "It has my name on the outside but there's nothing inside. Weird."

Lazlo shrugged. "Maybe whatever it was fell out in the mail." He went into the kitchen, followed by a slavering Fizz hankering for his supper, leaving Tiger studying the envelope. There was no return address and her name "Tiger Rose" was printed on the front in block letters. No address, hand delivered. A shiver went down Tiger's spine but she shook herself. It's nothing. She crumpled the envelope and went into the kitchen to help Lazlo prepare their supper.

ACROSS THE STREET, Grant Waller watched them go inside the house, and through the large picture windows either side of the door, he saw Tiger picked up the envelope, saw her confusion.

Yeah, me, too, Tiger. Grant had watched earlier, less than an hour ago, as Dex Loomis had delivered the letter to the door. Dex had seen him watching and saluted him sarcastically as he drive away. Then, the call.

"Nice to see you're still stalking Tiger, Mr Waller. Good work. Just don't get in my way."

"What is it you're doing, Loomis?"

"What do you care? I'm paying you, remember? At the end of all of this, Tiger will be out of both our lives, and you'll be a rich man. What do you care happens to her? Or what I'm doing?"

"I don't, but I'm a journalist, remember? I'm curious as to why you're doing what you're doing. Who is Tiger to you?"

Dex had just laughed and ended the call, leaving Grant listening to dead air and feeling frustrated. He looked back over to the house now and saw Tiger walk out of view. He started up his car, knowing by now that Tiger and Lazlo's evenings were a relaxed affair, home-bodies both of them. Grant drove to a fast food drive-through, picking up way too much greasy, salty food and going back to his hotel room. He dumped the food and the cup of soda on the desk, and took his coat off.

If Loomis wouldn't ante up what his motive was, then it was up to Grant to figure it out. For the first time in years, he felt the old feeling of excitement return to him. Research, following leads, digging up long forgotten secrets. He had a hunch that Tiger and Loomis were connected in a way that only Loomis knew about—just... how? He couldn't believe it was something so prosaic as Tiger having turned him down for sex. Loomis had now put his whole career on hold to pursue whatever he was planning for Tiger... why all the theater? Why not just kill her if that's what he wanted? Tiger and Lazlo's security was laughable for an ex-movie star. She just didn't want the intrusion.

"God help you, Tiger, if you let Loomis close." Grant sucked down a long swig of cold soda and opened his laptop. Start at the beginning. Get Tiger's story. Get Loomis's story. Work the problem, follow the clues.

This could be the story of your life...

SARAH CALLED Tiger later that evening. "I think you were a hit," she laughed. "Johan was so embarrassed he didn't recognize you."

"Ha, tell him I'm glad he didn't. That was the whole point of retirement."

"Huh."

"'Sup?"

Sarah chuckled softly. "I just... I always thought you might change your mind about retirement, I don't know why. When you talk about acting, there's so much... love... in your voice for it."

"Acting I love," Tiger said, thoughtfully, "it's just everything that goes with it in that world."

"Well, we have the stage now... you could start a little company."

Tiger smiled to herself, putting a hand on her belly. "I know, but let's just get the coffee house up and running, then the film showings, then we'll talk about it. I'm working on my own little company at the moment." As she said it, a sharp twinge of pain hit her and she sucked in a breath. It passed as soon as it had come and she shook her head, dismissing it. Her body was changing was all, and she didn't take much notice of things like that.

"So... come on. Don't leave me hanging. What did you think of him? Johan?" Sarah sounded as if she were trying to play it cool.

Tiger grinned. "I liked him very much, Saz, very much. And you say he's an interior designer?"

"I know, a straight one. Unheard of. I'm just kidding. And he's volunteered to help out. Help out, he says, not interfere, but I'm sure we can pick his brains for design tips."

"Anything will help. Can you believe we're nearly ready to open?"

"I cannot. Jeez, Tiger, I don't think I was even this excited when I opened the first coffee house."

They chatted for a while longer, then said goodnight. Tiger got up and went to Lazlo, who was working at the desk in the corner. She slid her arms around him. "You tired?"

He turned his head to kiss her. "Can you give me ten minutes?"

"Of course, baby. I'll just be upstairs... waiting. No, seriously, take the time, I'm going to shower and get ready for bed."

"Be up as soon as I've finished this."

TIGER WENT UP to their room, stripping out of her clothes and dumping them into the laundry basket. It wasn't until she was almost stepping into the shower when she stopped, turned, and went back into the bedroom. Her eyes scanned the room. Something was different, changed from the usual layout of the room. No, not the layout... the bed was where it always was, against the far wall, the sheets the same. It was perfectly made—that was more Lazlo than it was Tiger and she teased about his perfect 'hospital corners' all the time—and both the night stands were as they always were. On Lazlo's side, his alarm clock, his watch and a photo of Tiger. On Tiger's side, a picture of Lazlo in a frame Daisy had gifted her at Christmas, a box of tissues, the small antique clock that had belonged to her mother...

Tiger went to the nightstand and picked up the clock. The hands had stopped moving at eleven-thirty-nine. She felt her heart clench for a brief second. The same time the accident had happened, the horrific car wreck that had killed her parents. That time was burned onto her memory but this... it was coincidence, right? She checked the clock battery and pulled it out. She would have to buy a new one...

She turned the tiny switch to move the time, but the hands didn't move. "What the hell?"

She tried again, then peered inside the mechanism. Was something stuck? Tiger shook her head. She couldn't change the hands, and so she pulled out her drawer and dumped the clock into it, feeling irked. It was just coincidence but it still bothered her.

Distract yourself. It's nothing. Tiger nodded to herself and went to take a shower, enjoying the feeling of the hot water on her skin. She smoothed her hand down her belly. Maybe she should go get it all confirmed. "Put on your big girl pants," she murmured to herself. She wondered when she would start to show, and was still thinking about it when she dried her hair and went to her closet to grab a clean robe. She stopped, seeing what was hanging in the back and grinned to herself.

A HALF HOUR LATER, she was waiting for Lazlo, sitting up in bed, candles lit, and as he walked into the room, Tiger smiled lazily at him. "Come unwrap your gift, husband."

Lazlo chuckled, taking in the sight of her in her silk robe. He hooked a finger into the belt of the robe and slowly pulled it open. Underneath, Tiger was wearing the supple leather harness that he'd bought her before; his smile widened and desire ignited in his eyes. "Beautiful..."

"And all yours." Tiger wriggled with pleasure as Lazlo traced a fingertip from her throat down her body. The harness was so comfortable, so well-fitted to her curves that she felt wildly sexy in it, the way the buttery-soft straps crisscrossed her breasts and belly and framed her navel. Lazlo bent down now and pressed his lips against the curve of her belly.

"All mine," he murmured, his lips against her skin. His hands slid around her thighs and gently parted them and he buried his face in her sex, his tongue lashing around her clit.

Tiger shivered with pleasure as his tongue worked on her, and she tangled her fingers into his hair. She closed her eyes, giving herself completely over to the sensations he was sending through her entire body, forgetting everything else.

Lazlo's fingers bit into the soft flesh of her inner thigh, almost painfully, but she urged him to give her more pain. Lazlo obliged, his fingers digging into her, forcing her legs apart until her hips ached. He made her come once with his tongue, then flipped her over onto her stomach and, using the silky tie from her now discarded robe, bound her wrists tightly behind her back.

Tiger grinned, her face pressed into the pillow. Lazlo turned her head so she could breathe, so he could steal a kiss. "All. Mine." He said with a growl that made her sex flood with moisture. She heard him stalk over to the closet and rummage in the box on the floor. A second later, the tip of the crop flicked hard against the back of her thighs and she laughed, a half-shocked, half-ecstatic sound.

"You like?"

"Oh, yes...ah!"

Lazlo had flicked it against her buttocks, then he roughly kicked her legs apart. "Your cunt is so wet, baby..."

Tiger moaned with arousal. "For you, baby, only for you...oh..." Lazlo flicked the crop against her tender, swollen sex and she squealed. "Again!"

He repeated the action and she begged him to strike her harder. The flick of the crop against her clit was exquisitely painful and beyond pleasure. Tiger almost felt drunk as Lazlo continued to use their toys on her. She gasped as he thrust a dildo into her vagina, hard, at the same time as he eased his cock into her ass and fucked her hard. She was almost delirious, her body plundered, her shoulders aching, her wrists raw from the bindings.

Tiger's orgasm hit her full force and she almost screamed as came, calling out Lazlo's name again and again. As she panted for air, he released her wrists and massaged them, kissing the red welts on them. Tiger turned over and held out her arms, wanting to hold him.

Lazlo blew her a kiss. "Just let me deal with the condom, baby, I'll be right back."

He always used a condom when they had anal sex, and so Tiger waited patiently for him to return. She was still breathless and smiled at him when he returned. She loved to look at him naked, and now she asked him to stand still for moment, so she could admire his body.

He was so tall, so broad in the shoulder, his abs well-defined, his stomach a rippling washboard. His cock was already hardening again and she sat up, wanting to taste him.

But as she moved, a tearing pain ripped through her stomach and she gasped, bending double. Immediately, Lazlo was at her side. "Baby?"

The pain passed but it took her breath away. "I'm okay. Just my body getting used to having another human inside it."

Lazlo didn't look convinced. "Tiger, enough of delaying. You're seeing a doctor, an OB/GYN this week, right?"

"Fine." She felt a little disgruntled, but she knew he was right. "Will you come with me?"

"Of course, do you really need to ask?" Lazlo rolled his eyes, then chuckled and kissed her forehead. "Are you okay?"

"I really am. Just a twinge."

"OB/GYN. This week."

CHAPTER NINETEEN – NO TEARS LEFT TO CRY

MEDICAL CENTER, The Island, San Juan Islands, Washington State

THE OB/GYN, Dr. Palmer, gave her a glare. "Why did you delay coming to see me?"

Tiger sighed. "I really don't have a good excuse."

"No, you don't. But, you're lucky, everything seems to be going nicely. You say you think you're about ten weeks?"

"Possibly more."

"Hmm. I would have thought you'd be showing by now, but it may just be your baby is small. We'll arrange an ultrasound as soon as possible. Unfortunately, because of our limited equipment here on the island, our own ultrasound is out of action for a few days, but come back in a week and we'll get it done."

"We could go to the city if you think Tiger should be scanned sooner." Lazlo's arm was around the back of Tiger's chair, and she felt him stroke her shoulder.

"No, no, I don't think that's necessary, but it is of course your prerogative." Dr. Palmer smiled kindly at Tiger. "You don't care for hospitals, I can see that."

"I don't but this is about our child, not me," Tiger smiled back at him. "Whatever I need to do, I'll do. At last," she added with a grin at Lazlo. "Before you could say it."

He kissed her cheek. "I get it."

LAZLO TOOK her out to lunch afterward, and she could see he was relieved that she'd finally been checked out. "I'm sorry, Laz, I was being childish about going to the doctor."

"Not childish, just stubborn," he joked but touched her face with his finger. "I get it, you know. After Indy was stabbed by Carter, after she'd finally been released from the hospital—both times—the last thing I ever wanted to do was see the inside of a hospital. I still hate it. The smell just reminds me of…"

"…horror. Pain. Grief." Tiger's voice was gravelly and Lazlo nodded, his eyes serious.

"Yes. Your parents…"

"I had to identify their bodies. There was literally no one else to do it. I was eighteen and… Jesus." She closed her eyes but the images still floated in her vision. "They told me Dad had died instantly. He was burned all over. He didn't even look like a human anymore. It was his wedding ring, fused onto what was left of his ring finger. That was all I had to remember him by. I can't remember anything else but that when I think of him."

Tiger breathed in a shaky breath and Lazlo swept a hand over her hair. You don't have to talk about this if it's too painful."

"It is but it helps. I never did with Apollo. One of us having that in our head is enough." She felt herself take in strength from having Lazlo there as she recalled the worst day of her life. "Mom… Mom didn't die instantly, and she managed to crawl away from the wreckage before the fire started. But she had so many internal injuries… her face was perfect. Untouched. She looked peaceful. They told me she had breathed in too much smoke, that she had suffocated before the internal bleeding could get her, but that she wouldn't have survived anyway."

Tiger shook her head. "In a way, it was worse seeing her so perfect, so Mom, that it seemed all I had to do was shake her and she would open her eyes and be okay. Like, Dad's death was final, nothing anyone could have done. Closure. But with Mom... something has always bothered me about it."

She leaned against Lazlo and he drew her close, his lips against her temple. "If you want to look into their deaths more, we could do that. Get in touch with the cops, the coroner."

Tiger considered, then shook her head. "No. I would hate to drag all of this up for Pol again and with our baby coming, life has moved on. We're different people. And as for my...suspicions—to call them that—they are just a manifestation of my grief. I have nothing to base them on and why cause myself more pain when I should be celebrating the happiest time of my life? No, thank you, baby, but this is our time now. Us."

Lazlo nodded but said nothing more and Tiger was glad. She knew she was right about this, knew that today had been a turning point in their lives. Now the baby was the most important thing.

GRANT WALLER COULD HAVE HAD no idea that Tiger and Lazlo were talking about the very reports he was looking at now. The deaths of James and Christina Rose nearly fifteen years ago were certainly well reported at the time. James Rose, a judge, who was known for being particularly harsh on the abusers of woman and children, and of drug dealers, was immolated when their car was run off the road. Lucky for him, the medical examiner had concluded he was already dead when he began to burn. Christine Rose had lived long enough to crawl from the wreck but had died shortly afterward, knowing she was leaving two children behind.

Grant read through the medical examiner's report but it didn't tell him anything he didn't already know. The cops had looked at the accident as if it might be murder for a while, but nothing had come from their investigation.

He shoved the papers back into the file and handed them back to the clerk with a mumbled thanks. No, he was sure he would have to look at the Rose's past to find whatever was driving Dex Loomis.

And as for Loomis himself... the only Dexter Loomis he could find on the West Coast had been a child who died in infancy. That old trick. Dex Loomis wasn't who he said he was, but then again, Grant had known that from the start.

He stalked down the city sidewalk until he found a coffee house, snagged an Americano and found an empty booth. He took out his notebook and studied what he'd already found out about Loomis. He was a mid-range producer at one of the biggest studios, someone who worked behind the scenes rather than dealt with the stars. Loomis had never—and Grant found this hard to believe—worked on a film with Tiger, nor Massimo Verdi, who could be seen as another link. Grant wrote down the name 'Teddy Hood'—he, too, was friends with Lazlo Schuler, and at this point, Grant would take any lead he could. Loomis had been 'hand-picked' by one of the higher-ups at the studio, but there seemed to be a disconnect shortly after. Maybe Loomis had blackmailed his way in?

But who was Dex Loomis? A creep, thought Grant now, and he felt a strange pang. How are you any better, Grant? You assaulted a woman, hurt her, and now you're getting all... what? Indignant? Concerned that Dex Loomis is stalking Tiger? Why should you care?

"I don't fucking care," he mumbled to himself now, startling a woman at a table next to him. He raised his hand in apology and half-smiled to himself. Who was he now?

It was dark when he walked back to his apartment. Now that he'd been in Seattle for a few months, he'd become almost fond of the city, and certainly, the apartment Loomis' money had bought him felt almost like home now.

He took the elevator rather than the stairs. He'd order pizza—there was plenty of beer in his refrigerator—and do some internet research.

Grant pushed his way into his apartment and was about to close the door when it was slammed inward, knocking him down. "What the fuck?"

But there were two of them, and they were on him, and despite his own fitness and strength, he didn't stand a chance. For the next few minutes, they beat him everywhere, kicking him in the head until he tasted blood. A heel of a boot connected to his head beside his right eye, and it felt like his eyeball exploded.

Finally, blessedly, he felt them release him and the door slam behind them. He knew what this was. A warning. A 'don't fuck this up for me' threat. Dex Loomis was playing hardball.

Grant lay there for what seemed like hours. His entire body was wracked with pain, his mouth full of blood, his head screeched with agony. Eventually he rolled onto his side and slowly, painfully stood, staggering into his bathroom.

He barely glanced at himself in the mirror, knowing what he would see, and instead cranked on the shower. He pulled off his clothes and stepped under the hot spray, wincing as it hit his battered body. Fuck. He could go to the police, he supposed, but he would wager he wouldn't survive the week if he did. He wondered if Dex knew Grant was looking into his background... but, how could he?

No. This was about the time he'd seen Dex on the island. Don't tell or you're a dead man. Well, okay then. I won't say a word, Dex. You do what you have to do. Grant watched the blood drain away in the shower. He finally checked out his wounds in the mirror and groaned. His right eye was blood-red, the stark blue of his eyes standing out against it.

Fuck you, Dex. I'll leave you alone to do what you want to Tiger, but I'm going to take you down one way or another. Grant dressed in clean clothes and went back to the hallway, dead-bolting the door. His blood was spattered everywhere. An idea came to mind and he grinned to himself. He went back to his bedroom and packed his backpack with everything he needed, then scribbled a note and left it on the table. He turned on the radio as loud as it would go, then left, leaving the door ajar, the blood still on the floor. Whether anyone would be convinced by his 'suicide' note, he didn't care. From now on, his backpack full of the cash Loomis had given him, Grant Waller no longer existed.

Two can play that game, Loomis, Grant thought as he took the back way out of the building and disappeared into the inky Washington night. In two hours, he was on his way to Los Angeles.

20

CHAPTER TWENTY – WITH OR WITHOUT YOU

Los Angeles

TEDDY HOOD HID a yawn as his makeup artist touched up his face. "Do I really need makeup to do these interviews?"

Milly, the makeup artist, grinned. "There may be photos and b-roll and you want to look pretty, Ted."

Teddy snorted with laughter. "Lost cause."

"Well, I know that..." Milly giggled and ducked away from his playful swipe. "But we don't want to scare the journos, do we?"

"Don't we?" Teddy picked up his tablet. "How many more?"

"Just one," his assistant told him. "Oh, actually, maybe two. Some guy turned up late, begged for five minutes."

"Who?"

"Said his name was Tiberius? Guy Tiberius? Works for The Baltimore Sun. Dude, he looks like he was jumped or something, his face is a mess. Kind of felt sorry for him."

"Is he credentialled?"

"Yup."

Teddy shrugged. "Then fair enough. He'll be the last though, Jess is expecting me home."

As he said her name, his phone lit up with a call from Jess, his beloved wife. "Hey baby."

"Hey, gorgeous, I was hoping to catch you. Laz just called me."

"Oh, yes?"

"They're pregnant!"

Teddy's eyebrows shot up. "Wow."

"I know, right? Buy anyway, Tiger's coffee place is opening very soon, and they wanted to know if we'd go for the ceremony. Indy has already said yes. Can you get some time off?"

"Hey, I'm free as a bird after this, you know that. Can you get the time off?"

Jessica chuckled. She owned her own law firm, and she and Teddy juggled their time to spend as much as they could with their growing brood of children. "Hell, yes. And DJ said she's more than happy to babysit for the whole time."

"Ha, not a chance. We'll take them all, but yes, we should go. I've always liked Tiger."

He looked up as a beaten-looking man was ushered into the room. "Babe, I have to go."

"Okay, sweets. I love you."

"Love you, too. Call Tiger back and say yes. Give them both my love and congratulations."

Teddy noticed the journalist watching him intently. He shoved his phone into his pocket and shook the other man's hand. "Hey, man. I don't think we've met before. You look like you could use some painkillers. Can we get this man some water, some Tylenol?"

"I'm fine."

But the man's face was a mess of bruises and wounds and Teddy felt uncomfortable for him. "Please, just take it easy, dude."

"I need to talk to you. In private."

Teddy rocked back but he saw the desperation in the other man's eyes and nodded. "Okay."

"Ted, no." Both his assistant and Milly looked concerned, but he waved them away. He poured out a glass of water from the set on the table beside him and handed it to the man, who despite his words, took it gratefully.

"Mr. Tiberius, is it? What's up? How can I help?"

Guy Tiberius took in a deep breath. "Mr. Hood, I'm grateful that you saw me. I need some information about a producer here in Los Angeles. Someone you might know."

Teddy was really confused now. "What?"

"I think he may not be who he says he is... and I think he might be dangerous."

"DEX LOOMIS?" Jess frowned at Teddy when he told her about the strange meeting he'd had. They were having a late supper together, pasta off plates balanced on their knees. Most of the children were already in bed; their oldest child DJ was out with friends.

The evening was warm and balmy, and they sat out on the deck, the rhythmic sound of the ocean below them. Jess picked at her pasta. "I have to say I've heard the name, but I couldn't pick him out of a lineup. Why did this guy think you would know anything about him?"

"I have no idea. When I told him I didn't know Loomis, he asked me if I could give him an in somewhere. The whole conversation was weird, and I think he might have been concussed."

"How did he even get credentialled to interview you?"

Teddy shrugged. "He was harmless enough, just odd."

"Did you promise him anything?"

"Hell, no... except he mentioned Tiger. He said he was trying to figure out the link between Tiger and Dex Loomis. When I pressed him, he didn't say any more."

Jess grimaced. "Dude, I think you're better off leaving that well alone. I mean, we could ask Tiger, but doesn't it seem like an inexperienced journo digging for a story that doesn't exist?"

"It does," Teddy agreed. "Maybe he was reaching. Should we really bother Tiger with it?"

"We could ask her if she knows of a Dex Loomis, but I doubt it. I work with the studios all the time, and I've barely heard of him. Tiger's been out of the loop now for almost three and a half years."

"I think you're right. I'm sure they have better things to do."

BUT TWO DAYS LATER, Guy Tiberius called again to ask if Teddy could help him gain access to the right people and out of kindness—and a desire to get the man off his back—Teddy contacted somebody he knew at the studio where Loomis worked and asked her about the man.

"Loomis? Yeah, he's midlevel. To be honest, I haven't seen him around for weeks now, but that's not unusual. He's not big time. What about him?"

"This journalist wants to know who he really is. Apparently, he's convinced Loomis isn't who he says he is."

"Who is in this town? Give me the guy's number. He's probably just another crazy, but I don't owe Loomis anything. Dude's a creep."

Teddy felt relieved as he gave Tiberius' details to the woman. "Thanks, Bree. At least I can get this guy off my back. Hey, listen... do you know if Loomis ever worked on a film with Tiger Rose?"

"Tiger? No, no way. Tiger's last film with us was over a decade ago, more fool us, and Loomis hasn't been working here that long. Listen, dude, if you speak to Tiger, tell her we need her back. The list of actors I'm looking at for my next movie is pitiful. Don't suppose you're free in the latter part of next year?"

Teddy laughed. "No can do, Bree, sorry."

"Dang it. Well, never mind, later, dude."

"Later, babe, and thanks again."

TEDDY PUT the man out of his mind until Jessie again brought up the trip to the San Juan Islands to see their friends. One night in bed, as he stroked his wife's incredible body and kissed her, he asked her if she's talked to Tiger about Dex Loomis.

Jess nodded. "Briefly. I asked if she'd heard of him and she said no. I think she's pretty distracted with the Wharf opening and the baby. I've actually never heard her so happy, Ted. It's wonderful." She chuckled softly. "How did we never think to set her and Lazlo up together? It seems so obvious now."

"I don't think either of them would have gone along with that. It happened how it was supposed to happen, let's just be grateful for that." Teddy was distracted by the rise of Jessie's breasts as she breathed and she grinned at him now.

"Perv."

"You know it." He rolled her onto her back. Even after three children, Jessie's body was incredible—long legs and full breasts—and she smiled up at him now.

"Put that big cock inside me, Hood," she ordered and he laughed, hitching her legs around his hips and thrusting into her.

They made love slowly, taking their time, muffling the louder of their cries because the children were asleep. Even after all this time, they were not just lovers but best friends, and when they had both come, they showered together and went to bed, chatting easily.

Just as Jess was about to fall asleep, Teddy shook his head. "I don't want to sound like a broken record..."

Jess groaned. "Not that journo again."

"I just can't stop wondering why he's putting Tiger and that Loomis guy together. It's bugging me."

Jess sighed and turned over to face him. "Babe... if it bugs you, call Tiger. Call Lazlo. They'll only tell you what I did. Personally, I would be asking questions about this journalist. What's a guy from the Baltimore Sun doing out here asking questions about a lowly producer?"

IN THE MORNING, Teddy's worst fears were realized when he, at last, called The Baltimore Sun directly and was told that they had never heard of Guy Tiberius. Jess's expression when he told her made him feel wretched. He called Lazlo and explained everything.

"A journalist?" Lazlo's voice was like ice. "A journalist asking about Tiger." He sighed. "Ted... I'm going to text you a photo and I want you to tell me if this is the guy."

Teddy's phone bleeped with the message and he sighed as he opened it. "Oh, God damn it... why didn't I recognize him? I have to say; his face was mashed in and he looks a hell of a lot different, but yeah. That's him. Guy Tiberius, my ass. It's Grant Waller."

THE ISLAND, San Juan Islands, Washington State

TIGER WAS PAINTING the very last piece of reclaimed furniture she and Sarah had found in an antique store. They had decided to give the Wharf a homey feel by painting the mismatched chair and tables and using local sources to fill the place as much as they could.

And now it was exactly one week before the opening. Sarah had gone to the coffee place where they were sourcing their beverages from, and now that /the contractors had completed their work, she was alone in the old movie house.

Finishing up her task, she got up and went to wash her hands and the dirty paintbrush. As she stood at the sink, Tiger felt a wash of fatigue come over her and her head spun. Jeez, get a grip. She dried her hands and went to sit down on the couch in the staffroom. Yes, she had been working hard but not until she was exhausted—neither Sarah or Lazlo would have put up with that, and she, too, wanted to do everything she could to protect her unborn child.

But just these last two days, there had been more pain and she wondered if she should go get checked out again. She still hadn't scheduled the ultrasound scan—much to Lazlo's annoyance. She shook her head now. Damn stubborn woman. When the dizziness had passed, she got up and returned out into the main room. She jumped slightly as she heard someone bang on the door but smiled when she saw it was Sarah's boyfriend, Johan. She went to let him in.

Over the past few weeks, he had been of immeasurable help and had become a good friend. "Hey, you. Sarah's not here, but come on in."

"I don't want to intrude; I thought she'd be back by now." Johan smiled at her, holding up a bag. "I got some warm cinnamon rolls. Pity to waste them."

"Ha, she snoozes, she loses," Tiger grinned at him. "Come on. Ironically, I only have instant coffee until Sarah gets back. Will that do?"

"Of course."

She nodded towards the staffroom and he followed her in. "May I say something? No offense meant?"

"Of course."

"Tiger, you look tired. Beautiful as always, of course, but tired."

"I am, a little. It's just the baby." As she spoke, she felt another pain and let out her breath.

"You okay?" Johan was by her side in a second. Tiger nodded.

"Yeah, just growing pains. The baby's, not mine." She made the coffee and handed him a cup. She turned to join him at the table and a searing, agonizing pain ripped through her belly, and she dropped her cup, gasping, bending double.

This time the pain did not abate. "Tiger? Tiger!"

She heard Johan's cry of shock, but it sounded like it was coming from the end of a very long hallway. Tiger's eyes wheeled to the back of her head and she barely felt it when Johan caught her. She felt him lift her into his arms and carry her and then everything went dark.

21

CHAPTER TWENTY-ONE – SAY YOU WON'T LET GO

THE ISLAND, San Juan Islands, Washington State

LAZLO AND SARAH ran through the corridors of the hospital, Sarah barely keeping up with Lazlo's long stride. Johan had called Sarah, panic in his voice. "Tiger's collapsed. I'm taking her to the medical center now... can you reach Lazlo?"

Sarah had called Lazlo, trying to remain calm so she wouldn't terrify him, but Lazlo had simply barked, "I'll meet you there."

He felt like he couldn't breathe, but Lazlo smoothed his face into a bland expression when he saw Johan waiting for them. The other man was pale. "The doctor is in with her. They're waiting for you."

Lazlo nodded and went into the room. The doctor looked up. "Mr. Schuler?"

"Lazlo?"

The wash of relief when he heard Tiger's voice was overwhelming. "Tig?"

He went to her side. She was pale, too pale, and her lovely face was creased with pain. "There's something wrong with the baby."

She clutched his hand, her eyes imploring him. Lazlo's chest clenched again and he bent down to kiss her forehead. Tiger held his head against hers.

"Now, let's not jump to conclusions, Mrs. Schuler." The doctor was updating her records and checking the heart monitor.

"Oh!" Tiger gasped and he turned around. "I'm bleeding, I can feel it."

Lazlo glanced down the bed to see blood pooling—a lot of blood. Tiger gave a strange sound and fell back on the bed, her eyes closing. Lazlo went into full panic mode. "Doctor!"

The doctor pressed a button. "She's bleeding out. We need to get her into surgery right now."

Lazlo held Tiger's cold hand as they raced down to the surgical wing, but when a nurse stopped him, gently refusing to let him go any further, all he could do was stare after them as they wheeled his Tiger, his love, into a room she might not make it out of.

He stood frozen outside the doors until a kind nurse told him it would be a while until any news, and why didn't she get him some coffee? He refused politely and instead walked slowly back to where he'd left Sarah and Johan. Sarah looked tear-stained, Johan's arm comfortingly around her. Lazlo went to sit by them, but before he took a seat, he held his hand out to Johan. "Thank you, man. Thank you for bringing Tiger to the hospital. I'm not sure she would have made it otherwise."

Johan stood, shaking the proffered hand. "I'm just glad I was there when it happened." He nodded to Sarah. "I was waiting for Sarah to get back from the coffee stockist..."

"I was late," Sarah wiped her eyes. "Laz, is she going to be okay?"

"I don't know. She thinks it's the baby and she started bleeding. Badly. She's in surgery now." He sat down heavily next to Sarah, and Sarah took his hand. Johan put his hand on Lazlo's shoulder.

"I'll go get us some coffee."

It was a couple of hours later that the doctor came to find them. "She's stable. It was an ectopic pregnancy, Mr. Schuler. It started out this way, and eventually this was bound to happen. We've stopped the bleeding and she should be okay. We'll keep her in for a few days." He looked at Lazlo sympathetically. "I am sorry about the fetus, but it would never have been viable. I'm sorry."

"Thank you for saving her," Lazlo said, his voice cracking. "Can I see her?"

"She's in recovery for now, but yes, in an hour or so when we've moved her to a room."

"Thank you."

TIGER OPENED HER EYES, and she felt the emptiness right away. She put her hand on her belly and knew her baby was gone. "Oh, God damn it."

Her voice wasn't more than a whisper, but she heard a chair scrap on the linoleum floor and then Lazlo came into her view. "Baby."

He said nothing but leaned his forehead against hers and they cried together, silently. Tiger pulled him onto the bed with her and he drew her close, cradling her in his arms. "I'm so sorry, Lazlo... I'm sorry I lost our baby."

"Don't ever say that again." His voice was harsh, but she knew it came from a place of love. "It was a one in a million chance and we got unlucky." He kissed her tears away, smoothing her hair back from her face. "I love you so much and we have all the time in the world to have kids. Hundreds of them."

Tiger half-chuckled, half-sobbed. "Maybe not hundreds..."

"But we'll have our family, baby."

"Maybe something could have been done if I'd seen the doctor sooner."

Lazlo shook his head. "No. The doctor explained it all to me. There was no way this... embryo was viable."

Tiger gave a little moan of distress. Embryo. But she knew why Lazlo was saying that. It was infinity more painful to think of their loss as a baby. To name it. Thank God they hadn't even begun to pick out names. Thank God.

. . .

SHE SLEPT FITFULLY until the nurse gave her a sleeping pill. Over the next few days, Tiger grew restless waiting to be released, and when finally the doctor discharged her, she made Lazlo drive around the island for a while, taking in the fresh air before they went home.

Fizz seemed subdued, as if he understood something had been lost. Instead of jumping up at Tiger, he climbed onto the couch next to her and curled up, his furry head resting on her leg.

Later, after dozing on the couch with Fizz, she went to find Lazlo. He was in the kitchen, his back to her, staring out of the window. Tiger went to him, snaking her arm around his waist but before she could speak, she noticed the window. Or rather... the lock on the window.

"When did that get there?"

Lazlo followed her gaze. "While you were in the hospital. I had a security team going over the house, tightening things up."

Tiger stared at him, her heart thumping painfully against her ribs. "Why?"

"Sweetheart, sit down. I need to tell you something."

Tiger sat down, her eyes never leaving her husband. Lazlo's expression was grim. "Laz, you're scaring me."

Lazlo sat down and took her hands. "Baby, a few days ago Teddy Hood called me. It seemed he was being plagued by this journalist who called himself Guy Tiberius. Tiberius was asking questions, desperate to know about this producer guy called Dex Loomis. Does that name mean anything to you?"

Tiger shook her head. "No, not at all. Should it?"

"Tiberius claimed he was trying to find a link between you and this Loomis guy. He didn't say why."

Tiger frowned. "Well, I never heard of the guy so what does it matter?"

"Tiger, Guy Tiberius is Grant Waller."

Tiger felt as if she had been punched in the stomach. "No."

Lazlo nodded. "Teddy said he was acting... obsessively. He didn't recognize him right away because Waller had changed his appearance and had been beaten so badly his whole face was distorted. Teddy feels awful that he didn't realize who he was."

Tiger shook her head. "He's..."

"Obsessed with you. Yes. Hence the extra precautions. Now, the last thing I ever want to do is dictate terms to you, but I've been here before. We let our guard down and Indy almost died. So, I'm not taking any chances with your safety."

"I understand." Tiger felt chilled to the bone. "Fuck, I thought Waller would have more sense."

"Listen, he attacked you in a crowded hotel with security out the wazoo. The guy's not right in the head. I hate, hate to ask you this, but do you know how to use a gun?"

"No, and I don't want to." Tiger stood. "Non-negotiable. No guns in this house. Anything else I'll agree to, but no guns."

Lazlo sighed. "Fine, but until he's detained, no going out alone."

"Jesus." Tiger wrapped her arms around herself. "This is all we fucking need right now."

Lazlo cracked a half-smile. "Potty mouth."

"Sorry. Hormones, probably."

Lazlo stroked her face. "I'm so sorry, babe, but until we find him... if it makes you feel better, the police are on it."

"It doesn't, but okay." She leaned her head into her hands for a moment. "Do you think Waller hurt Apollo?"

"It's certainly a possibility. He seems... unhinged." Lazlo looked beyond angry. "If he comes within five miles of you, I'll..."

"Do not finish that sentence." Tiger looked up and grabbed his hands. "Do not. It won't come to that."

NEITHER OF THEM could sleep that night and Tiger knew Lazlo was listening to every creak and noise the house made, on full alert for an intruder. He'd outlined his plan to her. "At the coffeehouse, when it opens, either I or Johan will be there with you and Sarah. Now, don't be giving me that look—it's not that I don't think you or Sarah couldn't defend yourself. It's me and Johan—or a damn bodyguard. Pick."

She'd rolled her eyes but couldn't argue. The thought of Grant Waller out there and obsessed with hurting her... no. Fuck him. He wasn't going to ruin the happy life she had here. "Fine."

But the tension remained even as they held each other in bed. She finally fell asleep knowing Lazlo was wide awake.

He shook her awake a couple of hours later. "There's someone in the house."

Terror seized her heart, but there was something wrong with this picture. Lazlo didn't look scared—he was smiling. "Come with me."

He led her down the stairs, seemingly not worried about the intruder in the house. In the kitchen, moonlight streamed through the window and at the end of the room, a figure was in shadow.

"You brought her."

"Of course."

Confused, Tiger allowed Lazlo to take her hand and put it in the hand of the intruder who stepped into the light.

Tiger screamed as Grant Waller smiled at her and Lazlo laughed. Grant raised the knife in his hand. "Now, let's cut that baby out of you..."

"Tiger! Tiger, wake up! It's okay, you're okay... baby!"

Tiger opened her eyes and realized she was screaming. Lazlo was holding her, his eyes showing his alarm. She panted for air, trying desperately to calm down.

Eventually her heartbeat slowed and she slumped into Lazlo's embrace. "I'm sorry... I had a bad dream."

"It's my fault. I scared you with all that talk of Waller."

"No, baby, it's alright." She rubbed her face, feeling foolish. "I'm not a child, I needed to know. Damn nightmares."

"Want to tell me about it?"

"Not really." She shuddered, reliving the horror of it. Lazlo kissed her.

"Okay now?"

She nodded and leaned her head on his shoulder. "But I don't want to go back to sleep." She looked at him. "Have you slept at all?"

"Not really."

She sighed. "Well, darling, I can't distract you with sex at the moment. Can I interest you in a midnight feast and a good bottle of bourbon?"

Lazlo chuckled. "Good idea."

They went downstairs, followed by a confused Fizz, and camped out in the living room. They lit candles, snagged a bottle of booze, and played cards. It completely distracted Tiger from her nightmare.

As dawn broke over the island, Tiger finally fell asleep in Lazlo's arms as they snuggled on the couch together.

IN A HOUSE A FEW BLOCKS AWAY, Dex Loomis watched them. He had a hard time taking his eyes off of Tiger as she lay sleeping in her love's arms. She had no idea about what was coming and that made Dex Loomis really very happy.

Very happy indeed.

22

CHAPTER TWENTY-TWO – NO LIGHT, NO LIGHT

THE ISLAND, San Juan Islands, Washington State

SARAH HAD INSISTED on postponing the opening of the Wharf until Tiger was fully recovered from the keyhole operation to remove the ectopic pregnancy, and so it was another six weeks before the Wharf finally opened its doors to its customers.

To both Tiger and Sarah's relief, it was a full house although that might have been helped by the presence of both India Blue and Massimo Verdi. Tiger hugged her friends. "Thank you so much for coming."

"The place is gorgeous," India told her with a smile, then lowered her voice. "You okay?"

Tiger nodded. "Wasn't meant to be." She touched her hand to India's bump. "How long now?"

"A couple of months. I have to admit, I'm a little nervous. Not about the birth, but afterward."

Tiger smiled at her friend. "I don't think you would be ready if you weren't. Come and meet Johan, Sarah's boyfriend. He's a sweetheart."

Apollo, Nell, and Daisy turned up soon after, and Tiger was busy juggling showing them around the movie theater and tending to the customers who would come day after day—she hoped.

The day seemed to disappear and before long, as most customers began to drift away, the pace quieted down, and Tiger and Sarah started to clear up.

Tiger gathered a bunch of trash bags and headed out to the dumpster. As she hauled the bags into the trash, she felt the hair on the back of her neck prickle. She let go of the lid of the dumpster with a clang and spun around. There was no one behind her and she scanned the trees at the edge of the road for any sign of movement. Paranoid, much? She shook her head and turned to go back inside, hoping Lazlo wouldn't be annoyed with her for going out alone. She sighed. She hated this, all of it. Just when her life had settled into something she never dreamed it could be...

Tiger walked to the back door, but before she went inside, she glanced to the end of the alley, catching movement in the corner of her eye. She saw the figure of a man, cast in shadow, standing, facing her—at least that what his stance suggested. Was he staring at her? Her skin prickled again, and she grabbed the door handle and tugged the door open, slipping inside. She locked the back door. It was probably nothing—the man might not have even been facing her way, probably just someone having a smoke.

Lazlo was talking to Johan when she went back to the main room, and she slipped an arm around his waist. Lazlo smiled down at her. "Here she is."

"I was just saying to Lazlo that this is really a great thing you and Sarah have achieved here."

Tiger beamed at him and was surprised to see two spots of pink appear high on Johan's cheeks. "Thanks, dude. Listen, why don't you and Sarah escape and I'll finish up. There's only a little clearing up left to do."

"I can help."

"Nah, I'll put Laz to work."

Lazlo grinned down at her. "Such a hard taskmaster."

Tiger winked at him. Sarah, who looked exhausted, came over then and was grateful she could go home. "Are you sure?"

Tiger shooed her and Johan out of the coffee house. "See you tomorrow."

She lowered the blinds on the large picture windows and the door and turned back to Lazlo. "Well... that was a day."

Lazlo held out his arms and she went into them, tilting her face up for him to kiss her. His lips were soft at first then, as she pressed her body against his, the kiss deepened. Lazlo lifted her up and she wrapped her legs around his waist as he carried her to the huge, squashy couches in the corner of the room.

"About time we christened this place," Lazlo said as his fingers unzipped her jeans and he tugged them from her. Tiger smiled up at him, desire flooding her body as Lazlo removed her underwear and buried his face in her sex.

She sucked in a sharp breath as his tongue found her clit. They hadn't made love since her surgery, and she realized now how much she had missed the feeling of him touching her. She stroked his hair as he licked and teased her clit until she was shivering, almost at her peak. "Laz, I need you inside me..."

Lazlo unzipped his pants and freed his rampant cock, pushing her legs apart roughly and thrusting into her, his eyes alive with pure lust, pure love. "You're so beautiful, Tiger..."

They made love, fast and almost animal-like, completely focused on the other. Their kisses were feral, Tiger tasting blood as Lazlo crushed his mouth against hers. God, this was all she ever wanted, this man and moments like this.

LAZLO COULDN'T TAKE his eyes off her as she writhed beneath him. As she came, he watched her back arch up, and he ran a hand over her soft belly as it curved up towards him. The flush of her pink skin and the dewy sheen of her sweat was magnetic to him.

He came, hard, pumping thick, creamy cum deep inside her and as they recovered, she wanted him to stay inside her for a while.

Eventually, they cleaned up the place, giggling like lovesick teens, and went home. As they walked up to the house, a movement at the side of the house caught his eye and he stopped, automatically moving Tiger behind him.

"What is it?"

He didn't answer right away, scanning the dark trees at the corner of their home. "No. Nothing. Sorry, baby, my bad."

They went into the house, and Tiger smiled at him. "It seems to be catching. The paranoia, I mean. I was taking some trash out earlier—"

"—alone?"

Tiger rolled her eyes at him. "Yes, alone. I don't need a babysitter twenty-four hours a day."

"Sorry."

"But—and don't be smug—I got the yips, too. We're turning into tin-foil-hat people."

Lazlo shrugged. "Waller's in the wind and obsessed with you. Vigilance in this scenario isn't paranoia."

"If you say so. Anyway, enough about that jerk. Let's go to bed, baby, I'm bushed."

$\sim$

LOS ANGELES

THEIR PARANOIA WAS MISPLACED THOUGH. Grant Waller was nowhere near the island as the Wharf opened for business. He was still in Los Angeles, sofa-hopping with some friends. Someone from Loomis's studio had called him, directed by Teddy Hood, who had since refused to take his calls. Grant had risked one more call and it was immediately clear Teddy now knew who he was. "Leave Tiger alone, Waller, or God help me, you'll regret it."

Well, damn. But the lackey from the studio still called him. "You want to know about Dex Loomis?"

"I do."

Most of what she told him he already knew. Loomis was in his early forties, unmarried, and had been recommended to the studio by a higher up. No one knew much about him, and Grant could find no record of Dexter Loomis anywhere before the studio job. "Who was the higher up?"

His contact hesitated, then told him, dropping the name of a major producer. That was his only link and he'd have to finagle a meeting with the man. Trouble was... that producer in particular was in hiding having just been outed a serial abuser of young men. That was a clue. Maybe Dex had been one of his lovers and had threatened to out him unless he helped him get an in at the studio.

Grant called around, calling in some favors, and found the treatment facility the man, Edgar Higham, was being 'treated' at. More like a spa, Grant snorted to himself when he heard the news. All these creeps coming out of the woodwork, always issuing a non-apology apology, 'I am sorry you were offended' bullshit—all of them booked themselves in for 'treatment.'

"Bull crap." Grant shook his head. "At least I did my time." As if that excused his attack on Tiger.

Something was changing inside of Grant Waller. A feeling that was new to him. Shame. He wasn't a good man, he knew that, but thinking back to the anger that had consumed him when he had attacked Tiger... he could hardly believe it. And now, he knew that his life would never be what he had wanted it to be. He would always be one of those creeps. An abuser. Nothing he could do now could even begin to make up for what he had done. Nothing.

But maybe I can bring Dex Loomis down, at least. Give something, however small, back to the world. Grant found the address of the treatment center, rented a car, and set off.

～

THE ISLAND, *San Juan Islands, Washington State*

· · ·

INDIA WAS asleep when her water broke and she woke, startled by the sudden rush of wetness. It was too early. The baby was only seven months...

Fighting the panic, she shook Massimo awake. "Massi... my water just broke."

"What?" Massimo sat up, alarmed, his eyes startled, his hair sticking up in every direction. "Okay, just breathe, baby, we'll get to the hospital."

By the time they had reached the medical center on the island, India's contractions were coming fast and she panted through the excruciating pain. The OB/GYN examined her. "Well, this baby is in a hurry, it seems. We'll get you settled, Indy, don't worry."

"Isn't he or she too early?"

"Well, yes, but don't worry. It's not uncommon for babies to be born at thirty-four weeks, and there's always the possibility that the dates were a little off. Is this your first pregnancy?"

India shook her head. "No... I had a child seventeen years ago." She swallowed hard, trying not to remember back then. The daughter of her rapist, of the man who had tried and almost succeeded in killing her... twice. The daughter of the man she had killed in order to save her life.

India felt Massimo's hand on her shoulder. "Doc... is there anything we can do? Can labor be stopped?"

"Not now. Now the water is broken we need to get the little dude or dudette out." He smiled at them. "You're dilating normally, India, and both your and the baby's vitals are good. Hang in there. I'll be back soon."

India clutched at Massimo's hand the second they were alone. "It's going to be okay, right?"

"Of course, it is," Massimo's voice was soothing to her frazzled nerves. "Should I call Lazlo? He'll want to know."

"Yes, please." She felt better, knowing that of the two of them, Massimo at least was calm. She stroked the bump on her belly. For so long, she had been conflicted about this child, but now all India wanted was for him or her to be born healthy. Safe and healthy. Her first daughter had been happy, had lived a happy, safe, secure life with her adoptive parents right up until the illness had taken her, and while India knew the risks of bringing a life into the world that she might, one day, have to lose...

"Stop overthinking," Massimo said to her, breaking into her reverie. "We don't know that it was your genes that gave your daughter the illness that killed her. It might have been...him."

"I know." She looked up at Massimo, into his bright green eyes. "Baby, this is it, you know. We're about to be parents."

Massimo's smile was brilliant. "I know. I can't wait."

23

CHAPTER TWENTY-THREE – ALIVE

THE ISLAND, San Juan Islands, Washington State

LUCIANA PRIYA VERDI was born six hours later and although tiny, the doctors told her exhausted but elated parents that she was doing well, that she was more likely to be eight months than seven, that she was breathing well. "We'll keep you both in for a couple of days to make sure everything is okay."

India cradled her daughter in her arms, unable to look away from her tiny perfect face. She already thick dark curls on her little head, so like Massimo's, but she had India's delicate features: the almond eyes, the chubby cheeks. "She's so beautiful." India couldn't stop crying, from both happiness and the hormones racing through her system.

Massimo, too, was beside himself, taking endless photos of his wife and child, texting them to his mother in Italy, his siblings in Rome, to Gabe, India's brother in New York.

Lazlo and Tiger arrived at the hospital as India was about to give birth, and waited in the relative's room for news. Massimo brought them to see the baby as soon as they were allowed by the OB/GYN.

Lazlo's eyes were huge as he took in the sight of his new niece, and India felt Tiger's conflict, joy for India and Massimo, sadness for the loss of her own child. India handed Tiger the baby to hold, watching her eyes fill with tears as she gazed down at Lucy. "She's perfect."

"Isn't she?" India took Tiger's free hand. "Soon, this will be you, I just know it."

Tiger, overcome with emotion, kissed India's cheek. "I'm so happy for you, darling, I mean it. These are happy tears."

India squeezed her sister-in-law's hand. "I know."

LAZLO ALSO FELT COMPLETELY STAGGERED by the love he felt for his niece. He clapped Massimo on the back, then changed his mind and pulled him in for a hug. "Congratulations, man. I mean it."

Massimo, who always wore his emotions on his sleeve, grinned, his eyes glistening with tears. "Don't tell India, but she scared the crap out of me, going into labor this early. I thought, God, not this, don't take this away from us." He looked apologetically at Lazlo. "Sorry, that was insensitive."

"Not at all," Lazlo assured him. "What happened to us was dumb bad luck. The good news is that Tiger is okay, and we can try again when we're ready. I know the wait you two have had. I'm so happy for you, man."

THE DOCTOR TOLD India to try to rest, but she couldn't take her eyes off her daughter for long. Massimo had fallen asleep in the chair next to India's bed and she grinned at his soft snoring. She got up and lifted the sleeping child from her crib. She was grateful that Lucy hadn't needed to be hooked up to any wires or breathing apparatus, that she seemed perfectly healthy. The baby slept well, and India held her closely to her, skin-on-skin, wanting that bond to be as strong as she could make it.

She breastfed the baby when she woke, wriggling and fussing for her food, and the love she felt for her daughter was like nothing she had ever felt before. India looked over at Massimo, who had woken up and was watching them, the love in his eyes deep and limitless. She smiled at him. "Can you believe this little bean is ours?"

Massimo got up and came to her, wrapping his arms around them both. "I can." He pressed his lips to her temple. "We made it, Indy. We made it."

TIGER LAY awake but it wasn't out of sadness. She kept thinking about her tiny niece, about the happiness of her parents, and it made her happy. She was growing used to the thought that she and Lazlo wouldn't be parents anytime soon, but in her heart, she knew they would be. One day.

"Penny for them."

She turned onto her side and looked at Lazlo and told him what she had been thinking. He nodded. "You know it."

"How does it feel to be an uncle?"

He smiled. "Overwhelming."

Tiger stroked his face, scratching her fingertips on his stubble lightly. "Laz... if I say something, will you promise not to take offense?"

"Sure. What's on your mind?"

"It's just... I believe in fate. I think our baby... the pregnancy—it's less painful to think of it that way—wasn't meant to be. Not until we are completely free from... outside forces who may not wish us the best."

"That's quite the run-on sentence. Just say his name."

"Grant."

Lazlo kissed her. "We'll deal with that little pissant, but I'm not putting our lives on hold for one second because of him."

Tiger smiled at him gratefully. "Good. That's good. Fuck him."

"Quite." He drew her close to him. "Nothing's going to hurt us now."

. . .

A week later Tiger was at the coffee house early, and although she was surprised not to see Sarah already opening up, she shrugged and unlocked the door, shutting it behind her. She opened the drapes and turned on all the coffee machines. For the next hour she was busy with setting up for the day and chatting to the delivery boy who brought their baked goods from one of the independent bakeries on the island.

As opening time drew near, she checked her watch. It was unusual for Sarah to be this late. Tiger tugged out her phone and was about to call her friend when she saw Johan at the door. She went to let him in. "Hey, you."

"Hey, Tiger. I'm sorry I have bad news. Sarah's sick. She felt rough last night and spent most of the night throwing up."

"Oh, poor thing. Tell her not to worry, I can cope alone."

"Well, actually, she sent me to help out, if that's okay?"

Tiger was surprised. "Really? You can spare the time?"

"I can. I'm between contracts at the moment."

Privately, Tiger wondered if Johan was independently wealthy as he always seemed to be 'between contracts,' but that really wasn't her business. She liked the man a lot, but she'd never spent any time with him alone and she felt a little awkward. Still, it would be difficult to turn down his offer of help without seeming churlish, so she merely smiled and nodded. "If you like."

To his credit, Johan was a fast learner and he seemed comfortable with dealing with people, even if his conversation was a little stilted, and he wasn't as warm as Tiger would have hoped.

He's shy, she thought to her surprise, and Tiger's theory was confirmed when she saw him go bright red as a gaggle of young female grad students ordered coffee and hot chocolate from him. They eyed him appreciatively, and Tiger grinned as he came back to the counter with his cheeks aflame.

"You made some fans," she nudged him with her shoulder and he rolled his eyes.

"They're young enough to be my kids," he shook his head as he made the hot chocolate.

Tiger looked at him curiously. "You've never mentioned family before, Johan. Do you have kids?"

He shook his head. "No. Until Sarah, I never met a woman I wanted to have kids with."

"What about your parents? Are they still with you?"

Johan was silent for a time and although he appeared to be concentrating on his work, Tiger could see the hesitation in his eyes when he finally looked up at her. "No. My father left when I was a kid. My mom died a few years ago."

"I'm sorry."

Johan nodded a little stiffly. "Thank you. Excuse me a moment, I'll just go serve these drinks."

Tiger wondered if she had upset him, but when he came back, he smiled gently at her. "I'm sorry, it's difficult to talk about."

"It's okay, I shouldn't have pried."

"You didn't, it's a perfectly normal question. We're still getting to know each other. Are your parents still with you?"

Tiger shook her head. "No. They died in a car wreck when I was eighteen."

"Then I'm sorry, too. We both of us... well. My mother... she died in a suicide right after my father left the family."

"Oh, God, that's horrible, Johan." Tiger put her hand on his arm, but regretted it when his face flushed pink. Oh, no. Johan's eyes grew soft as he looked at her.

"Thank you." His voice was almost a whisper. Tiger withdrew her hand gently and turned back to her work to diffuse the weird tension between them. Lazlo had teased her about Johan having a crush on her, but she hadn't really seen any evidence of it.

Until now. She knew that look. Shit. That was the very last thing she needed right now.

To her vast relief, Johan moved away to clear some tables and a sudden influx of customers meant that for the next couple of hours, they were too busy to feel anything but busy.

When Tiger saw Lazlo stride in the door just as evening fell, she beamed at him. "You'd better not have gone to see the baby without me."

He laughed. "No, I've been working. Tomas Meir has been in touch again."

"Did you tell him yes?" Tiger was excited as Lazlo nodded, smiling.

"I did. We still have our lawyers hashing out some things, but yeah. I'm now a partner in the Quartet Recording Company."

Tiger whooped and went to him. He picked her up and spun her around. "Another piece of our new life, baby."

"What are we celebrating?"

Lazlo put Tiger down and turned at the sound of Johan's voice. "Oh, hey, man..." He looked a little confused when he saw Johan carrying a tray of dirty cups. "Did I miss something?"

"Sarah is sick. Johan's been helping me out."

Lazlo nodded, his smile fading. "Oh, I see."

Johan nodded, gave Lazlo a friendly smile, but Lazlo's eyes had narrowed and Tiger noticed. She didn't ask him about it until much later as they drove home together. "What's up with you and Johan?"

Lazlo sighed. "Nothing. I mean, he's a good guy, he saved your life, and yet..."

"And yet?"

Lazlo smiled at her sheepishly. "He just... he has a crush on you and it's irksome. Understandable, but irksome." He smiled to soften his words but Tiger felt uncomfortable.

"I know." She sighed, shaking her head. "I finally saw it today, but it feels so wrong to say it. So vain."

"Not if it's the truth."

"I'm sure it'll pass. He told me some stuff about his family today. Pretty tragic stuff." Tiger told him what Johan had said about his parents. Lazlo nodded.

"Rough stuff. Still... do you ever get the impression he tells you what he wants you to know and nothing more? I mean, we've known the guys months now and that's the first time we've heard even one thing about him. We know he's an interior designer, but to be honest,

I saw no evidence of that, did you? When we were building the Wharf?"

Tiger thought back. "That might not be anything. After all, both Sarah and I were pretty set on what we wanted. You could say he was just respecting boundaries."

"Maybe."

Tiger put her hand on Lazlo's thigh. "Let's not talk about Johan anymore. I'm going to call Sarah after supper and see if she's okay."

BUT SARAH DIDN'T ANSWER her call, and it wasn't until almost bedtime that Tiger got a text message from her.

Hey, gorgeous, I'm sorry I didn't answer your call earlier. This flu has wiped me out. I hope Johan wasn't a nuisance? Ha ha. He's volunteered to help out again tomorrow—I don't think I'll make it, I'm sorry.

Lazlo was reading the message over her shoulder and he grunted. "Tell him not to bother. I'll be your coffee serf tomorrow."

Tiger grinned as she texted back. Hey honey, feel better soon. Tell Johan thank you, but Lazlo's marking his territory and coming to help me. MEN. :D Love you, T x

"Hey." Lazlo protested when he read her message, but then laughed. Tiger put her phone down and tickled him.

"You are such a jealous little mochi."

"Mochi?"

Tiger shrugged. "Whatever. Jelly belly boy."

"Not jealous."

"Bullshit."

Lazlo laughed and hugged her to him. "I'm only human."

Tiger looked up at him. "You never need to be jealous of anyone, Mr. Schuler. I'm yours, forever."

DEX LOOMIS SMILED as he received the text message. Tiger still had no idea, none. He put down Sarah's phone and picked up the tray of food and drink, balancing it carefully as he descended down the wooden stairs.

Sarah sat on the bed and looked up at him with terrified eyes. The handcuff around her right wrist that fastened her to the wall jangled as she tried to reach for him.

Dex put the tray down carefully, just out of her reach. "Now, are you going to behave this time? Because if I get another plateful of food in my face, Sarah darling, it'll be the last you see for a while."

"Why? Why are you doing this? Johan..."

"My name isn't Johan and I think you know that, my sweet Sarah."

He sat down on the bunk next to her, taking her face in his hands. "Don't think this is because I don't adore you. Because I do. But you're not the reason I'm here on the island. I need her alone, Sarah. I need her isolated."

Sarah shook her head at him. "But why? Who is Tiger to you, Johan? Who?"

His smile was humorless as he pinched her chin between his fingers until she jerked her head away. "Because," he said softly, "because she is the reason. She is the reason my father abandoned me. She is the reason my mother killed herself. Tiger Rose will know hell, Sarah. She will come to see it, because that what her existence means to me. And she will know hell before she dies, Sarah. She will know hell."

24

CHAPTER TWENTY-FOUR - SECRETS

THE ISLAND, San Juan Islands, Washington State

TIGER ENDED THE CALL, frustrated. Johan was insisting that Sarah was too sick to be visited, to answer the call, but she had to give it to him. He sounded out of his mind with worry. "They're talking about taking her into isolation, Tiger, but she refuses to go to the hospital. They think she might have pneumonia."

"I should come and help you."

"She won't see anyone," Johan sounded as exasperated as Tiger felt. "I'm so sorry, Tiger, look, why don't you hire someone, temporarily? I'll pay for them myself."

"No, don't be silly, it's fine. Just tell Sarah I love her and to get well before she even considers coming back."

"I will. Call me if you need anything."

Something was off, but Tiger couldn't figure out what it was. At dinner that night, Lazlo sensed her mood and asked her what was wrong. She told him about her conversation with Johan. "I'm probably being an idiot but something seems off. Sarah really can't talk on the phone?"

She sighed and out down her fork, pushing the plate of food away from her. "I'm sorry, baby, I have no appetite."

"You're not getting sick, too?" Lazlo swept a hand onto her forehead, but she shook her head.

"No, I'm fine." She gave a short laugh. "I guess this is what it's like when you love people. You worry."

"That we do. Look... why don't we take a little drive around the island, and if we happen to pass Sarah's house and the lights are on..."

Tiger grinned at Lazlo. "Sneaky. I like it."

THEY WAITED UNTIL AFTER DARK, then got into the car. Lazlo took the coastal road until they drove into the part of town where Sarah lived. As they turned down her block, Tiger put her hand on Lazlo's arm. "Stop. Park here and turn the head lights off."

Lazlo frowned but did as she asked. Tiger pointed up the street. "Look."

Lazlo looked in the direction Tiger was pointing and saw Johan coming out of Sarah's house. He got into his car and turned it around. He switched on his headlights, illuminating Lazlo's car, and instinctively Tiger and Lazlo slid down in their seats until Johan had driven past them.

Then Tiger sat up and looked out to make sure the car had gone. "Where the hell is he going at this time night?"

"Alright, calm down, Sherlock. He might be running to the pharmacy to get some medicine for Sarah."

Tiger chewed her lip. "I'm going to go knock on the door."

"What?"

"I know what he said Sarah said, but what if... I don't know. I'll just feel better if I know she's okay for myself. You keep watch."

Lazlo sighed. Tiger was clearly on a tear. "Fine."

They got out and walked down the street to Sarah's house. It was in darkness. Tiger knocked at the door and they waited. Nothing. She went to peer into the windows but shook her head. "I can't see anything."

"You'll wake her up." Lazlo checked the street, suddenly nervous. Tiger was right, something was hinky about all of this.

Tiger suddenly started around the house. "What are you doing? Tiger!"

She shushed him and beckoned. "Sarah told me her backdoor was tricky. You keep watch."

He suddenly realized what she was going to do and grabbed her arm. "Are you serious? You're going to break in?"

"Yup." Tiger flashed him a grin. "Like I said, keep watch. I just want to check she's still alive in there."

She opened the backdoor easily and flashing him a final grin, went inside.

"Fuck, fuck, fuck!" Lazlo hissed, shaking his head. But he had no choice now but to keep watch, and when less than five minutes later, he saw Johan's car travelling back down the street, his heart leaped into his mouth.

He went to the door. "Tiger! Tiger, Johan's back... Tiger!"

Tiger appeared in the hallway and scooted towards him. Behind her, the front door began to open and the light in the porch shone through. Lazlo grabbed Tiger and pulled her out of view as the main lights came on, and they scooched down outside the backdoor, hardly breathing. Had Johan noticed anything? They listened for any clue, and then Lazlo edged her around the side of the house away from the backdoor. They heard Johan's footfall on the decking and peeked around the corner. He was standing, staring out into the garden. The way he stood so absolutely still sent a chill down Lazlo's spine. In his hand, a tire iron. Lazlo closed his eyes, feeling sick. Another few seconds, Johan would have found Tiger, and if he had mistaken her for a burglar... no. No.

He pulled Tiger away, and they silently crossed back across the front of the house and down the street. As they got into the car, Lazlo breathed a sigh of relief, but Tiger put a finger to her lips and shook her head, signaling for him to get down again.

A second later, they heard Johan's car again, disappearing away from the house again. Tiger sat up then. "Follow him," she said softly, but her eyes were hard, and Lazlo nodded.

As he turned the car around and began to go in the direction Johan has driven, he glanced at his wife. "What? What is it, Tiger?"

She turned her gaze to him, and he saw her eyes were huge with alarm. "She's not there. She's not in the house. The bedrooms were empty. Every room was empty, Lazlo. Where the hell is he going this late at night? And where the fuck is Sarah?"

DEX DIDN'T NOTICE the car following until he was almost at the site, then as he saw it slow down when he did, he caught a brief glimpse at the license plates. Lazlo's car. Fuck...

Making a show of pulling over, he picked up his phone and pretended to answer a call. They had no choice but to pass him and glancing out of the corner of his eye, he saw Lazlo turn away from his view. So, they were following him? What the hell?

Realization hit him. They had been at the house. He'd been in such a hurry—he'd had to turn back to collect some clean clothes for Sarah, fresh underwear, clean jeans. He wasn't that much of a monster that he would deny her those things. It hadn't occurred to him that anyone would have been in the house, even though he'd felt a draft blowing through. That back door of Sarah's. Tricky.

Had it been a mistake to take Sarah out of the game so early? He'd bided his time and actually enjoyed dating her while he worked on the bunker. Maybe he'd jumped the gun, but now that it was built, he wanted to know he could keep someone there for an extended period before...

It was a shame. He liked Sarah a lot. She was beautiful and kind and funny... and expendable. Dex watched the rear lights of Lazlo Schuler's car disappear up ahead. He waited to see if they would turn around and come find him, but after twenty minutes, he knew they had given up. Good. But his story about where Sarah was would have to change and fast. He still wasn't ready to put his plan into action yet.

He drove back to the compound where he had built the bunker. Bunker, he scoffed to himself. Three rooms underneath the soil, completely soundproofed and inescapable for anyone but himself. Somewhere bodies could be hidden never to be found again. It had taken months to be built, but luckily, before he'd been a producer—and after all, what the hell was that job, really?—he'd learned the trade from one of his many johns back in Chehalis.

God, what his name again? Glenn? Garrett? Yes, that was it. He'd been one of Dex's regulars, a hulking bear of a man, married to a woman, so deeply closeted that he had to pay Dex to fuck him on the rare occasions he got away. Dex used that to his advantage back then. Garrett got him a job on his crew, house building, and the young Dex had learned the first of many trades.

Which meant, when Dex came calling a few months back, looking for materials and know-how, Garrett had been amenable. He was now the town mayor and definitely didn't want anyone to know about his bisexuality. He didn't even ask questions when Dex told him he wanted a secure, underground bunker, which would have made anyone else raise their eyebrows.

Anyone without a secret that could be exposed. Without a word of complaint, Garrett gave him the know-how and the materials Dex needed and didn't ask any questions.

Dex pulled the car up to the hidden entrance of the place and got out. He wouldn't stay long. He couldn't abide Sarah's tearful pleas to let her go or her constant question of why. Why was he doing this to her?

I'm not doing it to you, dearest Sarah. It's not you I want to hurt. You are just... collateral.

An idea came to him then, and before he went into the small room where he was keeping Sarah, he went to the kitchen. He opened the cupboard where he kept the medications he had been hoarding for a while just in case he needed an out for himself.

A few moments later, he unlocked the door. Sarah sat on the bed, her face red and drawn from crying. Dex flicked a look at the handcuff on her wrist. Thankfully she'd stopped trying to resist it. How would he explain the bruises?

"Here. Drink this." He handed her the glass of juice, and as always, expected it to be tossed back in his face. Instead she drained the glass in one gulp.

"Can I have some more? Please, Johan? The water tastes strange."

It was all he could do to keep the smirk off his face. You think the water's bad? "Of course," he said smoothly. "You know, this needn't be unpleasant for either of us, Sarah."

He went back out the kitchen and poured another glass of juice, sweeping the last of the pills into it. Such a shame, but he had to be sure.

AN HOUR LATER, he checked Sarah's pulse. Weak but still there. He shook her, slapped her face, but she didn't wake. A small stream of drool leaked out from the corner of her mouth... and Dex smiled.

TIGER AND LAZLO had driven home, both feeling confused and troubled. They'd sat up talking through all the possibilities of where Sarah could be, how shady Johan was being... and didn't come to any conclusions.

Eventually Lazlo stroked her face. "Let's go to bed, sweetie. This isn't doing anyone any good. There could be a completely rational explanation for all of this. In the morning, we'll go back and ask Johan to let us see her. Then we'll know."

Tiger had agreed, but as they lay in bed, Tiger cradled in Lazlo's arms, she couldn't sleep. There was a churning in her gut, a dread that she couldn't identify.

At four a.m., her phone rang. Sarah's number. "Sarah?"

"Tiger?" It was Johan. Tiger sat up, Lazlo waking beside her. Johan sounded upset.

"What it is, Johan? Where's Sarah?"

"She's in the hospital, Tiger. She was so upset earlier... we'd argued. I thought she was too sick to go out, but she insisted. I didn't know... she took something, Tiger. She was unconscious when I found her.... They don't know if she's going to make it..."

25

CHAPTER TWENTY-FIVE – MISERY IS THE RIVER OF THE WORLD

THE ISLAND, San Juan Islands, Washington State

TIGER'S HAND was in Lazlo's as they walked through the main door of the medical center. "We've been here way, way too often lately," Lazlo said darkly, but Tiger felt numb.

Sarah was in a coma. She'd taken too much cold medication, that's what Johan had said, but he had no idea if it was on purpose or not. "Why would Sarah try to..." she couldn't get the words out. None of this made any sense.

Johan looked beside himself when they found him. "They're pumping her stomach now but she won't respond to treatment."

"I don't understand how she could go from sick in bed to missing to here." Tiger hadn't meant the words to come out so harshly, and she regretted it when she saw the guilt in his eyes, the glint of tears. "Sorry, Johan, I didn't mean it like that." *I did...* She pushed the thought away. He was obviously upset, but she couldn't help the suspicion in her heart. What the hell was going on?

"Can we sit?" Lazlo steered Johan into a chair and shot a look at

Tiger. "Now, let's all be calm. Johan, why don't you tell us what's been going on?"

Johan drew in a deep breath. "She's been really sick, a virus. She refused to go to the doctor, said it would pass. I noticed a couple of days ago that she'd stopped throwing up, but she looked so... defeated. I asked her if she felt okay and she swore blind it was just a virus, that she was in pain but ready to come back to work. She planned to come back tomorrow, said she was going out to stock up on cold medication, and that she was over the worst of it. We argued. I told her that I thought she should take it easy. She accused me of trying to control her.

Tiger, Lazlo, I've never seen her like this. She's usually calm and collected, but I don't know. Maybe it's the lack of sleep or something else. She went out last night when I was in the shower, took her car. As soon as I saw she was gone, I went out to all the pharmacies on the island. I came back to the house periodically to check if she'd returned; she wasn't answering my calls. Then, as I went out to check the Walgreens on the other side of the island, I got a call. A guy had found her collapsed on the street. I went there immediately and found her unconscious. In her car, there were empty medication packets. God."

He bent forward with his hands over his face. Tiger shot a look at Lazlo's face; he didn't seem to be buying it, either. But before they could question him further, the doctor came to see them. "We pumped Ms. Knowles' stomach, but I'm afraid she is still unresponsive. She must have taken a large dose of whatever she took. Perhaps in her fevered state, she didn't realize what she was doing, but we won't know how bad the damage is until she wakes up. If she wakes up. I'm sorry to be the bearer of bad news, but she is very sick indeed."

"Doctor... Sarah, she's alone, she has no family. Please, if you can tell us anything more..."

"That is all at the moment. Mr. Lamas already explained he was Ms. Knowles only next of kin. I'll come update you if we have any more news."

Tiger sat back down, her shoulders slumping. She knew she should comfort Johan, but there was something so off about this whole thing that she couldn't bring herself to.

HOURS PASSED and there was no further news. They were allowed to go to Sarah's room, and Tiger couldn't help the small gasp of distress that escaped her lips at the sight of her friend so pale, so ashen. Johan sat down, taking Sarah's hand in his and pressing it to her lips.

After a while, Lazlo stood. "Look, I'm going to take Tiger home for now, Johan..."

"Wait," Tiger stood up, "Maybe we should go to your place, pack a bag of essentials for Sarah." She held her breath waiting for him to object, to want to hide whatever had been going on in that house. But Johan nodded, digging in his pocket for the keys.

"Here. Thank you, that would be helpful."

Tiger nodded stiffly and she and Lazlo left. The drive to Sarah's house was silent as they were both lost in their own thoughts.

But when they got there, Tiger looked at Lazlo. "Check everything."

He nodded, the look in his eyes as fierce as hers.

An hour later, Tiger let out a cry of frustration, and Lazlo ran a hand through his hair. "Damn it."

"There must be something..." Tiger looked around the bedroom, but it looked exactly how Johan described it, as if there had been someone sick in bed for a few days. The trash can was loaded with used tissues and on the nightstand, empty boxes of cold remedies and half-drunk bottles of water.

"Come on. Let's not get bogged down in conspiracy theories. Sarah's safe, if not well. Let's pack her bag and we'll go back to the hospital."

Tiger turned to look at her husband, and he gave her a soft smile. "We just don't have any evidence he's lying, baby."

"I know. God, maybe I'm just... Jesus, Lazlo, this is awful."

"It is. Let's not make things worse by imagining something that might not be."

THEY DROPPED off the bag at the hospital. Johan came to meet them. "She hasn't woken up and there's no news."

Tiger felt a pang of pity for the man at last. He did look devastated. "You call us if you need anything. If Sarah needs anything. Promise."

"I promise." Johan rubbed his eyes. "Look, the coffeehouse."

"We'll handle that, Johan, don't worry about it."

Johan nodded. "Thank you."

AT HOME, Tiger and Lazlo showered together, then went to bed. It was early afternoon but they were both exhausted, so when the phone rang a couple of hours later, it took a minute before the sound penetrated Tiger's sleep.

"Hello?"

"Tiger."

Tiger frowned. "Who is this?"

"We need to talk."

A prickle of fear went up her spine. "Who is this?"

The caller hung up the phone and left Tiger mouthing dumbly. Lazlo opened his eyes. "Who was that?"

Tiger looked at him for a long moment, then dashed to the bathroom, throwing up into the toilet over and over. Lazlo came to her aid immediately, rubbing her back, holding her hair back from her face.

"Baby, what is it? Who was that?"

Finally, the vomiting stopped, and Tiger began to cry softly. Lazlo wrapped his arms around her and asked her again who the caller was.

"He didn't say," she managed to get out. Her entire body was trembling. "But I think... oh God, Lazlo... it was Grant Waller."

26

CHAPTER TWENTY-SIX – WHITE FLAG

SEATTLE

GRANT HAD no idea why he had suddenly decided to be the good guy and warn Tiger about Dex Loomis. Why his personality had suddenly done a one-eighty from wanting desperately to hurt Tiger Rose for putting him behind bars to warning her that Dex Loomis was coming for her and she was in grave danger.

Maybe it was because Loomis's goons had ransacked the motel room he had been using for the past month. He'd come back from talking to Edgar Higham, who had been remarkably talkative... and bitter. And now Grant knew Dex Loomis' real name.

A quick trip to the public records offices upstate, and he'd found everything he needed. And he'd found the reason Dex Loomis hated the Rose family.

As soon as he'd returned to his motel room and seen it ransacked, he'd cleared right out of there. Luckily, he'd taken his laptop and phone with him and merely had to grab his personal items—the few things the assholes hadn't smashed, that was.

The new motel was more upmarket with security at the gates and the main desk. He asked for a room away from the road and made sure they understood that he wasn't to be disturbed.

So, he dumped his stuff and went to take a shower, order some food, get some rest. In the morning, he sat at the desk in the room and wrote notes, a lot of notes. This whole situation was as fucked up as anything could be and it would make a great story. A great story.

His immediate response had been that if Dex Loomis carried out his plan to kill Tiger, then the story was going to go global. But... sense prevailed. The police would have way too many questions for him in that case. Too many.

But if he were to uncover both the plot to kill Tiger as well as the story... not only would his reputation be at least partially recovered, but he'd have Tiger's gratitude and that would be even more satisfying to him. To have her owe him. He could use the leverage that would give him to get his life back on track, that was for sure.

For the next couple of days, he gathered more information about Dex Loomis. A tip got him down to Chehalis and more questions gave him another name. The name of the mayor of a small town just outside Chehalis, the town Dex Loomis had grown up.

Garrett Squires didn't exactly look friendly as Grant shook his hand, and the mayor dismissed his secretary and closed the door behind her. "Like I said on the phone, Mr. Waller, I don't have a lot of time."

"That's okay, Mayor Squires, I don't need much. I just need to know about your friend Lincoln."

Squires sighed. "Look... I don't know what I can tell you. Yes, Linc was my lover—a long time ago. I'm talking twenty years ago. I have a family now. A wife. I don't know what I can tell you."

"Lincoln now calls himself Dexter Loomis."

"So?"

Grant smiled. "I want to know why he recently contacted you."

That shocked the mayor. "How did you find out about that?"

"I'm a journalist, Mayor. Why, after all this time, did he contact you?"

Mayor Squires rolled his eyes. "Believe it or not, he wanted construction advice."

That threw Grant. "Construction advice? What the hell?"

"I take it that's a surprise to you? Maybe you thought he was hitting me up for money?"

"Dex Loomis—or Lincoln—doesn't need money, Mayor. He's independently wealthy; apparently, he found a richer man than yourself who set him up for life. No, I'm more interested in why he's obsessed with Tiger Rose."

Squires looked uncomfortable then. "Is she James Rose's kid?"

"I think you know she is. You knew James?"

"Vaguely."

"He spent a good deal of time in your town before he married Tiger's mother. Isn't that right?"

Squires just stared at him and Grant knew he had him. "And after he married Tiger's mom. He spent a lot of time here, didn't he?"

The mayor sighed. "Yes. Yes, he did."

"With his other family. His wife. First wife, excuse me. And his first-born child, Lincoln."

Squires nodded, rubbing his face. "If Linc found out you knew this..."

"How did Lincoln's mother die?"

"She was a suicide. After James left for good one day. He never even said goodbye, just upped and left. He chose his new family. Angela never got over it. She killed herself three days before Linc's sixteenth birthday. At the funeral... Linc was just silent. Wouldn't let anyone in. Then he just left for a while, and when he came back, he was beyond angry, but we could never understand why."

"He found out about James Rose's other family?"

"I guess. Man... what kind of man does that?"

Grant smiled bleakly. "I don't think either Tiger or Apollo know about their father's bigamy."

"It doesn't stop Lincoln from wanting payback, I assume." The mayor sighed. "Look, Linc could always be obsessive about things.

There was a time when I had to consider a restraining order, but despite that... I'd hate for anything to happen to him."

Grant was quiet for a moment. "Do you think he's capable of murder?"

The mayor looked Grant steadily and nodded. "Without a doubt."

GRANT WAS STILL THINKING about what Garrett Squires had told him and was distracted as he unlocked the door to his motel room. The next thing he registered was that he was flying across the room and being slammed against the wall. For a second, he thought it was Dex's goons again, but when he heard a different voice, an angry deep growl in his ear, he knew he was wrong.

"What the fuck are you doing in Seattle, Waller? No don't answer... I know exactly what you're doing..."

He was shoved to the floor now and had a chance to look his attacker in the eye. Lazlo Schuler. Grant tasted blood on his lip and wiped it, waiting for the next assault.

"If it's any of your business..."

Lazlo grabbed him by the lapels and hoisted him up. Grant was a big man, but he had nothing on Lazlo's size and strength. "If you come near her, if you even think her name, I will end you. Understand? If you had anything to do with Apollo's hit-and-run, I will end you."

"I had nothing to do with that." Grant managed to spit out the words finally, and he saw Lazlo's look of disgust as his spittle hit the other man's face.

Lazlo released him and stepped back. "Get out of Seattle, Waller. There's nothing for you here."

Grant smirked. "And what if what I'm doing here will help Tiger?"

Lazlo's fist connected with Grant's temple, hard. Jesus, the man could hit. Grant blinked as he tried to clamber back to his feet.

"I told you... don't even think her name. Nothing you could say would ever convince me that you had anything but the worst intentions for Tiger. She's my wife now and she's protected..."

Grant started to laugh then. "You have no idea what's about to hit you. None, asshole. I could help you... but screw you. Screw that bitch. She deserves everything coming to her."

He was expecting to get hit again and he wasn't disappointed. Lazlo's boot connected with his face. His nose shattered, pain exploded through him, and everything went dark.

27

CHAPTER TWENTY-SEVEN – BEAUTIFUL PEOPLE, BEAUTIFUL PROBLEMS

THE ISLAND, San Juan Islands, Washington State

TIGER WAS angry and frustrated with herself. She hated that she'd had such a visceral reaction to Grant Waller's call to her. *It's always the same... you think of the best comebacks after the event,* she thought to herself. *Why hadn't she simply told him to go fuck himself? God, she hated that he still had this much influence on her state of mind. It's been three, almost four years. You're married, happy, loved. Safe.*

So why the hell was he calling her? When Tiger went to work the next morning to open up, she kept glancing around her even though Lazlo had been with her. He'd insisted on hiring a guy to be with her at the coffeehouse when he was at work and when he'd suddenly had to go to Seattle a day later.

Luckily, the Wharf was busy enough for Tiger to be able to distract herself. Johan had stopped by and even though her suspicions of him hadn't be completely assuaged, she was grateful to have someone she knew close by.

He told her Sarah was still unconscious. Johan looked

exhausted and Tiger made him sit while she made him some sandwiches and hot coffee. "I know I shouldn't leave her alone unless she wakes up, but I had to come shower and get some clean clothes."

"You can't be there all the time. After work, I'll go sit with her for a while."

"Are you sure? I just need a few hours of sleep."

Tiger patted his shoulder. "Of course, I am."

So, LATER, WITH HER 'BODYGUARD' in tow, she closed the coffee house early and drove to the hospital to sit with her comatose friend. She studied Sarah's still face, wondering what had driven her friend to take too many pills. Maybe she'd just lost count of what she had taken and when. It happened. Look at Heath Ledger. An accidental overdose.

Tiger couldn't imagine her life now without her friend. She held Sarah's cold hand and kissed the back of it. "Please be okay, Sazzle. You are my sister, and I love you. Please don't go."

Tiger felt drained. So much had happened in such a short time, both joyful and devastating. Lazlo, Fizz, the new coffeehouse, getting married... then Apollo's accident and losing the baby. Maybe she was just reeling from everything, and that's why she got so suspicious of Johan. The man had done nothing but be loving to Sarah and a good friend to Tiger.

She felt shame now. "God damn it, pull yourself together, woman."

She entwined her fingers with Sarah's and closed her eyes. She listened to the steady bleep-bleep of the machines and to Sarah's regular breathing, in, out, in out...

THE HOSPITAL CORRIDOR was cold and empty. Flickering strip lights gave it a sinister cast, the pallid yellow of the lights dimming so that the end of the corridor was in darkness, and Tiger knew if she went into that blackness, she would never come out of it, but her feet disobeyed her brain's instruction not to move.

The doors on each side of the corridor were closed and as she walked, she tried to look into each room but all she saw was walls covered with blood and a sea of bodies, some whose faces she recognized as those she loved. Lazlo... Apollo... Nell... Sarah... Daisy, oh God no, not Daisy...

Tiger felt the blood in her own body drip down from the many wounds on it. Where they'd come from, she didn't know, but she knew nothing would stop the bleeding. Now, at the end of the corridor, she saw a figure emerge from the darkness. His face was ever-changing, slipping from Grant Waller's pasty mug to Johan's soft, bland good looks, but the one constant was the rictus grin, way too big to be a human mouth, and now he opened it wider and wider, a ghastly maw filled with too-sharp teeth...

TIGER SHOCKED herself awake and panted quietly. A fine sheen of sweat clung to her forehead and she wiped her sleeve over it.

"Are you alright?"

Tiger tried not to shriek as Johan leaned into the light from the corner of the rom. She gaped at him. "God, you startled me."

"Sorry. You were asleep when I came in and you looked so peaceful, I didn't want to wake you."

"That's ironic." Tiger got her breath back. "What time is it?"

"A little after eight p.m. I got here only a short time ago. Has there been any change?" Johan wasn't looking at Tiger now. He moved his chair closer to the other side of Sarah and took her free hand. Tiger felt guilty.

"Not that I know. I'm sorry I feel asleep."

"Don't be." Johan stroked Sarah's face. "It's hard to believe she'll ever wake up, sometimes."

"She will. Don't think like that." Tiger was painfully reminded of having a similar conversation with Nell a few months earlier when Apollo had been hurt in the hit and run.

"Sorry. I just... I love her, you know?" Johan looked desolate, and Tiger got up and went around to him, hugging him. He patted her hand as she did, and they stayed like that for a few moments.

"Hello."

Tiger looked up and smiled. Lazlo stood in the doorway, halfway in shadow. Tiger's smile faded when she saw his expression. She let Johan go and went to Lazlo. "We're just feeling a little hopeless. And useless."

"Tiger has been a comfort," Johan said softly, and Lazlo nodded, albeit a little stiffly. "Why don't you take Tiger home, Laz? I've got this from here."

IN THE CAR on the way home, Lazlo was quiet, and Tiger felt tension deep in the pit of her stomach. "He was upset. I was making him feel better."

"So, one moment he's shady as all hell, and the next you're all over him?"

Hot anger flushed through her. "I was not all over him. I gave a friend a hug. That's what I do. What anyone would do, Lazlo."

She turned away from him, tears prickling her eyes. What the hell? Lazlo was never like this. He knew he had no reason to be jealous.

Didn't he? Suddenly it struck her. How well did they really know each other? God, that hurt to think, but really, it had been less than a year and they'd gotten married, gotten pregnant, and lost a child in that time. It was frightening.

They didn't speak as Lazlo parked the car, but as Tiger opened their front door, he caught her hand. "I'm sorry, baby. I'm just... I don't know."

She nodded, allowed him to pull her into his arms. "Are you okay?" She looked up at him and he nodded, his eyes unreadable. He pressed his lips to hers.

"I am... I just need you."

Tiger kissed him again. "I'll make you feel better, baby."

They were interrupted by an excitable and hungry Fizz and they both laughed. "Passion killer," Lazlo grumbled at the dog, but he went to feed him as Tiger went upstairs.

Soon, he joined her in the bathroom, opening the shower door and slipping inside with her. Tiger turned to face him and press her damp body against his. "I love you," she whispered over the hiss of the water and then Lazlo's mouth was urgent on hers.

Tiger reached down to stroke his cock against her belly. "Take me," she said, her eyes on his. "Right here, right now."

Lazlo lifted her up easily in his strong arms and she curved her legs around him. He thrust into her and they began to make love unsteadily in the slippery shower, but soon they were so excited, so aroused, they didn't care that they were slipping everywhere. Eventually, Lazlo tumbled her out of the shower and fucked her on the cool tile of the bathroom floor, then again in bed, his body dominating hers at every second, and Tiger loved him for it.

"I'm yours," she murmured to him as he went down on her, nipping at her clit with his teeth before lashing his tongue around it, "Oh, Lazlo... I'm yours forever..."

THEY BOTH FELL ASLEEP, exhausted in the early hours of the morning, and it wasn't until she awoke, thirsty, a few hours later that she noticed the scuff on Lazlo's knuckles. Had they been too rough? Tiger frowned, but shrugged to herself.

IT WASN'T until the police turned up in the morning that she discovered how Lazlo had gotten the bruises and cuts. The officers seemed half-amused by the fact they were there, talking to the husband of Tiger Rose, but still, they had work to do.

"We've had a report that you assaulted Grant Waller at his hotel, Mr. Schuler."

Lazlo was stony-faced as Tiger gaped at him. "I had a conversation with Mr. Waller. It may have taken a turn, yes. He was harassing my wife."

"We know. We know his history." The officers exchanged a look. "He's not pressing charges... this time, he says. But we had to get your side of the story."

"You're not arresting Lazlo?"

"No, ma'am."

Tiger felt her body slump with relief. "He called me. Wanted to talk. Given what he did to me..."

"We're applying for a permanent restraining order. I went to his motel to tell him that, but he seemed to, um, take against my presence."

"He says you assaulted him before he could get a word out."

"And you believe him?"

One of the officers smirked. "Not particularly. Look, we're obliged to follow up, to caution you against any more contact with him."

"That's the last thing we want," Tiger said vehemently, and the officer smiled at her.

"I understand. Well, thanks for your time, Mr. Schuler, Miss Rose."

"Mrs. Schuler now," Tiger said softly.

"Mrs. Schuler. Thanks again."

TIGER CLOSED the door behind the police officers and slowly turned to face Lazlo with a stern expression on her face. "Lazlo Schuler...you bad, bad man."

But she couldn't help the grin that spread across her face, and she laughed. Lazlo looked a little taken aback by her reaction, but then he grinned sheepishly. "Sorry. I went caveman on his ass."

"My own Neanderthal." She kissed him. "But thank you. You did what I have wanted to do for years, and I know that's not the moral or adult thing to wish, but... he took something from me. Something you gave back to me."

"What?"

"Self-respect. If someone like you loves me, there's nothing I can't do." She kissed him. "And if you report me to the Sisterhood for saying that, I'll never forgive you."

Lazlo grinned. "I promise not to. I love you, Tiger Rose. Tiger Rose Schuler."

Tiger chuckled. "That's my name now. I'd like to keep Rose for a second name—a link to my parents. With their name and your name, I feel complete."

GRANT WALLER LEANED against the side of the ferry boat. Lazlo's beat down of him was an annoyance, but he wished he hadn't reported it to the police. He would have preferred to fly under the radar while he worked on this, the biggest story of his career.

And God damn it... even despite Lazlo's aggression, Grant still knew the right thing to do was to warn Tiger about Dex Loomis.

Lincoln Rose. Man, the guy had held onto a grudge way, way too long, but he supposed that's what psychopaths did. He'd already tried to kill Apollo Rose, and now he had his sights set on Tiger.

What the hell are you waiting for, Dex? She's there, unprotected, working in a God damn coffee house. Why didn't he just shoot her through the damn window?

Unless... it was far too personal for a mere assassination, clearly. Dex wanted to make Tiger suffer, but how the hell would he get past her guard-dog husband?

Christ. Grant shook his head. He for the life of him could not figure what Dex's plans were. All he knew was, Tiger Rose was in trouble, and unless she listened to him, she was going to end up dead.

And to his endless surprise, Grant had decided he couldn't live with that.

28

CHAPTER TWENTY-EIGHT – BADBYE

THE ISLAND, San Juan Islands, Washington State

TIGER LOOKED up as Johan came into the coffee house. "I've been sent to drive you home," he said with a smile. Tiger was surprised.

"Lazlo came to the hospital. Told me to go home and get some sleep. Asked me if I could take you home first."

Tiger nodded. "Okay, that's fine. Just let me finish up here. How's Sarah?"

Johan seemed distracted. "What? Oh, sorry, no change."

"You okay?"

His smile was thin. "Yes, thanks. Just tired."

"I won't be a sec, then we can go."

Tiger went into the backroom and switched on the dishwasher. She turned to grab her bag and stopped. The back door was open, banging slightly in the breeze from outside. Her skin prickled. She was certain she had shut it, but now she pushed it closed and locked it. Stupid woman, leaving it open... it still bugged her that Grant Waller was so close, was in Seattle, although they had heard nothing more from the police. Hopefully he's gotten the message and gone back to whatever bridge he was living under.

She smirked to herself as she went back to the main room.

"Something funny?"

Tiger looked up. There was something off about Johan this evening but she shrugged it off. I'll take him at his word: he's tired. She followed Johan out to his car just as her cell phone rang. Lazlo.

"Hey baby. I hear you're on Sazzle-watch."

Lazlo laughed that deep, throaty chuckle she loved; the sound of it always gave her butterflies. "I dropped by and Johan looked like he was ready to drop. The docs say Sarah is showing signs of waking up."

Tiger gave a little gasp. "Really? Johan said there was no change." She shot a look over at Johan who was concentrating on the road and didn't look at her.

"Well, he probably didn't want to get your hopes up. It's still up in the air. He's with you?"

"Taking me home as per your orders."

Lazlo was silent for a time and Tiger frowned. "What?"

"No, nothing. I'm glad you have someone with you. I'm still not convinced we shouldn't have kept the bodyguard on."

Tiger groaned. "No, thank you. I've spent years getting away from that life."

"Fair enough. Just make sure Johan sees you to the door, would you? Seeing as he's with you."

Tiger picked up on something in his voice that she didn't understand. "Are you okay?"

"I am, baby. I'll be home soon. I love you."

"Love you, too."

She ended the call and put her phone in her pocket. Johan was silent beside her. "Lazlo says the docs..."

"They said she might be waking up, not that she was going to." Johan turned to her and smiled, but Tiger noticed it didn't reach his eyes. "I didn't want to give you false hope until something was confirmed."

"Okay." Tiger was feeling so uncomfortable now, but she breathed a sigh of relief as they turned into her street. "Would you like to come in for a drink?"

Say no, say no. To her relief, Johan shook his head. "I'm beat. Raincheck?"

"Of course. Thanks for the ride."

"I'll call you when there's news of Sarah."

"Thank you."

TIGER WENT INTO HER HOME, still a little bemused. Why hadn't Johan told her about Sarah? It felt like he was hiding something from her or that he didn't consider her good enough to tell...no, that wasn't it.

Tiger sighed and took her coat off. She would make dinner for her and Lazlo, something from scratch, and maybe that would ease her discomfort. There were too many strange things happening lately and it bugged her. She wanted the life that seems always just out of reach—Lazlo and her and Fizz and their family and friends, all happy and safe.

She decided to make a lasagna and began to cut up onions and peppers. She switched the radio on to keep her company as she chopped the vegetables, and sang along softly with it. As she gathered the peel from the onions up to throw into the compost bin, she turned and gasped.

Behind her, Grant Waller was standing in the doorway of her home. For a second, neither of them moved, then dropping the peelings, Tiger darted for the back door.

He caught up with her before she got there and as his hands gripped her shoulders, Tiger screamed, turning and lashing out at him.

"Tiger! Tiger! I'm not here to hurt you..."

But in her panic, she couldn't hear him, and it took Grant covering her mouth with his big palm and wrestling her to the floor before he could speak again.

For Tiger, every memory of his previous assault was running

through her mind, and she bucked and kicked until Grant managed to stifle her. "Tiger! Calm down, I'm not here to hurt you. I'm here to help you."

"Mmmmm-shit..." She murmured as he released her mouth. "Get off of me."

"I can't. Not until you listen to me. Will you please just listen to me for five minutes, then I'll go and I'll never bother you again, I swear. But what I'm about to tell you could save your life."

Tiger finally took in what he was saying. Grant was panting hard with the effort of restraining her and she slumped in his arms. He loosened his grip and she crawled away and he didn't stop her. As she turned to face him, she saw him put his hands up. "Five minutes."

"You broke in."

"Yes. I'm sorry about that, but I had to."

Tiger panted for air, trying to quell the desire to scream again. "What do you want?"

"It's about the man you know as Johan, Tiger. I first met him as Dex Loomis."

Somewhere that name rang a bell, but Tiger was more concerned with getting her nemesis out of her house. "So?"

Grant stared at her, and she saw something she never had in his eyes before now—sympathy. "Tiger... his real name is Lincoln Rose."

Tiger blinked. "What?"

"He's your brother."

"What the actual fuck? Are you insane?" Tiger scrambled to her feet and Grant stood up with her again, his hands outstretched to stop her running or coming for him.

"He's your father's first born. Your father had another family before he married your mother... bigamously."

Tiger's temper got the best of her then. "Get out. Don't you dare try and drag my father into this. This is some sick shit you're making up..."

But somewhere inside her, she knew it wasn't. She felt tears prick her eyes.

"Tiger," Grant's voice was quieter now, softer, "I'm sorry. I'm sorry for what happened, for what I did. I have no excuse. But I'm telling the truth now. Dex, or Lincoln, or Johan... he wants payback for your father abandoning him. For his mother committing suicide because your father left them. Look..." He reached into his jacket and Tiger braced herself for a weapon. Instead, he pulled out a sheaf of papers. "It took me weeks to find all of this, but it pretty much lays it all out. Dex Loomis wants to harm you. I'm pretty sure he was the one who hit Apollo with that car. Dex, or Johan, had wormed his way into your lives in a way that means he earned your trust. So, when he comes for you, you'll have no idea." He stopped and took a deep breath.

"Why should I believe you?" Tiger's voice shook but she stared at him steadily. He looked smaller somehow than what she'd built up in her head. His face was heavily bruised, no doubt from Lazlo's beating, and he looked seedier, tired and older despite not being that much older than her.

And why the change of heart? Why try and protect her now? She asked him as much now.

"I'm not a good man, Tiger, I know that. I know I can never make things right for what I did. Believe me when I say I disgust myself. I don't flatter myself this will go anyway toward making up for it, but you need to know the truth about your family. Your father... was a bigamist. Your half-brother is a psychopath who wants you dead. He will never, ever stop, Tiger. Please... is there any way you can believe me?"

Tiger stared at him for a few long moments. Somewhere inside her, although it was painful, there was part of her that did believe him. That somehow, she had known about her father, her beloved Papa. God. She opened her mouth to speak when the door behind her opened and Grant's eyes grew wide.

Tiger turned to see Johan... Lincoln... her brother standing in the door, his eyes riveted to Grant. In his hand, a gun. His eyes flicked to Tiger's and he smirked. "Hi, sis..."

"Tiger, run!"

Grant launched himself at Lincoln as Tiger darted across the kitchen, but she skidded to a stop when she heard the gunshot. She turned and saw Grant slowly sinking to his knees, blood blooming across his t-shirt. In horror, she gazed at him and he shook his head. "I'm sorry... I tried..."

He slumped to the floor and Tiger raised her eyes to see Johan/Lincoln aiming the gun at her. His eyes were cold. "Don't even try to run, Tiger. I will shoot you without a second thought." He strode across the kitchen and grabbed her arm, jabbing the muzzle against her belly. "Time for us to get to know each other, sis. Let's go."

LAZLO SAW Sarah open her eyes and he smiled. The doctor was leaning across her, checking her vitals as she blinked, her eyes wheeling around. They finally landed on Lazlo's face and her eyes grew big. "Lazlo..." Her voice was barely a whisper, but urgent. He took her hand and leaned closer.

"It's okay, honey, I'm here. God, Sarah, we were so scared. Johan has been beside himself..."

"...no, listen to me..." She was shaking her head hard and the doctor frowned.

"Try not to..."

"Listen to me!" Even though her voice was scratchy, the urgency in it was unmistakable. "Johan... he's crazy.... Lazlo... he's going to kill Tiger..."

Her head dropped back, her eyes closed, and the machines flat-lined, and as Lazlo stared at her in horror, pandemonium broke out.

29

CHAPTER TWENTY-NINE – JUMPSUIT

*THE ISLAND, **San Juan Islands, Washington State***

TIGER LAY in the back seat of Johan's—Lincoln, she told herself, Lincoln—car, her wrists and ankles bound, duct tape across her mouth. The horror of what was happening to her was sinking in and she felt hopeless. Grant Waller, of all people, had been telling the truth, and now she was in the hands of a man who shared half her DNA and who obviously had no compunction about murder.

Keep him calm. Talk to him. That's your only shot. Before they'd left her home, he'd made her swallow some pills, the gun pressed against her stomach, and she knew then this is what he had done to Sarah. "Why? Why hurt Sarah?"

"I needed a dry run."

God, he was a bastard. She thought about going for the chopping knife she could see on the kitchen counter, but the muzzle of the gun was cold through her t-shirt, and she knew she'd never make it.

So now, as Lincoln drove into the night, Tiger felt her head feeling muzzy and her concentration slipping. Try and remember details, she thought, anything that might help someone find you. She managed to ease her ring off of her finger to drop in Lincoln's car—evidence she had been in it. Not her wedding ring—she couldn't bring herself to part with that, especially if...

God. The thought of never seeing Lazlo again made her lose heart, and an involuntary whimper escape her, muffled by the gag.

"We're nearly there, Tiger."

Lincoln's voice was almost tender, but it terrified her. He sounded as if he were telling her it was almost over and maybe it was. Oh, Lazlo, I'm sorry... I love you...

LAZLO STOOD outside Sarah's room as the doctors tried to resuscitate her. His heart thudded with anxiety and his cell phone was glued to his ear. Tiger wasn't answering, and it was all he could not to run out of the hospital right now. But leaving Sarah on her death bed? Tiger would kill him...

"We have her back," the doctor, sweating and breathless, found Lazlo.

"Is she conscious?"

The doctor shook his head. "No, but she's stable... Mr. Schuler, you look like you're about to collapse."

"I'm fine, listen... I have to go. What Sarah said before she flat-lined... it might mean my wife's life is in danger."

The doctor nodded, his expression one of concern. "Of course... should we call the police?"

"Please do... and protect Sarah. If Johan is the psycho she says..."

"Go." The doctor nodded. "We'll keep her safe."

LAZLO BROKE every speed law as he drove back to his home, and when he saw the front door standing open, his heart shattered. Oh, God, no...

He ran inside. "Tiger!" There was no answer but he skidded to a halt when he saw the blood on the floor of the kitchen. His knees gave way and he fell to the floor. "Oh, no, no, no..."

"Schuler."

Lazlo spun around at the sound of the man's voice. Slumped in the corner of the room, his clothes soaked with blood, was Grant Waller. "What the hell?"

Lazlo went to the stricken man, but Grant held a hand up. "Please... we don't have long. He took her, Schuler. He took Tiger. Lincoln Rose..."

Lazlo blinked, confused. "Who?"

"You know him as Johan..." Grant coughed and a stream of blood erupted from his mouth.

"Jesus." Lazlo went to fetch a cold cloth for the man. It was clear Waller was dying. He wiped the man's mouth.

"He's her brother. Half-brother. Her dad was a bigamist. Tiger didn't know." Grant's voice was getting weaker. "He's going to kill her, Lazlo. He's insane. Talk to a man called Garrett Squires in Chehalis. He knows more than he's saying... Schuler..."

His breathing was hitching and catching, and Lazlo knew he was almost gone. "What is it, Grant? What do you want to say?"

"Tell her... tell her I'm sorry... tell her..." Grant's eyes grew distant and a long, final breath escaped his mouth. He was dead.

Lazlo stood and cussed, not knowing what to do. He went out to his car and called the police as he set off—in what direction he didn't know.

The police assured him they were on their way. "There's a dead guy in my house. The man who kidnapped my wife shot him." God, that was painful to say...

Tiger. Please, fight, please. Hold on.

Tiger had no idea where they were as Lincoln dragged her from the car. She landed on soft ground, grassy, and Lincoln picked her up and threw her over his shoulder. Although it was dark, she was surprised when they seemed to be going below ground, and she finally realized they were in some sort of bunker. Her heart sank. It had to be well hidden, not visible from the road. Somewhere no one could find them easily.

Tiger screwed up her eyes. Was it really this hopeless?

Lincoln dumped her onto a bunk bed, and she winced at the pain in her shoulders as her bound wrists were caught under her. He made no move to untie her. The room they were in was bare bones, made out of inexpensive cement blocks. She had the incongruous thought that she hoped they weren't too deep underground and that any support beams did their job. The single bunk was the only furniture in the room, but in front of her stood a tripod with a camera aimed directly at the bunk.

Lincoln gave her a cold smile. "Here's how this is going to go. I'm going to tell you everything, all about our bastard father, all about the hell he brought down on me and my mother. What your mother did to us. You're going to listen to it all. Then," he patted the camera, "I'm going to put a bullet into your belly and watch you slowly bleed to death. This thing will record it both for my own enjoyment, and so I can send it to Lazlo so he can relive your murder over and over."

He came over to her and Tiger cringed away from him. He pinched her chin between his fingers. "I can't see any resemblance between us, sister." He ripped the tape from her mouth and Tiger gasped at the sudden pain.

"Why didn't you tell me? We could have been family." The thought made her sick, but she had to keep him calm. Tiger had no doubt he would carry out his vile plan, that she would die here.

Lincoln laughed. "I think not. Do you know how long I've had to watch you, Tiger, being feted, being held up as some sort of paragon? To be so protected. When you retired, I finally saw my chance to get payback, but you disappeared. It took me paying Grant Waller to hunt you down. He was a fool. When he attacked you, I couldn't believe it. I wanted to be the one to hurt you, not him."

Tiger's eyes narrowed. "And you killed him. I'd say you were even."

Lincoln smirked. Tiger studied him, trying to find any features of her father in his face. She could see nothing. "How do I know if you're telling the truth? You could just be saying my father was yours."

"I could, but what would be the point? What would be the point of all this?"

"You wouldn't be the first obsessive I've dealt with."

"Don't flatter yourself, Tiger. I wouldn't fuck you even if you weren't my sister."

"Right back at you, asshole."

Lincoln chuckled. "The fact I had to fuck a woman, even someone as nice as Sarah, to build a cover was maybe one of the worst things about this."

"You're gay?"

"No. I'm asexual. Sex doesn't drive me, but I've recognized in my life that sex gets things done. It can be used." He sat down in front of her. "After all, isn't that basically what you do? Actors, actresses, they're mostly selling sex, even if it's not explicit. Look at that face of yours... the epitome of beauty. Do you really think the people who went to your movies were there to see the characterization of the parts you played? No. They either wanted to fuck you or be you. I just want to kill you."

Tiger suddenly felt calm. "My father and mother were killed when I was eighteen. You don't think that was enough payback?"

"Oh, I know all about that." He was openly laughing at her now. He sat back in his chair, his eyes never leaving hers. "All about it."

Tiger went cold. "What?"

"Who do you think drove them off the road, Tiger?"

Tiger felt like she had been sledgehammered in the chest. "What? You're lying."

Lincoln's smile grew wider. "I think you know I'm not. Your father —our father—died straight away and he burned real good, Tiger. Your mom... she crawled out of the car. Tried to get away but her injuries... God, she was beautiful woman, too, Tiger, looked just like you. Stunning eyes. When I held my hand over her nose and mouth, they got real big."

Tiger couldn't help the gasp of horrified grief. "You murdered her?"

"I suffocated her. She might have made it, and I couldn't have that. She saw what I did."

Tiger couldn't stop the tears from flowing then. Her Mommy... "I hope you rot in hell, Johan, Lincoln, Dex, whatever your goddamn name is."

"I'm already there, Tiger. Where our father put me. My own mother... she couldn't cope when he left for good. With no goodbye. No word, ever. So... I had to give her peace."

"You said... oh, God, you told me she committed suicide."

"Because that's what the official record says. An old trick, drugging someone's juice with too many pills, but very effective. Worked on Sarah. Sadly, not well enough it seems."

"She's waking up. She'll expose you."

Lincoln nodded. "Yes. Which is why I built this place. No one will find us here, Tiger, at least, not in time. This isn't going to be a long, drawn-out thing."

"You won't get off the island. They'll have police everywhere at the harbor."

"Oh, Tiger... you think I haven't made plans in advance? Why do you think I bided my time for so long? I weaseled my way into island life, into your life, Sarah's life. I know everything." He leaned forward so his face was inches away from hers. "Even the face you make when you come."

Tiger's temper flared and she headbutted him, connecting enough that he jumped back. "You fucking little bitch."

"Suck it, douchebag." Tiger was a little satisfied that she'd had even the smallest effect. Lincoln stood up.

"Enjoy the night, Tiger. It's the last one you'll see. Next time I come into this room, I'm going to kill you."

He left the room and a second later, the lights went out, leaving Tiger in pitch darkness.

CHAPTER THIRTY – DECODE

THE ISLAND, San Juan Islands, Washington State

LAZLO WAS BARELY HOLDING it together. As the police questioned him, all he wanted to do was get out there again to find Tiger. But he had no clue where Johan had taken her. The harbor was on lockdown and the sea planes had been grounded, but it was still feasible that Johan could have gotten Tiger off the island.

The police didn't think so, however, and a fleet of them had been sent out to scour the island. Lazlo directed them to Sarah's place, the Wharf, everywhere.

In the meantime, he was asked to stay in one place, and with no better place to go, he went back to the hospital and hoped Sarah would wake again and tell them more, give them some clue to where Tiger might be.

At the lead detective's request, Lazlo had read through the papers they'd found on the floor of the kitchen, spattered with Waller's blood. It was true: Johan a.k.a., Dex Loomis a.k.a., Lincoln Rose was Tiger's older half-brother. Waller had dug up everything he could on the Rose family—both of them. Jesus, what a fucking mess.

"Lazlo!" Lazlo turned from the window he was staring out to see Apollo, still in a wheelchair, being pushed by one of the policemen towards him. Behind him, a tear-stained Nell carried Daisy in her arms.

Lazlo went to them, hugging Apollo and Nell. "I had them come get you as soon as I knew."

"What the hell happened? They told us Tiger is missing and that some dude is claiming to be our brother?" Apollo looked pale and drawn, terrified for his sister.

The Chief of Surgery, alerted by the drama, came to meet them. "We've set up one of the private rooms for your use. If you need anything, just ask."

IT WAS hell waiting for any kind of news. Lazlo felt pulled between both a grieving, terrified Apollo and Nell, and checking in on Sarah. Every cell in his body was screaming at him to leave the hospital and find her, but the police wouldn't let him.

The morning after Tiger's abduction, he stared out of the window of the hospital room where Sarah lay asleep. "Where are you?" He whispered it out into the ether, his ears straining for the answer he knew would never come. God, Tiger...

"Lazlo?"

For a scintilla of a moment, Lazlo thought it was Tiger's voice, answering his plea, but then reality set in. He turned to see Sarah's eyes open, and he went to her side. "Hey... hey, Sarah... Nurse? Sarah's awake."

The nurse came in as Lazlo held Sarah's hand. Sarah's eyes were wide. "Lazlo... Johan..."

"We know, Sarah. I'm sorry, but it was too late. He's gone...and he has Tiger."

Sarah moaned, and the nurse shot Lazlo an irritated look, but he didn't care. "Sarah, I hate to ask this as soon as you're awake, but every second counts."

"Mr. Schuler..."

"No, it's okay," Sarah struggled up into a sitting position despite the nurses' protests. "Lazlo... he took me somewhere on the island. A bunker. He had it built... hello."

She looked past Lazlo's shoulder to see the detective in charge of the case come in.

"I'm sorry, I didn't want to intrude, but..."

"Every second counts." Sarah nodded. She looked exhausted but more alert than last time. "Like I said, he took me to this place. It was dark and I was blindfolded, but I can tell you that it was about a twenty-minute ride from my house."

"How did he get you in the car?"

Sarah smiled sadly. "He told me he'd arranged a surprise for me. I'd been sick..."

"So, you were sick?"

"Yes, for a few days. Flu. I was really sick. At first, he was so attentive, but then he seemed to change, become moody." She shook her head. "Have you time for this?"

"Anything you can tell us," the detective said, gently. Lazlo nodded.

"Please, go on."

"As I say, he got me in the car, asked me to put the blindfold on. Said it was a surprise. You know... I thought he was going to propose, and this was just his way of doing it. I couldn't have been more wrong." Her voice broke and she looked away for a second before clearing her throat. "But it was a twenty-minute ride. He didn't let me take the blindfold off when we got out of the car, but soon we got out onto grass—soft land. I heard birdsong. Then we were going down some stairs. It smelled new, but musty, like a construction site just after the building is completed, you know? It's underground. That's all I know about where it is."

The detective nodded and went out, barking orders into his cell phone. Lazlo held Sarah's hand as she apologized for not knowing more. Lazlo stopped her. "Sarah, how would you have known? You've given us more information than we had and—"

He stopped suddenly, something occurring to him. Sarah looked at him curiously. "What?"

"We followed him.... From your place. Tiger had her suspicions; she thought something was hinky about your illness, about how Johan was keeping her from you."

"He was?"

Lazlo half-smiled at her. "You know Tiger. We went to your house one night, and Tiger, well, broke in. Sorry. That tricky back door. When we couldn't find you, that's when we both suspected something. We followed him for a while and he pulled over..." He got up. "Sarah, will you be okay if I go find the detective?"

"Go, go. I'm praying you find them."

INSTEAD OF SPENDING time finding the detective though, Lazlo simply left the hospital. His gut was telling him to follow the same road they had followed Johan's car that night. He would bet the farm that Johan had been close to where he'd built his bunker.

Lazlo shook his head now. Months, months he'd been planning this, obviously. The patience, the psychopathy it would take... Jesus. That kind of obsession he couldn't fathom. He followed the same route they had that night. From Sarah's house—still being combed over by the police—he followed the road Johan had taken, keeping an eye on the clock. Sarah said Johan had driven for roughly twenty minutes.

Lazlo pulled the car over to the side of the road twenty minutes later. He vaguely recognized it, but then again, this stretch of road bordered fields, and it was hard to differentiate. There were a few places where he could see tracks that led into the fields, and he set out on foot to traverse the ones he could see. He didn't want the car to draw attention to his presence if he came across the bunker—if possible, he wanted to take Johan by surprise. Lazlo didn't have a gun—Tiger had refused to have one in the house—but before he'd left the hospital, he'd stolen a scalpel.

He didn't care if he had to kill Johan personally to save Tiger—he would do it.

He thought back now to when his sister, India, had been forced to kill her stalker or die herself. He'd always been supportive of that but wondered how it had changed Indy to have to take a life. Now, he knew. It wasn't about morals, it was about survival, and he was damned if his love, his wife, his beloved Tiger would be taken away from him.

Lazlo fingered the scalpel in his pocket but hesitated before he set off. He'd sneaked past the police to come here, but now his common sense prevailed. They had the resources to help him search the area, and so before he set off, he called the lead detective.

The detective wasn't happy with him, but promised to send people out. "You really should have told us before you got there. Don't put yourself in danger, Mr. Schuler."

"Would you put yourself in danger for the person you love, Detective?" Lazlo waited for his answer.

A silence. "I understand." The detective sighed. "Just... wait for us."

Lazlo told him he would, but they both knew he was lying. When Lazlo ended the call, he looked up and around.

Tiger... hold on. I'm coming for you.

31

CHAPTER THIRTY-ONE – LEAVE

LINCOLN'S BUNKER, The Island, San Juan Islands, Washington State

TIGER HAD NOT SLEPT, not wanting to waste a moment if the night was all that was left of her life. She spent the time both thinking of Lazlo, her brother, her family, her friends, and trying to figure out a way to escape. The duct tape around her wrists was tight, but she kept moving them despite the fact she felt the skin buckle and fray and blood drip from the red rawness of them. At dawn, she felt the tape give slightly and it spurred her on.

She hadn't quite freed herself when Lincoln returned and made her drink some water. To her relief, he didn't check her bindings, nor did the water taste as if he'd drugged it. Her eyes were riveted to the gun he'd stuck into the waistband of his pants. Why was he putting off killing her?

She asked him that, and he gave a humorless chuckle. "So many questions. Why am I delaying the inevitable?" He pulled the gun from his waistband, flicked the safety off, and shoved the muzzle against her belly. She could feel the coldness of the muzzle through her thin shirt and tensed for the bullet.

"Bang, bang, bang." He laughed then as she flinched. "That. That right there is why I'm delaying. The torture of it for you. Knowing it's coming." He pulled the gun away, putting the safety on. He waved it above his head. "There are six bullets in here. You're getting five of them, Tiger."

She narrowed her eyes at him. "Why not all six? Really go for the jackpot?"

He snickered. "I need one in case my plans go south. Just in case. Or if your husband decides to come for me."

Tiger's body went cold at his words. "Leave him out of this. This is between you and me. You're already killed my parents and hurt my brother. If you shoot me, your job is done."

"When, Tiger. When I shoot you. I'd tell you to get some rest, but there really isn't any point. The next time you see me, I'm going to kill you."

"You said that the last time."

Lincoln's mouth hitched up on one side. "Sassy. I like that. But it won't save you."

He left the light on this time when he left the room and Tiger didn't waste time. She pulled and pulled at the loose duct tape on her wrists and finally, she felt it snap. The relief that flooded through her was palpable, and she rubbed the raw skin gently, blowing on the wounds to soothe them. Then she tackled the tape on her ankles, tearing it carefully so she could use it again if she needed to. For what, she didn't know, but right now, the only tools at her disposal were the tape and the camera on its tripod.

She could tell it wasn't on, which surprised her. Why wouldn't he watch her, make sure she wasn't doing exactly what she was doing right now?

Arrogance. Johan—Lincoln's—certainty that she was helpless gave her a glimmer of hope. Tiger got up from the bunk and went to the camera, second-guessing herself, checking she wasn't incorrect. She gave a sigh of relief when she confirmed the camera was off. She lifted the tripod—it wasn't weighty, but still, it was better with nothing. If she could catch Lincoln by surprise, she might be able to distract him long enough to get out of this room.

Tiger glanced up at the light on the ceiling. It was a bare bulb that she could smash, but even with the tripod, she couldn't reach it. Her eyes dropped to the bunk. It was made of a heavy iron, and she could try to move it... but the sound would surely carry and alert Lincoln.

She went to it and risked picking it up. God, it weighed a ton and she wasn't sure if she could even move it at all, let alone enough make a sound.

Fuck. She looked back up at the light. If she stood on the edge of the bed, she might be able to smash the light, but she would have to be careful not to overbalance.

"Fuck this." She would risk it. If at least she knocked the light out, she'd stand a chance.

She grabbed the tripod and climbed onto the bunk. If she stood on the iron headboard, she could just about reach...

Steadying herself as best she could without the wall to support her, she swung a few times but each time, she missed by a few centimeters. She hissed in frustration. She heard movement outside the room and with one last desperate swing, the tripod connected to the lightbulb.

It smashed, sending tinkling glass to the floor. With her swing, the bunk moved, and Tiger fell, slamming her knees into the broken glass on the floor. An involuntary yelp escaped her, but she rolled onto her back and got to her feet as the door burst open.

It was a millisecond that she had and she took it, going for Lincoln with the tripod, slamming it into his chest, knocking him down.

"Fucking bitch!" He grabbed at her foot as she tried to get around him, and Tiger jabbed the tripod at him again. Lincoln grabbed it before it could smash into his face and twisted it, hard. Tiger threw herself away from Lincoln, feeling the camera split from the tripod. She was between Lincoln and the exit now and she ran. She heard the first gunshot and the bullet pinging off the wall behind her.

"Tiger!"

Another gunshot. That's it, she thought zigzagging down the long corridor.

Then everything went dark and she stumbled on the first step, slamming down onto the concrete staircase. Another gunshot briefly lit up the corridor as she turned over, breathless.

"You won't get out, Tiger, it's useless to try."

"Fuck you!"

She heard his laugh, getting closer, closer... she turned and scrambled up the stairs. The tripod was in her hand, and she lashed out blindly as she realized the door was locked.

Locked but made of wood... "Help! Help me!" She screamed it at the top of her lungs hoping that someone, anyone would hear. She felt Lincoln closing in on her, his breath hot on her neck and he grabbed her, dragging her back down the staircase.

With one, last desperate move, as Lincoln pressed the gun to her belly, Tiger struck out with the tripod. For a moment time froze, then she felt something spatter on her.

Lincoln made a gurgling sound, and she knew she must have injured him. A brief glimmer of hope ignited inside her, but then, a sudden flare of light and pain, so much pain. The light from the muzzle flash lit up the scene as he shot her. Even in her agony, her terror, she saw that his throat was slashed open, probably by the exposed screw at the tip of the tripod. When he'd wrenched the camera off, Lincoln had given her a weapon and she had used it.

Still, now, Tiger knew it was all over. Lincoln was firing indiscriminately, each time the place lit up, each time brought her new pain. Tiger rolled over onto her side, crying out as another bullet struck her hip.

"Just... die..." She heard his gurgled cry, then heard him fall, his body crumpling to the floor.

Silence. For a second Tiger heard nothing, her ears ringing from the sound of the gunshots. Her abdomen was in agony, her hip shattered, and she could feel hot blood pumping from her, but she was alive. She felt around on the floor, searching for the gun. By her reckoning there was one bullet left. She dragged her body up the stone stairs, to the door. She felt around for the handle, tracing the path to where it was locked.

She had no idea if it would work but she had to try. If she didn't get out of here, she would die—that much was clear. The good news was she could feel fresh, cold air. It meant she couldn't be too far down. She pressed the gun against where she thought the lock mechanism was and, drawing in painful breath, she pulled the trigger.

LAZLO WAS LOSING HOPE. Even after the police arrived to help him search, he thought that they might never find Lincoln Rose's bunker and that they would be too late if they did. He trudged around the fields and the trees, looking for any sign. A couple of times, tire tracks had made him almost giddy, but they had come to nothing, and now, not helping, a storm had blown up and rain pummeled the ground, washing away any clues.

Where are you? Lazlo felt the desperation in every cell in his body, mentally hearing the tick of the clock as Tiger's life slipped away. Baby... please...

"Lazlo!"

Over the clap of thunder, he heard the lead detective calling him. And he turned, ducking under a tree—not that sensible in a storm, but he wasn't in his right mind—and the detective came up to him. "We have to move out." The detective looked pale and shocked, and Lazlo shook his head.

"What? No..."

"Lazlo, there's been an incident down at the harbor... they think someone set devices. The ferry port, some of the places on Main Street. The Wharf... there are fires..."

"He did this," Lazlo shouted back at him. "It's a distraction technique."

"Maybe... but we have to be there. Look, we're getting reinforcements, but they're coming by helicopter, and because of the storm... Lazlo, I'm sorry."

Lazlo couldn't believe they were leaving. "We can't just abandon her! That's my wife..."

"I'm sorry, but we've found nothing to suggest she's here. She could be anywhere. Lazlo, I'm sorry, we have to go."

Lazlo watched helplessly as his police backup moved out and left him alone. "Fuck!" He screamed it out into the storm. He was soaked through by the rain, and twilight was beginning to set in, but there was no way he was giving up. He knew with every fiber of his being that she was close. He felt her... "Tiger... please... help me out here. Give me a clue."

And that's when he heard the gunshots.

32

CHAPTER THIRTY-TWO – BORN TO DIE

THE ISLAND, San Juan Islands, Washington State

TIGER COULD NO LONGER FEEL the bottom half of her body. She had to use every bit of her upper body strength, but even so, it took an age to pull herself up each step and when she reached the stairs Lincoln had cut into the mud, the torrential rain had turned them into a slippery nightmare. Tiger had slipped back down them, and now she was exhausted from the effort and from blood loss.

She didn't want to give up, didn't want to die out here alone, but her body wasn't obeying her will anymore, and she started to cry. *I don't want to die here...*

Black spots appeared at the corners of her vision and she knew the end was near. *Oh God, Lazlo... I should have loved you better...*

Her chest felt tight, her breathing was becoming shallow, and Tiger closed her eyes. *Accept this. You are going to die here...*

She lost consciousness and didn't hear the love of her life calling her name.

. . .

LAZLO STUMBLED towards the sound of the gunshots, praying he wasn't delusional enough to have imagined them, but still terrified that it meant Tiger was dead. Almost sliding on the muddy ground, he moved through the trees and into a small copse. He saw the hole in the ground immediately, his heart leaping, then saw the small, crumpled figure at the bottom of it. "Tiger!"

Lazlo didn't think—he just had to get to her. He slid down the side of the small opening, seeing the doorway to the bunker, but then all his attention was riveted on his wife. He scooped her into his arms, and then moaned in horror as he saw the gunshot wounds in her belly and her hip. Her clothes were soaked with blood, her eyes were closed, and as he held her, her body was limp. With trembling fingers, Lazlo felt for her pulse.

Alive. His breath came out of him in a rush. Her heartbeat was weak, but it was there. Lazlo pressed his lips to hers. "Stay with me, baby."

He looked around and saw how much trouble they were both in now. The rain had made a slick of the steps cut into the turf, and with Tiger a dead weight in his arms, it would make it impossible for Lazlo to carry her out.

Dead weight.

"No... no. Come on, baby, this isn't the way this ends." He kissed her again, and for the next few minutes, he tried his best to clamber out of the hole. He failed every time.

God...

He looked back into the bunker. There could be something in there that could help. He assumed that either Lincoln had left or...

Lazlo carried Tiger into the bunker and laid her gently in the doorway, noticing the shot-up lock. The entrance to the bunker was in darkness, and he used his phone to light his way. At the bottom of a few steps, he saw him. Lincoln Rose was on his back, his eyes open and staring, his throat slashed. Lazlo stared at the corpse for a long moment, kicked the man to check he was really dead, but it was obvious. Tiger had killed him, he was sure.

"My beautiful bad ass." He kicked Lincoln's body to one side and hurried down the corridor, searching the two rooms he found. In the furthest one, he saw a bunk with one sheet. It would have to do.

Somehow, he managed to use the sheet to get Tiger up to the open ground, and once he had her there, he picked her up and carried her back to the car. They were both caked with mud, and Lazlo stripped down to his bare skin, throwing his dirty jacket in the trunk and using his relative clean shirt to put against her wounds. Tiger stirred as he pressed the fabric to her stomach and to his joy, she opened her eyes.

"Am I dead?"

Lazlo couldn't stop the tears then. "No, baby, you're still with me. Please... stay with me..." His voice broke and he touched his forehead to hers. "I don't have time to explain. I need to get you to hospital."

"Okay." Her voice was faint and her eyes closed again, and Lazlo laid her gently in the back and got into the driver's seat.

"Hang on, baby... please..."

LAZLO DIDN'T REMEMBER any of the drive back to the hospital. All he could recall was almost driving right into the emergency room and yelling at people to please, please help him. He had Tiger in his arms and he couldn't even remember the weight of her as he staggered into the emergency room, then the emptiness he felt when they took her from him, rushing her into surgery. He stood, covered with mud, oblivious to the bemused stares of those around him.

Eventually, someone touched his shoulder, and he turned, numb, to see the detective. "Lazlo... you found her."

Lazlo nodded. "She's been shot. He shot her. He shot her and she killed him. She tried to get out, but the mud and the rain..."

He was aware he was rambling and the detective called another doctor and they steered Lazlo into a chair. "He's in shock," the doctor said, but Lazlo shook his head.

"No. I just... I can't think. Will they tell me if she's okay?"

The detective explained what had happened to the doctor and he nodded. "I'll go get an update. In the meantime, we'll check you out, Mr. Schuler."

"I'm fine."

But he wasn't. His mind was in a state of confusion, and the fear, the terror that Tiger wouldn't make it was all Lazlo could think about.

The world moved around him as he waited for news on her condition, and when Apollo and Nell were brought down, he told them in a monotone what happened. Hours wore on and although the surgeon sent a nurse out to update Tiger's family, all they could tell them was that "we're doing all we can."

Lazlo excused himself and went to call India, needing to hear his sister's voice. India told him the news had broken nationally. "We're flying out. We're on the way to the airport now."

It was on the tip of his tongue to tell her not to come, not to inconvenience herself and Massimo, especially with such a young infant, but something stopped him. Lazlo need her right now, needed his sister desperately, and so found himself thanking her instead. "I'll arrange a car."

"Laz, don't worry, we'll see to that."

He gave a humorless laugh. "It'll give me something to distract me."

"Oh, Laz..." India's voice was soft. "You deserve so much more than this pain. I'll be there soon. She's going to be okay... I know it in my bones."

Lazlo was grateful for India's words, but he wished he could feel so hopeful. Third time unlucky was all he could think of—he'd nearly lost India, then his friend Jess, and now Tiger's life hovered in the balance. The dread inside him was almost overwhelming.

He went to arrange a car to pick up India and Massimo from SeaTac, then went to see Sarah.

Sarah was sitting up in bed, and to his relief, she looked much better. The ashen tone of her skin was less and her eyes were clear. But they were full of sadness and he went to sit with her. "Is there any news, Lazlo?"

He shook his head and Sarah sighed. "I'm so sorry, Laz. I should have seen it. I should have seen through him, but..."

"Love is blind."

She nodded. "And I did love him. He was the first man I loved since Ben died; he had me fooled completely. I feel so... wretched."

"He had us all fooled," Lazlo reassured her. "All of us. The depths of his psychopathy... Jesus, Sarah, Johan was insane. Insane. He deserved what happened to him. You didn't." He squeezed her hand. "How are you feeling?"

"Better. I mean, I'll be better when I'm not hooked up to these machines... but the docs are optimistic about my kidney function." She sighed. "Did you hear about The Wharf?"

Lazlo nodded. It seemed Johan—Lincoln Rose—had set devices at various places to divert attention away from him as he tried to escape the island. They were timed to go off at a certain time, causing explosions and fires. The lead detective guessed Rose had planned to kill Tiger, then use the bedlam that had ensued to escape the island without detection. The ferry port, a farmer's market, and The Wharf had all been damaged, with The Wharf almost completely gutted by fire.

Lazlo reassured Sarah now. "Listen, don't worry. You have to take care of yourself, and Tiger..." His voice cracked, but he cleared his throat, "Tiger will pull through, and while you're both recovering, we'll get the best people in to remodel everything. You will have The Wharf back, I promise you."

He stayed with Sarah for a little while longer, then went back to sit with Apollo and Nell. Nell was finding coffee for them, and Lazlo found Apollo staring out of the window. He was out of his wheelchair now, but still used crutches, and to Lazlo, he looked older.

Damaged. So much damage. "Pol?"

Apollo turned a tear-stained face to his brother-in-law. "Hey, Laz. How's Sarah?"

Lazlo updated him, then went and put his hand on Apollo's shoulder. "She's going to be okay. Tiger. I know it."

"I see the conflict in your eyes, Laz. I know things are bad." Apollo sighed and rubbed his eyes. "Just... she practically brought me up, you know?"

"I know."

"Excuse me?"

Both of the men turned and saw Tiger's surgeon standing behind them. He smiled at them. "I have news. Very good news."

TIGER OPENED her eyes and sighed. No pain. She was either dead or on some very, very nice medication. Her throat felt dry, but she risked trying to speak. "Lazlo?"

She heard a chair scrape and then he was in her field of vision, looking so beautiful, so utterly delighted to see her that she smiled. "Handsome. Wanna hop in beside me?"

Lazlo laughed. "That's the morphine talking. God, Tiger..."

His lips were fierce against hers then, and as if remembering she was in a hospital bed, he drew away and Tiger pouted. Lazlo stroked her hair. "How do you feel?"

"Bulky." She put her hands over the heavy dressings on her abdomen and felt the cast on her right leg. "I got messed up, huh?"

Lazlo gave a choked laugh, tears in her eyes. "Only you could underplay it like that. God, Tiger... you almost died."

"But I didn't. And that motherfucker is dead, I made sure of that."

"Bad ass."

"You know it. How's Sarah?"

"Better. Worried about you."

Tiger pulled his face closer for another kiss. "I'm fine. I'm fine now."

Lazlo sighed and leaned his forehead against hers. "Promise?"

"I promise."

33

CHAPTER THIRTY-THREE – TE AMO

THE ISLAND, San Juan Islands, Washington State
One year later...

IT WAS ALMOST two a.m. before the party broke up. The Wharf, newly renovated, had been teaming with guests, customers, and friends, and now as Sarah shooed Tiger and Lazlo from the shop, she smiled at them both. "Go. I'll close up. You've both done more than enough today. More than today. I love you both so much."

Lazlo drove Tiger and himself home and they had no need for words. Hand-in-hand, they went into their home, greeting Fizz, who wagged his tail, jumping up for kisses and cuddles, then returned back to his basket. He seemed to sense that now was their time to be together.

LAZLO AND TIGER walked up the stairs together, smiling at each other as they entered their bedroom. It had been a long, hard year with Tiger's recovery slow and painful and the renovation of the Wharf taking longer than it should.

But now... Lazlo took Tiger in his arms and pressed his lips to hers. "I love you so much," he murmured and felt her lips curve up in a smile against his mouth.

"I love you, Lazlo Schuler."

His kiss became more urgent, and as they stripped each other's clothes off, Lazlo picked her up and carried her to their bed, kissing her lips, her throat, and moving down her body until his tongue found her clit. He lifted her legs over his shoulders as he heard her gasp, his fingers digging into her buttocks. She tasted like honey, and as he worked on her, his own body reacted, his cock stiffening, straining, so that even before he had made her come, he was desperate to be inside her.

"Lazlo... please..." Tiger made it clear she wanted the same thing, and so, smiling down at her, he moved up her body and thrust into her hard. Tiger wrapped her legs around him, arched her back so her belly and breasts pressed against him, her eyes never leaving his face. "You are my world... oh!"

Lazlo's pace quickened and he braced his hands either side of her head, giving himself the leverage to bury his cock deeper and harder into her with each thrust. She was his and tonight, he wanted to dominate her body in every way he could. She was so God damn beautiful, he thought now, every inch of her is perfection. He told her so as he fucked her, and when she came, a beautiful flush of pink colored her skin.

"Oh, I love you, I love you..."

Lazlo came hard, groaning her name over and over, burying his face in her neck as he pumped thick, creamy cum inside her. Tiger cradled his head against her, kissing his temple.

When they had caught their breath, Lazlo lifted his head and smiled at her. "All good things from now on."

Tiger smiled. "My love... I have a gift for you."

"You do?"

She grinned widely. "It's in the drawer in your nightstand."

Lazlo, bemused, leaned over and opened the drawer. A long box sat there and he took it out. "Shouldn't I be the one giving you a gift?"

Tiger chuckled. "Shut up and open it, doofus."

"Ah, romantic talk," Lazlo laughed, but he opened the box. His eyes grew wide and he looked back at her. "Tiger..."

She smiled, tears in her eyes. "Six weeks today. I had the doctor check me out over and over again before I felt I could tell you. We're having a baby, Lazlo..."

Lazlo felt his heart explode with joy and he splayed his fingers across her belly. "Our baby."

Tiger nodded. "Our baby," she agreed and kissed him until they were both breathless.

The End

Did you like this book? Then you'll LOVE Secrets of the Flame: A Holiday Romance (Saved by the Doctor Book One)

My last year of med school, the best year ever because of her—my future changed forever because of her ...

From the moment I saw her, I knew there was something between us not many people find.

Passionate nights, stolen kisses throughout our busy days; she and I had the same goals—goals that would end the special connection we'd found.

Leaving her behind proved to be the hardest thing I'd ever done.

Finding her one day in a Seattle hospital, tending to one of my best friends, proved that old flame had never completely gone out.

No longer the easygoing, easy-to-love girl I'd known years ago, she'd become guarded.

My only question—why?

Start Reading Secrets of the Flame

ALL OF ME EXTENDED EPILOGUE
A BDSM ROMANCE

When Tiger Rose and Lazlo Schuler travel to Paris for a very belated honeymoon with their young daughter Bettina, the couple take time to enjoy the time together after Betty is asleep, and relive some of their most erotic nights together.
Finding they are still just as uninhibited as ever, Tiger and Lazlo reconnect after two years filled with torment and pain, relieved only by the birth of their daughter and are delighted to realize that even though their love affair began so suddenly, it is still burning hot.
But Lazlo has a secret and as he struggles to keep it from Tiger, she becomes worried that perhaps she doesn't know this man she loves as well as she thought and, after she and Betty have a troubling encounter with a strange man, she begins to wonder if her Paris honeymoon is turning into a nightmare...

∽

TIGER GRINNED as her daughter's eyes grew wide. Betty—Bettina— was almost three years old now, but she had still not lost that sense of wonder that delighted her parents. Betty looked out of the plane's window now as the aircraft began to circle the city.

"Paris, darling. Are you excited?"

Betty nodded, completely engrossed in the scene below her and Tiger shot an amused look at her husband. Lazlo reached over and stroked Betty's hair. "Almost there, Betty Bug."

He touched the back of his fingers to Tiger's cheek and smiled. "Love you," he mouthed, and she smiled back, leaning across for a kiss.

"Love you more."

"Not possible."

Tiger chuckled. "Always have to have the last word."

"And rarely get it."

They both laughed now then as the announcement to fasten their seatbelts came over the speakers.

THE HASSLE and hurry of baggage collection and passport control distracted them from the excitement of arrival and Betty got a little fussy, scared by the huge crowds of people. Lazlo lifted her into his arms, hugging her tightly and in the security of his arms, Betty visibly relaxed. Tiger slid a woolly hat onto her daughter's dark, silky hair. "Just to keep you warm, Betty Bug."

THE CHAUFFEUR WAS WAITING with their name on a sign in Arrivals and soon they were safely tucked into the car, being driven to the Four Seasons Georges V, just off the Champs-Élysées. They had decided to go all out for their first trip abroad with Betty, and despite eschewing most of her old life as a Hollywood movie star, Tiger had always wanted to go back to the city she had fallen in love with after filming two or three movies there.

Also, she reasoned, after the few years they'd had, they deserved the best and it wasn't as if she and Lazlo couldn't afford it. Even though, on paper, she was just the owner of a (admittedly very successful) coffee house/movie theater on their island in Puget Sound, she had made her fortune in a decade long movie career. And

Lazlo was one of the best showbiz lawyers around. They never had to worry about money again but they lived reasonably simply.

But not on this trip. This trip, no expense was spared. They had the biggest suite in the hotel with spectacular views over Paris and—more importantly—a separate bedroom across the suite for Betty.

Because, although their days were all about showing their daughter the city and having fun with her, they were determined that the nights belonged to them.

As the hotel came into view, Tiger turned to meet Lazlo's eyes and saw the burning desire in them. Yes... after everything, this would be their time.

"Tonight," she whispered to Lazlo, who pressed his lips to hers briefly and smiled.

"Tonight."

BETTY WAS ALMOST FALLING asleep as she ate dinner in the suite, pushing French fries around her plate and yawning. But she hopped off her chair and went to the balcony. It was Fall in Paris and a cool breeze blew in. Tiger went to her daughter's side and lifted her so she could see over the balustrade, pointing out the Eiffel Tower. Lazlo joined them, locking his arms around them.

After a while, Tiger felt Betty's head drop onto her shoulder and felt her daughter's warm breath on her neck as she slept. She shot an amused glance at Lazlo, then turned and took her daughter to her bedroom, waking her long enough to brush her teeth ad change into her pajamas. Betty fell back to sleep almost immediately.

Lazlo was closing the doors to the balcony as Tiger returned to the main suite and Lazlo held his hand out to her. "Feel like a soak in the tub?"

"God, yes, please."

Lazlo chuckled softly. "I thought you might."

They undressed each other as the tub filled with hot scented water, then Tiger moaned with pleasure as they slipped into the warm water. "God, that's good."

Lazlo, grinning wickedly, slipped his hand between her legs and began to rub her clit. Tiger giggled softly. "And that feels even better."

Laying back against his chest, she closed her eyes as he stroked her into a mellow orgasm. Sighing happily, she moved around to straddle him in the water. "My Laz..."

They kissed, gently at first, tentatively like they had only just met, then Tiger slid her hands into his hair and her mouth became hungry on his. Lazlo gave a moan of animal desire and pulled her closer and she could feel his cock stiffening. She smiled against his lips and snaked her hand down to stroke his cock, then guided it inside her. She shivered with ecstasy as they began to move, his cock filling her as she rocked and impaled herself onto it.

"God, Tiger..."

Tiger felt him buck and then his cock was pumping his thick, creamy cum deep inside her and she kissed him harder. "That's just for starters tonight, my love."

THEY PLAYED AROUND for a little longer in the tub then, just as their fingertips started to prune, Lazlo lifted her out of the tub and they dried each other. Lazlo reached out and unclipped the long dark hair Tiger had piled up on top of her head, letting it fall around her shoulders like a cloud. He traced a fingertip down her face, his eyes soft. "I could tell you a million times how beautiful you are, Tiger Rose, and it still wouldn't be enough."

Her violet eyes shone up at him. "Right back at you, handsome. Take me to bed."

"Wanton woman."

"You know it." She laughed aloud as he threw her over his shoulder in a fireman's life and took her to the bedroom. He laid her down on the bed and Tiger rolled over onto her stomach.

Lazlo gave a throaty chuckle. "You read my mind." He went to their suitcase and pulled out a bag.

Tiger wriggled her toes in excitement as he pulled a short, thick crop from the bag. Lazlo raised his eyebrows. "Yes?"

"Yes!"

"Yes what?"

Tiger laughed. "Yes, please."

"That's better." He approached the bed, and she took a moment to appreciate her husband, so big and strong, his broad shoulders and hard chest, the stomach muscles that rippled as he moved. The slim hips, the thick, heavy cock standing so proud against his belly. His face, a face that looked like it had been sculptured by classic artists, straight from the Roman gods. He grinned, enjoying her scrutiny. "You like?"

"I love..." She purred the words then yelped as he flicked the end of the crop against her thighs.

"Louder."

"I love you..."

Crack! The crop came down hard across her buttocks and she groaned in exquisite pain. "More, please, Lazlo..."

The soft flesh of her thighs felt like it had burst into flames as he struck her again. "Roll onto your back and spread those beautiful legs for me, Tiger."

Moving slowly to not ruin the mood, Tiger did as he asked, parting her thighs and revealing her red, swollen, damp sex. Lazlo flicked the crop against each inner thigh then the tip of it caught her clit and she shivered and came, her back arching up, the soft curve of her belly irresistible to him. He splayed his fingers across it, circling her navel with a fingertip as he watched her catch her breath.

His cock was straining, salty pre-cum already at the tip and Tiger sat up and took him into her mouth, her hands at the base, massaging his balls, her forefinger pressing into the tender perineum in the way she knew he liked. He sucked in a breath through his teeth. "*Jesus*, Tiger..."

Her tongue swept over the wide crest of him, licking the pre-cum from the tip and sliding up and down the thick, long shaft. Each flick of her tongue sent an explosion of pleasure through him and before long, he was clutching at her hair as he came into her mouth and she swallowed him down.

As he recovered, Tiger pulled him onto the bed. "And we can do this all night long."

Lazlo grinned. "I'm glad you have a high opinion of my stamina. But then again, with you as an incentive..." He buried his face in her neck and nibbled at the skin of her throat, making her giggle.

"Silly man... I love you so much, Lazlo Schuler."

"You too, wifey. Now... if you'd kindly open those delectable legs for me..."

THE NEXT FEW DAYS, they rejected the idea of jetlag and went to every touristy place they could think of with Betty. The little girl took everything in with her quiet wonder, her violet eyes, so like her mother's, wide and curious.

On the fourth day of their vacation, they were sitting outside one of the many cafes that lined the Paris streets. Betty was holding court, wrapped in her warm jacket, a cup of hot chocolate going cold in front of her as she recounted everything they had done that day. Lazlo's phone buzzed, and he glanced at the screen. "Sorry, baby, it's work."

Tiger gave him a glare. "On our honeymoon?"

"Just this once, I promise. It's time sensitive."

Tiger gave a nod, knowing Lazlo wouldn't do this unless it was urgent. Lazlo got up and walked a little way away so his call wouldn't disturb the other patrons. Betty was drawing patterns in the foam on her hot chocolate now and Tiger rolled her eyes. "Betty, no. Honestly, child, if there's a mess to be made, you'll make it."

Betty grinned at her mother's mild tone—Tiger never got really irritated at her daughter for things like this but to Betty's credit, once she was told no, she was obedient. "Momma? Why does Daddy look cross?"

Tiger, wiping Betty's little fingers with a napkin, glanced up at her husband. Lazlo's forehead was creased and his body looked tense and stiff. He was having what was obviously a heated conversation and

Tiger frowned. Lazlo was generally laid back—unless his family was threatened—and to get het up about work...

"It's just work, baby," Tiger wanted to reassure Betty even if she was concerned herself, "Daddy's just making sure everything is okay at home."

Betty shrugged, satisfied but Tiger put some money down on the table and picked her up. "Let's walk around for a bit to get warm, okay?"

She signaled to Lazlo that they were walking back to the hotel and he nodded, indicated that he would follow. They weren't too far from the Champs-Élysées now and on the way, Betty stopped to watch a street performer. Tiger indulged her daughter, mostly so a lagging Lazlo could catch up. He was barely in sight down the street now. Tiger sighed. Maybe she should cut him a break. She knew he was a workaholic when she married him... *ha*. Had she? They married after only a few weeks of meeting and the last three years had been a sharp learning curve for both of them. A quickie marriage, pregnancy—the first an ectopic one which broke their hearts—then the horror of Tiger's attempted murder, with her left horribly injured. They'd been through it all. What did one phone call matter?

She hugged Betty close to her. "Shall we go, Bugs?"

"One minute more, Momma, please."

Tiger smiled, nuzzling Betty's soft cheek with her nose. She couldn't resist her daughter when she soft and pliable like this.

It only began to sink into her subconscious that they were being watched as the street performer finished his act. Tiger's eyes slid to the crowd opposite and saw the man staring straight at her. He was middle-aged, his brow furrowed, and his icy blue eyes bored into hers with a look of such anger it sent a thrill of fear through her.

She looked away quickly, a shiver of anxiety in her stomach. "Come home. Home time." She said it more firmly to Betty who nodded. Tiger glanced behind her to see Lazlo catching up with them and gave a sigh of relief. She risked another glance but the strange man had gone.

Thank god, another weirdo is the last thing we need...

As if her body agreed, her hip, the one shattered by a madman's bullet began to ache and when Lazlo reached to take Betty from her, she gave her up gladly for once.

Lazlo seemed to notice she was favoring her other leg as they made their way back to the hotel. "Are you okay?"

"My hip is aching, that's all. No biggie. Did you get things hashed out with work?"

Lazlo shrugged. "It is what it is." He smiled down at her, all the frown lines from earlier gone. "No biggie."

Tiger chuckled and tucked her arm in his. Who cared about work calls and weirdos when they were together, all three of them? As they went to their suite, Betty took herself off to her room to play and Tiger and Lazlo enjoyed a glass of wine on the balcony. Twilight was falling and the lights on the Eiffel Tower were twinkling like stars. "Could this city be more beautiful?"

"Nope. It is perfection," Tiger leaned back against Lazlo's chest, "Not that I don't love our little island but of all the cities we could escape to..."

"Right?" Lazlo gave a satisfied smile. "You know... we could always buy a place here."

Tiger shook her head. "Nah, I like staying here. And if we bought somewhere here, then, I don't know, it would somehow negate the fantasy of it. Am I making sense?"

"Yes and no. I get it." Lazlo pressed his lips to her temple. "Listen... they have all-night sitters here, you know."

Tiger turned to look at him, her eyebrows raised. "They do? Why do you say that?"

Lazlo grinned the lazy, desire-filled smile that sent butterflies scattering in her belly. He trailed a finger down her spine. "Because there's a club I thought you might like to go to... somewhere we can... play."

Tiger's smile spread slowly across her face. "You're a very, very bad man..."

Lazlo replied by kissing her hard, crushing his mouth against hers

so hard that she felt her teeth cut into her inner lip. She was breathless when he finally drew away and the violent desire in his eyes
made her gasp. "Lazlo..."

"Yes or no, Tiger."

Her entire body was reacting to the dangerous passion in him and
she nodded. "Yes... yes..."

So, much later, when the hotel's registered child minder had been
introduced to Betty and Tiger had her mind put at ease by the
woman, she and Lazlo were taken by cab to the club. Tiger had
slipped into a skin-tight red silk dress, no underwear, but as they
reached the club, she began to shiver both in anticipation and with
nerves.

Lazlo's lips were at her ear as they walked in. "Don't be scared,
baby. The upper floor is just a bar. We'll go there first, relax a little
and if you change your mind about... going down to the dungeon...
then we'll just stay in the bar."

Tiger felt her body relax. She was excited and horny but also...
she was a mother and her body was that of a thirty-six-year-old who'd
been shot and who had had major surgery. Her confidence had been
knocked—or would have been if Lazlo hadn't spent the last three
years worshipping her as if she were some sort of goddess.

But that was in private... from what Lazlo had told her, the club
was uninhibited and free, naked people everywhere. She could stay
clothed, it was her choice, but... if they were going to do that then she
wanted to go all the way. She just hoped she could find her courage.

Lazlo led her up a few steps into a bar, half-open on a terrace.
They found a booth at the back and Lazlo ordered drinks. "Champagne?" He raised his eyebrows at her but she shook her head.

"Something strong?"

"We have a delicious selection of cocktails, *madame*. I will bring
you a menu if you wish?"

"*Oui, s'il vous plaît.*"

The waiter nodded, his smile friendly. Lazlo ordered champagne for himself nevertheless and grinned when the waiter brought the cocktail Tiger had ordered—a long, tall glass of multi-colored spirits and syrups. "I'm sure you're risking a diabetic coma with that."

"Probably. I don't care, it's yummy." Tiger put the straw to her lips, grinning as she met Lazlo's gaze and sucked a long draft of the drink, wincing as the alcohol burned her throat. "Dang, that's strong."

"Just like your power of sucking."

Tiger grinned. "You know it."

"I do." Lazlo looked smug and Tiger laughed.

"You look very pleased with yourself."

Lazlo shrugged. "It's just nice to have a date night with my beautiful wife. That I found out abut this place is a bonus, and I thought you might enjoy it. If not, no harm, no foul. We'll have a drink and go home."

The effect of the cocktail was already making Tiger feel braver, and she slid her foot out of her shoe and up his leg until her toes curled into his crotch. Lazlo grinned at her as she felt his cock respond. "That feels so good."

He leaned over and kissed her, lingering over it, his tongue gently massaging hers. She was breathless when they broke apart, but she took his hand and slid it under her dress. "Make me come," she whispered, "right here, right now."

"My pleasure," he growled softly as his fingers found her clit and began to rub. Tiger didn't take her eyes from his as she pressed her groin against his hand. Lazlo slipped two fingers inside her and began to move them in rhythm with the thumb that was strumming her clit and when she came, he muffled her moan with a kiss.

His eyes were alive with desire as she trailed her lips along his jawline up to his ear. "Let's go downstairs, Laz. Let's do this."

AT FIRST GLANCE, the club downstairs didn't look much different to the upper floor bar, but as Tiger and Lazlo moved through, they saw more and more people naked, making love, spanking each other or moving against each other to the slow, sensual beat of the music. At one end of the biggest room, a DJ worked, topless, his gloriously hard body shimmering with sweat and a naked woman wrapped around him as he played the music.

Lazlo felt proud as he saw people admiring Tiger's body as she sashayed past them in her skintight red dress but he could see she only wanted him. A stunningly beautifully waitress, naked apart from a thong, stopped Tiger, spoke quietly to her and smiled widely. Tiger glanced back at Lazlo then laughed and nodded. With one easy movement, she pulled the dress over her head and the waitress nodded approvingly.

Lazlo's cock was pressing hard against his pants and Tiger nodded at him to follow her lead and undress. He didn't hesitate, and they walked to an empty table, dumping their clothes and pressing their bodies against each other, oblivious now to everyone else in the club.

Lazlo only had one focus now, and that was fucking his beautiful, sensational wife in every way. He steered her into a chair and pushed her legs apart, dropping to his knees. He buried his face in her sweet cunt, drilling his tongue deep inside her, sharp jabs, mimicking what his cock wanted to do, then lashing his tongue around her hard, swollen clit.

Tiger tangled her fingers into his hair, pulling on it hard. Lazlo's fingers dug into the tender skin of her inner thighs, harder until he could feel the muscles tense with the pressure.

"God, Lazlo..." Tiger slid down in the chair, pressing her groin against his face but then she pulled his head up. "Fuck me," she demanded, "right here, right *now*..."

Lazlo grinned and stood, tugging her legs around him and thrusting his straining cock deep inside her. Tiger clung to him as he moved, using all his strength to slam his hips against hers, his cock burying itself deep inside her velvety cunt.

The rest of the club, hell, the rest of the world melted away as they made love, the connection between them unbreakable. Neither cared that they had an audience—in fact, it made it all the more exciting and when they came, together, they heard a murmur of appreciation in their small audience.

"You look so beautiful when you come," he murmured to a breathless Tiger. He admired the way her full breasts rose and fell as she breathed hard, and he bent his head and sucked at each nipple.

"Lazlo..." Just the way she whispered his name made his heart pound, and he looked up and smiled at her.

"Yes, beauty?"

"Shall we... play?"

Lazlo grinned and stood, offering her his hand. "Come with me."

They collected their clothes from the table and walked hand-in-hand further into the club to one of the private rooms in the back. Lazlo closed the door behind them as he saw Tiger walk around the room, touching the cabinets full of sex toys, looking at the manacles attached to the walls, the floggers and crops in the rack in the corner. She grinned at him. "So many pretty things."

"Only one beautiful thing in this room and I'm looking at it."

"Cheesy."

He threw his head back and laughed. "I'm not sorry. Come here to me." He held his hand out but Tiger just grinned, taking one of the crops from the rack and stroking it against her palm.

"No, boy, you come here to me."

Lazlo obeyed, turned on by the look of fierceness on her lovely face. "Anything for you..."

"Anything for me... what?"

"Mistress."

Tiger grinned. "Damn right." As he came close, she grabbed the back of his neck and pulled his face down to hers but stopped short of kissing him. "Do you trust me?"

"With my life."

"Then put your damn hands in those manacles on the wall. *I'm fucking you* this time."

Lazlo grinned, a little confused, but did as she asked, laughing as she whipped the crop against his buttocks, then as he watched her, she withdrew a strap-on from one of the cabinets. She held it up.

"Are you game?"

Lazlo grinned. "Hell, yes, I'm game."

"Good." She strapped the phallus onto her own groin and Lazlo almost moaned at the sight of her. Christ, she was so beautiful, it was painful. Tiger came over to him, kissing his back, running her tongue down his spine. "Spread your legs, Lazlo."

He closed his eyes as he felt her reach around and cup his cock and balls, kneading them gently, sending both pleasure and pain shooting through his body. Then she was easing into his ass, the dildo well-lubricated. She moved slowly, careful, her hand working his cock. "Okay?"

He nodded. They had never tried this before, although they had anal sex a few times, it was never this way around and he was surprised how pleasurable he found it. Maybe it was the turn-on of Tiger being in charge that was doing it, but she made him come, shuddering and groaning her name. As he caught his breath, he heard Tiger slip out of the strap-on, casting it aside, and then she was sliding between him and the wall, grinning up at him. "Hey, baby."

"Hey, boss."

She chuckled, running her hands over his hard chest. "Did you enjoy that?"

"I did." He nodded up to his still manacled hands. "You going to let me free so I can touch you?"

She grinned widely. "Nope."

He groaned. "Torturer."

"That's why we're here..." She dropped to her knees and took his cock into her mouth then and he let out a deep, relaxed breath as she sucked him into a mellow orgasm.

Tiger freed his hands afterwards, and they went to the bed to catch their breaths and chill out. Lazlo wrapped his arms around her and they kissed then Tiger grinned at him. "I'm sorry to break the spell, but if I don't use the bathroom..."

"And we're not doing golden showers," he finished with a laugh. "Let's go find the bathroom."

They tugged their clothes over their naked, sweaty bodies. "And us respectable parents."

"Disgraceful."

They wandered out of the room and found the bathrooms along a darkened corridor. "Met you back here."

After Tiger finished, she went back through what she thought was the same door but soon found herself lost. She walked into what looked like a stall of showers and frowned. *Nope. Not this way.*

She turned and gasped in shock. A man in a mask stood behind her. "Are you here for the blood play?"

A cold shiver of fear went down her spine. "No, I..."

The man took his mask off and she felt the shock of recognition. It was the same creepy man who had been watching her and Betty as they watched the street performer. She saw the same recognition in his eyes. "I know you."

"No... excuse me."

She tried to step around him but he put an arm out, stopping her. "Don't be in such a rush."

He had an accent, but she didn't recognize it. His green eyes searched her face. "You want to play with me?"

With growing panic, she shook her head then her heart almost failed when she saw the knife. He brought it up and showed it to her, then slowly drew it down his chest. A faint red line appeared and a few drops of blood splashed onto the tile flooring. "It doesn't hurt... much. Just enough to be pleasurable. Let me show you."

Tiger backed off in a hurry but he grabbed her arm. "Don't be afraid."

The knife was inches from her stomach and Tiger screamed, unable to quell the terror inside her now. The man let go of her arm, his own eyes alarmed and the next moment, he was being slammed against the wall by a raging Lazlo.

"Wait, stop, stop, I thought she was into.... I'm sorry, I'm sorry... please, I misread the situation..."

Tiger, breathless, put a hand on Lazlo's shoulder. "Laz... it's not worth it. I'm okay, really."

Lazlo hesitated the released the man who disappeared back into the club. Lazlo held Tiger. She was trembling all over. "I'm sorry, I took the wrong door out of the bathrooms, and he was here, and he was watching me and Betty earlier and..."

"Woah, woah, woah stop, take a breath." Lazlo looked down at her. "He was watching you and Betty?"

"In the street. While we were watching the juggler... god, it doesn't matter. I'm sorry. This... our lovely evening is ruined."

"Hell no, it's not. But let's get out of here."

THEY COLLECTED their coats from the coat-check and went out into the cold Parisian night. Lazlo wrapped his arm around her shoulders as they walk and soon Tiger felt the tension of the brief terrifying encounter seep from her. She looked up at her husband, so handsome in his black wool coat. "I had a good time tonight, regardless of how it ended."

"Me too, baby." He grinned down at her. "Always finding trouble."

"Isn't that the truth?" She laughed. "At least, I think, in the end, that poor guy was more scared than I was. He meant no actual harm."

"Just some creep."

"Just a creep we'll never have to see again."

Lazlo kissed her temple. "Listen, let's get a cab. I'm freezing."

"Me too."

BACK AT THE HOTEL, Tiger thanked the sitter and Lazlo gave her a sizeable tip as he saw her to the door. Tiger checked in on Betty who was sound asleep. Tiger stroked her daughter's soft cheek and Lazlo returned.

"Look at her," Tiger whispered, her voice full of wonder, "can you believe she's ours?"

"I know. I can, though she looks so much like you, baby."

Tiger leaned back against him as they watched their child sleep, safe and happy. "Want another one?"

She felt Lazlo's silent chuckle rumble through his chest. "A whole bunch if you're up to it."

She turned in his arms. "Always, with you. Let's go to bed."

TIGER WOKE in the morning to the bed empty beside her. She heard voices from the other room and supposed Lazlo had gotten up with Betty. Tiger glanced at the clock. A little after ten a.m. Well, they had been up until late so she didn't feel guilty. She got up and slipped into her robe, padding into the bathroom to brush her teeth.

When she went out into the main room, however, Lazlo was alone and he looked up and smiled at her. "Hey you."

"Betty not with you?"

"Napping again. How are you this morning?"

She kissed him. "Good. I thought I heard voices is all."

"Ah. Phone call. Work again, sorry."

She smiled. "It's okay."

Lazlo made a face. "Well... I'm afraid you might not think so when I tell you I have to go out for a time this morning."

"Oh, Laz, a phone call is one thing..." Tiger shook her head, silencing herself. What did it matter? An hour or two? "No. Sorry, it's okay. Betty and I will have a playdate with each other until you get back."

"I am sorry." He came to her and wrapped his arms around her.

"Really, it's okay. In fact, Betty and I will go grab some hot chocolate somewhere. Maybe I'll take her to that toy store she had googly eyes for."

"Good idea."

So, later, Tiger bundled Betty into her coat and they took the Metro down to the toy store they'd found a few days previously. To both their dismay, however, it was closed. Betty's lips wobbled and her eyes glistened but Tiger hugged her closely. "We'll find another store, Bugs, don't worry. I promise."

They had hot chocolate in a small café, Betty appeased by a mountain of mini-marshmallows, while Tiger scrolled through her phone looking for another store. She found one eventually, and they took a cab there and spent a happy hour choosing some toys for Betty.

It was already getting dark by the time they left the store, storm clouds gathering over the city and as rain began to fall in torrents. Tiger whisked Betty into the shelter of a hotel restaurant where they ate French fries and burgers and kidded around.

As Tiger carried Betty out later, she suddenly stopped, her heart pounding. In the bar of the hotel she saw Lazlo talking with a blonde woman she didn't recognize. The shock was palpable but instead of going over to them, she continued on, carrying Betty out into the street where they caught a cab.

As they rode back to the hotel, Tiger called Lazlo on his cell phone. "Are you almost done working?"

"Sure, baby, almost. I've just got to talk to these guys a little while longer."

"Guys?"

"The band. They flew into Paris this morning unexpectedly."

"Oh."

There was a small silence. "Are you okay?"

There was a lump in her throat but Tiger still nodded to herself. "Fine. We'll see you later. We've had lunch by the way."

"Okay, babe, I'll grab something here. We can go out later with the lovebug, right?"

"Right. Bye."

"Bye."

Tiger put her cellphone in her bag. *The guys. The band.* Made up, apparently of one beautiful blonde. She couldn't believe he would be cheating on her. Not her Lazlo, not after everything they had been through, but...

No. Don't even go there. But even Betty noticed her sudden introspection. "Momma? Are you okay?"

She pulled Betty onto her lap. "Of course, bugs. When we get back o the hotel, we can play with your new toys, okay?"

BETTY LOVED her new toys but by the time Lazlo came through the door, she had fallen asleep in her mother's arms. Tiger nodded to Lazlo who kissed her cheek and took the sleeping child from her. Together they put her to bed in her room, Betty not stirring for a moment.

Lazlo followed Tiger back to their own room and Tiger sat cross-legged on the bed, watching him change into his jeans and sweater. "How did the meeting go?"

"Good. A lot of stuff arranged. Might have to meet with their representatives one last time."

"Where?"

"Where what?"

Tiger looked at him steadily. "Where will you meet them?"

"At the venue, like today, I expect."

Tiger felt her heart falter, and she looked away from him quickly. "Okay."

"Are you alright?"

"Why wouldn't I be?" She got off the bed. "I'll leave you to change. I don't feel like going out tonight, I'd rather just eat in if that's okay with you? Betty Bug is pretty wiped out after today too. We went all over the city."

She didn't wait to hear his answer, leaving him in the bedroom as she went back out to the main room. He didn't follow her and Tiger felt tear prick her eyes. Why was he lying to her if there was nothing going on?

Fuck you. She felt a surge of rage and wanted to go back into the bedroom and have it out with him... but... did she really want to know the truth?

"Oh, hey," Lazlo came out of the bedroom, "by the way, I've arranged for someone from one of the fashion houses in the city to come and talk to you about some new clothes."

Tiger frowned. "What?"

"My treat."

Okay, this was very, very odd. Since when had Lazlo cared about what she wore? "Laz... I don't need any clothes."

"Well," and now she noticed two spots of red high on his cheeks, "I thought, for our last night here, we might both dress up—Bugs too —and go out. I've already arranged for a new suit for myself." He studied her. "I mean, if you don't want to, I understand. I know you have plenty of beautiful clothes... I just thought, as we're in the Fashion capital of the world."

What the hell was this? Tiger stared at him for a long moment then nodded stiffly. "Okay. Whatever."

"Tiger..."

"I said okay." She figured it out. A guilt gift. *God, damn it.* She couldn't believe it.

The rest of the evening limped on with a palpable tension, with even Betty picking up on it and acting fractious and worried.

THE NEXT DAY the fashion people came, bringing with them a rack of the most gorgeous, beautifully tailored clothes but Tiger could barely get up any enthusiasm for them. "You choose," she said to Lazlo, finally, "I can't."

She saw him exchange an exasperated look with the representative and eventually he chose a stunning, figure hugging white dress with a delicate detail across the bodice. Tiger begrudgingly admitted it would suit her very well indeed but personally thought it looked a little bridal.

LAZLO WAITED until the rep had gone then turned to her. "Okay, out with it. What's wrong?"

"You tell me. What the hell is this?" Tiger nodded at the dress. "Got something you feel guilty about, Lazlo?"

Lazlo gaped at her. "What the hell are you talking about?"

Tiger drew in a deep breath. "Bugs and me... yesterday we went to that toy store, but it was closed. So, we went all over the city until we found one. Then, because of the storm, we went to the Fielding for lunch."

She watched as his expression turned from annoyed to understanding. "Oh."

"Yes. Unless the Fielding suddenly host rock concerts..."

"There is a very good explanation for this." Lazlo held his hands up but Tiger having held all of this in, wasn't finished.

"Yes. I saw *her*. Is she a good fuck, Laz? Or just different?"

"Wait a minute... what the hell do you think I was there for?"

"You say you were meeting a bunch of guys in a band but when I saw you, there was just one blonde woman."

Lazlo wait until Tiger had ranted then waited. "Tiger, that was Kym Clayton."

"Who?"

He rolled his eyes. "From The 9th and Pine. The guys I was talking about was the band. Bay, Pete and Kym. When you saw me, Bay and Pete had gone to do some phone interviews. That was all."

Tiger felt the anger drain from her. *Shit.* Well... she'd fucked this up, hadn't she? "Oh."

He raised an eyebrow at her, almost in jest but she could see the searing hurt and ager in his eyes. "You really think, after everything, after what we've been through, that I would want anyone else but you? That I would cheat on you?"

Tiger felt shame rushing through her veins. "I'm sorry."

"Not good enough, Tiger. Come on now... this, god, this hurts like hell that you would think that."

The hurt in his eyes was hard to look at. "I'm sorry. I just... I got scared. After what we did the other night, I thought, all bets were off. No, that's not it. I just got... I'm sorry, Laz." She went to him and put her hands on his chest. "I am sorry. I should have trusted you, I have no excuse except my own stupid brain fucking me up."

Lazlo was a frozen statue for a minute then his shoulders slumped and he touched her face. "I would never ever cheat on you, Tiger. Ever. When I found you, I found the home for my heart. You and Bugs and any other kids we have... you are my world. I've never been someone who cheated, ask anyone. Every one of my exes—and there haven't been that many—will tell you the same. We might have split, but it wasn't because of infidelity."

He half-smiled now. "I like to think it was because my heart knew you'd come along sooner or later."

Tiger's eyes were full of tears. "Cheesy," she said but her voice broke and Lazlo kissed the hot tears as they dropped down her cheek.

"Live with it, wifey. Cheese is all you get from here on out."

"Eww."

But they both laughed. Lazlo kissed her softly. "I'm sorry I didn't make it clear about the meeting."

"It's okay, I'm sorry for not coming over then and there. A lot of nonsense could have been prevented if I had."

"I swear, you can be at my side whenever I meet anyone. Even if it's Monica Bellucci," he added with a wicked grin and she laughed.

"Dude, with Monica Bellucci you get a hall pass. If you don't fuck her, I will."

"Ha ha." But they clung to each other despite the joking around. Eventually he let her go and Tiger went to the dress hanging up.

"I should try this on."

"I hope you don't look too good in it... it's a nice dress and I don't want to rip it off of you."

Tiger blew him a kiss and went to try the dress on. As she smoothed it over her hips, Lazlo followed her into the bedroom and she met his eyes in the mirror. "Yes?"

Lazlo let out a sign of pure desire. "God, yes... wear it tomorrow?"

"Done. Where are you taking us?"

His smile widened. "Now that is a secret."

BETTY WAS AS EXCITED as Tiger the next evening, dressed in her gorgeous little dress, all sparkles and netting. She looked like a little angel and Tiger hugged her tightly. "Betty Bug, where do you think Daddy is taking us?"

Betty shook her head, grinning at her father. Tiger looked over at Lazlo. He looked so gloriously handsome in the navy-blue suit and she smiled as he touched her cheek now. "Almost there, beautiful."

They were at the Fielding again, and Tiger gave Lazlo a bemused look as he was greeted by a representative of the hotel. "Everything is in place, Mr. Schuler."

They were taken up to the penthouse in the elevator and as they stepped out, Tiger gasped as a huge cheer went up. "Oh, my *god*." She clutched her chest as the scene before her sank in. Apollo, her beloved brother, was there with his wife Nell and their daughter Daisy; India and Massimo, Lazlo's brother Gabe, even their friends from California, Jess and Teddy. Tiger's best friend and colleague, Sarah came forward to greet them. "Hello, gorgeous people."

Tiger looked at Lazlo. "What is this?" But she was laughing, giggling, delighted to see all the people she loved in the same room. "What is this?" She repeated as Lazlo hugged her tightly then, as the crowd gathered around them, they were left alone in the middle of the crowd and Lazlo was getting down on one knee.

"Tiger Rose, I didn't do this properly last time but tonight, in front of everyone we love, I wanted to make it right. You are the love of my life, my beloved wife, the mother of our children, both living and passed."

His voice broke then and Tiger felt her eyes fill with tears. The fact he considered her a mother of two both made her heart swell and made her want to cry. Their lost baby. Lost to an ectopic pregnancy that was no-one's fault. He or she had still been their child.

Lazlo held her hand. "My love, my darling love, I know we've already said our vows once, to each other just you and I at City Hall in Seattle, that most romantic of places."

Tiger laughed along with the guests at that but Lazlo's eyes were steady on hers. "Darling… would you do the honor of marrying me again, tonight in front of our daughter, of our family, our friends, our loved ones?"

"I will," she said without hesitation then laughed as Lazlo stood and picked her up, twirling her around.

God, it was just like him to do something as romantic as this. She touched his cheek as he set her down. "You are the love of my life, Lazlo Schuler. Thank you for waiting for me."

"You and I, forever," he said, resting his forehead against hers and she nodded, smiling.

"For all time, my darling love."

LAZLO HAD ARRANGED everything and Tiger realized that even the band, The 9ᵗʰ and Pine, had come over especially for this wedding. All that time he said he was working... Tiger shook her head.

But then she got caught up in the moment, as she and Lazlo exchanged vows again, this time making them up on the fly, making jokes but meaning every single word with all their hearts. Betty was overjoyed to be their flower girl, enchanting everyone by dancing with her cousin Daisy around the happy couple.

Afterwards, the band played for them, and they even managed to persuade India to join them for an encore. India was pregnant with her and Massimo's second child and Tiger thanked her for coming even in her late second trimester. "Are you kidding? You think I'd miss my brother's wedding?" India hugged her tightly. "You've made him so happy, Tiger, thank you."

The night was a wonderful celebration and by the time Lazlo and Tiger took Betty and left in a shower of confetti, she knew she wouldn't be able to sleep a wink. Lazlo kissed her temple. "Thank you for marrying me... again."

"What a wonderful night, Laz, thank you so much." She looked down at their sleeping daughter then back at him. "Thank you for this wonderful life."

Lazlo kissed her and rested his forehead against hers. "And we've only just begun," he said, as they drove on into the Parisian night...

THE END.

CPSIA information can be obtained
at www.ICGtesting.com
Printed in the USA
BVHW040943150221
600148BV00008B/138